# Devil's Bait

DEBBIE BOEK

To Iva, Rachelle and Diane, for keeping me moving in the right direction.

# PROLOGUE
## Endwell, Connecticut 2009

"Please listen, Mrs. Walters, honestly, we're just trying to help."

"I do understand, but you have to leave now."

Her voice wavered and she was obviously terrified, but Scott wasn't sure if it was because of whatever spectral being was terrorizing them, or because of her husband. The woman kept nervously grabbing wads of her faded and over-sized housedress as she glanced sideways towards the front door. Her thin face was taut, her eyes were red and watery and Scott was afraid that she might start crying at any moment.

He looked over at Tim in frustration, but Tim just shrugged and raised his hands, ready to give up.

"Last chance, Mrs. Walters." Scott tried one last time, feeling more than a little desperate when he glanced up and saw a skinny, young boy sitting halfway down the wide sweeping staircase, watching them closely. He looked as haunted as his mother and, even from this distance, Scott could see the large, dark circles under his eyes, making them stand out sharply against his pale skin and dark hair.

The kid was young enough to still be wearing footie pajamas, but the fabric was so tight that the little red fire engines on it were somewhat distorted. He'd be too tall for them very soon, and Scott just hoped the boy would live to see that day.

"We know something is wrong in this house and we can help you and your family, please, just let us check it out."

"What the hell is going on here?" They all turned towards the loud, drunken voice coming from the open doorway and, out of the corner of his eye, Scott saw the boy scamper further up the stairs, into the shadows and out his father's view.

Sighing heavily, Scott walked over towards the man. They'd done their homework and knew of Mr. Walters' proclivity for heavy drinking, so they tried to arrive at the house early enough that it wouldn't be a factor, but were obviously too late.

Scott was tall and well-built, but this man was a bleary-eyed goliath and towered over him. Scott wasn't worried about his own safety, he could take the man easily enough, especially in the drunken state that he was in, but they needed his cooperation, so Scott decided to tread lightly.

"Hello, sir, my name is Scott Devereaux and this is my brother, Tim."

"And what the hell are you doing in my house?"

"Well, sir," Scott was trying to be as respectful as possible, but frustration was beginning to edge out into his voice, "we've heard that there are some odd things happening in the house and we would like to offer our services, free of charge, to look into them and, hopefully, get rid of whatever the problem is for you."

The man's narrow bloodshot eyes went from Scott to Tim to his wife, where they hardened into tiny slits. She cowered back and stared at the floor, nervously grabbing and releasing handfuls of the thin fabric of her housedress.

"I don't know what the wife's been telling you, but she does have a nasty habit of making shit up."

"She hasn't told us anything." Scott was worried that they may have placed the woman in greater danger from her husband than she was in from the house itself. "One of your neighbors mentioned that there are some problems with the house. Apparently, there have been strange things happening for years, even before you bought it. We just wanted to help out."

"Get the hell out of my house, any problem here, I can take care of it myself."

Scott and Tim realized that this angry drunk would never be agreeable to their looking into this further, at least not in his current frame of mind. And there was nothing that they could do for these people without their permission.

"Sure, we can give you our card and you can call another time, if you'd be interested in our help." Tim said, sensing Scott's frustration and trying to keep the conversation civil.

"No need."

"Please, take it." Tim extended his hand, the card held lightly between his thumb and forefinger. The behemoth slapped it away and it drifted lazily onto the floor. Tim was as tall as the other man and just as broad, but without the excessive paunch and doughy face. After a brief moment of indecision, Tim chose to stand down and, rather than punch the idiot's lights out, he took a deep breath and walked towards the front door.

As Scott walked past Mr. Walters, he paused and leaned towards him, trying to ignore the beer fumes seeping out of the man's pores, and spoke to him quietly, so that none of the others could hear.

The man's throat and face blossomed a deep red as he bellowed, "We'll see about that."

"What did you say to him?" Tim asked, once they were safely back in their car.

"I just told him that his wife had nothing to do with our being there, and that if he harmed her in any way that I'd come back and kick his ass six ways to Sunday."

"Nice touch, but I'm pretty sure it had the opposite effect on him."

"I'm afraid it may have, but I had to say something. I couldn't let him take it out on her."

"Nothing we can do about it now, Scott. It looks like we aren't getting in there this time either."

"Nope, and I really don't anticipate that they'll be reaching out to us anytime soon. Let's head out."

*         *         *

It was almost a week later when Tim discovered the news article about the family and turned his laptop so that Scott could see it as well. The headline read:

## SIX-YEAR-OLD FALLS DOWN FAMILY
## STAIRCASE AND DIES INSTANTLY

Scott looked over at his brother, his dark eyes were snapping with frustration and anger as he began to run his fingers through his thick brown hair.

Running his hand through his hair was Scott's tell when something affected him deeply. His only tell, as far as Tim knew, and it was the only way that he was able to gauge the full extent of his brother's feelings about the situation.

"The father or the ghost?"

"According to the article, the father was locked up in the drunk tank when it happened, so I'd have to go with the ghost. Scott, we tried, and you know that we can't save them all, so don't start beating yourself up about this."

"But, damn it, Timmy, we could've saved this one. We could have saved him, if they'd just let us."

# CHAPTER 1

The raggedy green and red paisley curtains moved slightly, although the window was closed and there was no discernible draft. They parted slowly as the arriving caravan came closer and pulled up into the circular driveway. Above the sounds of car doors slamming and voices rising in excitement, a disembodied sound of eager anticipation whispered throughout the room, then the curtains slowly returned to their original position.

"Are you sure this is the right house, Jeremy?" Emma Draper asked, staring curiously at the monstrosity in front of her.

"This is it, honey," her husband replied, a lock of his black hair falling over one eye as he reached into the trunk of the Lexus to retrieve his brief case and a couple of small boxes.

"The pictures didn't do it justice," she responded, her green eyes narrowed as she contemplated all of the work that was going to have to be done, just on the outside alone.

Jeremy smiled as he headed toward the front porch, amused at her reaction.

"Once the grass is mowed and the siding is repaired, you'll see what a beauty it is."

"And the shutters refastened, and the porch and woodwork scraped and painted, and I can't even begin to imagine what the inside looks like," she muttered, following along behind him.

Collin and James raced past her, taking the front steps in two leaps and then sprinting into the house behind Jeremy, arguing all the way.

Both of them looked like their father, they had his twinkling blue eyes and jet black hair and, since they were only fifteen months apart, were often mistaken for twins. They were full of boundless teenage energy and always on the move, so it was difficult to notice any of the slight physical differences between them. Collin took after his father more than James, he was smart and practical, and was always looking for answers and explanations. James was much more laid back and easy going than his older brother. They balanced each other out in a very good way.

Shelly followed more sedately, showing her maturity at the ripe old age of seventeen. She had her mother's thick, blonde hair, but Shelly's was much longer and hung midway down her back. Her eyes were the same vivid blue as her father's, but the sour look on her face was purely her own.

It was going to be quite a long while before she would even begin to be able to forgive her parents for this catastrophe that they had created. As a matter of fact, Shelly wasn't sure if she would ever speak to them again, since they still refused to appreciate how much this move had disrupted her life. This fall she would begin her senior year of high school, one of the most important times of her life, and now she would be doing it in a new town, at a new school, where she knew no one. It was just too unfair and completely unforgivable.

Emma watched her stalk towards the house with her cute little sundress swirling impatiently around her and just shook her head. She knew that Shelly would eventually get over this drama, but Emma also knew that life with her was not going to be easy until that day arrived.

She suddenly stopped walking, her eyes drawn to one of the upper windows. It was a warm summer day, but Emma felt like a shadow crossed over her and goosebumps rose on her arms as she stared up into the vacant darkness.

At that same moment, she became aware of the silence, there were no birds singing in the huge maple trees scattered throughout the property, no crickets chirping, no noise of any kind, other than the distance hum of traffic moving along back in town.

"Shake it off," she chided herself, rubbing her arms, trying to get rid of the feeling of unease that had crept over her. "It's a new house, new town, lotta stress, just shake it off and deal with it. There is nothing wrong here and no matter how creepy it feels, its home now."

Once inside, they were all a little stunned at how grand the house was. It truly had been a mansion in its day, with high ceilings, large, bright windows, big open rooms and beautifully crafted woodwork.

There was a large chandelier hanging in the foyer and prisms of light flashed off it as the sunlight poured in through the open doorway. The wide, sweeping staircase curved outward on both sides up to the second floor, so that the top step was almost as wide as the foyer itself. Hallways extended out from the foyer on either side of the staircase and there were large double doors opening onto the rooms along them. The doors were all wide open and, even though Emma had seen photos and the floor plan, the inherent beauty of the house was unexpected, to say the least.

The carpets were frayed, bulbs were burnt out in the chandelier and other miscellaneous items needed repair or replacement, but you could still envision how glorious it had been and, hopefully, would be again.

Shelly and the boys made their way up the stairs to check out their bedrooms and Emma headed down the hallway to the left, looking for the kitchen. She was impressed by how spacious it was and by the fairly modern appliances that filled it. As she was admiring the amount of cupboard space, she heard a creaking behind her and turned to find a door along the wall slightly ajar.

Emma opened it the rest of the way and turned on the light. She was immediately assaulted by a blast of cold air that smelled positively vile. She peered down the steps into the murky basement, but had no intention of going down there until Jeremy had a chance to clean up whatever was making that rotten smell. Emma tried to rub some warmth back into her arms and made a mental note to be sure that Jeremy also checked for broken windows while he was down there.

That was the extent of the exploring she was able to do before the moving van came chugging up the driveway. Pandemonium commenced as boxes were brought in and delivered to various rooms, sorted through, moved to other rooms and, eventually, the unpacking and re-assembly of furniture began.

*       *       *

There were loud sighs of exhausted gratitude when the moving men finally finished up and left.

"I'll run into town and see if I can find a decent pizza place," Jeremy offered. "Anyone want to ride along with me?"

The boys jumped at the chance and ran out front, arguing over who was going to ride shotgun. Shelly, as usual, did not respond.

While the men left to pick up dinner, Shelly skulked upstairs to her room. She had the only room on the third floor and, although she would never admit it to her parents, was very pleased with it overall.

It wasn't just a room; the entire top floor was hers. There was a small hallway which led to her bedroom and to her very own bathroom, for which she was eternally grateful since sharing a bathroom with her brothers all these years had been just awful, considering that they were such pigs.

The bedroom itself would definitely need to be painted. It was a pukish yellow color and she couldn't have that. The curtains were old and dusty with a disgusting paisley design that Shelly could not tolerate. She would insist that they be replaced once the room was repainted. Maybe she would even ask for a complete new bedroom set, something that would look better up here than the old one that she'd had since she was a child.

Shelly knew that she would be able to get her parents to cave quite easily to some of her demands right now, because she was continuing to make them feel so guilty about the move. It was, after all, the least that they could do for her.

The house, and particularly her floor, reminded Shelly of the mansions from olden times that she'd seen in movies or read about in books. She could envision this whole floor made up of several small rooms for the maids to live in. Fortunately for her, the bedroom was now just one large, open, airy room. It was enormous and had a big bay window that looked down the street and almost all the way across town. For several minutes, she just knelt on the cushioned window seat and stared into the distance, wondering what this little town had in store for her.

Shaking herself from her reverie, Shelly moved around the room, putting her little treasures in their new places. One box contained all of her toiletries and she was extremely excited to be able to carry the whole box down to her bathroom, where she could put them out anywhere that she chose to.

Once those items were unpacked and put away, she wandered down the hallway. There were two sets of stairs, the main staircase led down to the second floor where her parents' and brothers' bedrooms were. Shelly decided to explore the other staircase in the far corner of the hallway, it was very narrow and enclosed and led down directly to the kitchen at the back of the house. She saw her mother cleaning out the cupboards and quietly snuck back up the stairs without being seen. This hidden stairway was going to come in very handy if she wanted to sneak out with no one being the wiser.

Returning to the hallway, she noticed a small door in the ceiling, which she assumed led to the attic. Shelly jumped up and pulled on the little rope handle that was hanging down from the trap door. The steps to the attic appeared and she pulled them all the way down and stepped up.

The minute her head and upper body entered the attic, she was hit hard by a very cold draft and a horrid smell that made her want to gag. It was dark and dreary and the only things that she could make out were covered in dusty, old sheets. The smell hit her again and she wrinkled her nose in disgust and decided to go back down to her room, hoping that whatever it was wouldn't make her room stink, too.

Heading back into her room, a creaking sound startled her and Shelly turned quickly. There was nothing there but the hair on the back of her neck stood up. She listened closely for a moment, but heard nothing further. Her heart slowly stopped hammering in her chest when she saw that the closet door had opened slightly.

"Old houses," she chided herself, "you'd better get used to it."

Their previous home had been old enough to have some quirks of its own, including floors that were not quite level and doors that wouldn't stay shut. It made her nostalgic for a moment and she was afraid that she might cry, but then she let her anger and frustration seep back in and started unpacking the rest of her belongings with a fury.

Meanwhile, Emma was trying to clean up the kitchen a little so that they could have a place to eat. After locating and opening the boxes with the dishes, she was scrubbing down the cabinets with hot, soapy water so she would have a place to put them.

The cabinets were not as bad as she expected and Emma had made her way through about half of them when she felt the hair being brushed off the nape of her neck. She shivered as the fingers running over the collar of her blouse tickled the skin beneath it.

She smiled and leaned her head back, expecting her husband to nuzzle her throat like he always did when he snuck up behind her. When nothing happened, she turned and was very surprised to find herself alone in the big kitchen.

"Jeremy," Emma called hesitantly, scanning the room. There was no response and nowhere that he could be hiding. She rubbed the back of her neck as a wave of uneasiness fell over her again and then peeked into the hallway outside the kitchen door, but there was no one there either.

Emma tried to get back to work, but couldn't forget the feel of her hair being brushed off her neck, and she could have sworn that she felt fingers running along the collar of her shirt. She shivered again and found herself constantly stopping what she was doing to look around the room to be sure that she was still alone.

Fortunately, the boys returned with the pizza and soda a few minutes later and Emma was able to forget about the incident and relax as they shared their first dinner in their new home.

It was late by the time they were done and Jeremy and Emma made sure that everyone had at least a sleeping bag on their bed, since the boxes with the sheets and blankets were mixed in with the dozens of other boxes strewn around the house, and no one had the energy to try and find them.

She was exhausted from traveling and unpacking all day, but sleep did not come easily for Emma. Even snuggled up inside a warm sleeping bag, there was a deep coldness in her bones that she couldn't shake, and watching the dark shadows twist and turn against the walls of her new home, she continued to shiver violently off and on until the wee hours of the morning.

* * *

The next few days flew by as they tried to get the house livable, although there were times when Emma wondered if they would ever get to that point. She could swear they had a gremlin living with them. She would hang pictures and then find them on the floor the next morning, with the glass in the frame broken, of course, or sometimes she would unpack a box and go back to find one of the items and it had somehow managed to end up in a cabinet or drawer in a completely different part of the room.

It was a little frustrating, but she figured either Jeremy or one of the kids were moving them to where they thought they should be. Once Jeremy went back to work and the boys stopped trying to help so much, she would be able to get everything back where it belonged.

"Well, hon, what do you think? Do we have it in good enough order that we can go get the animals now?" Jeremy asked.

"I thought we were going to wait for the weekend."

"I have to drive into town anyway, to get my apartment together, so I may as well do that, spend the night there and then bring everybody back tomorrow."

Emma finished wiping off the dish that she held in her hand, put it in the strainer and started nervously twisting her ring.  Even though she understood that an hour and a half drive every morning and evening would put a strain on Jeremy, she was still struggling with the whole apartment issue. The plan was that he would stay in the city all week and only spend the weekends and vacations with the family, and that was still not something that Emma could readily accept.

She felt his hands on her shoulders, gently rubbing the knots out, and leaned her head back against his chest with a heavy sigh.

"Okay, I know this has to happen, but I'm going to miss having you around."

"Seriously, Em, I'm never home until 7 or 8 at night anyway, so it's not like things will change that dramatically."

"But I like having you in my bed at night, keeping me safe and warm. And I like having you around to talk to, you know, adult talk."

He smiled. "I'll miss you too, but it will make the weekends that much more exciting, right?"

"Sure." Her answer was cut short as a piercing screech echoed down the back stairwell.

# CHAPTER 2

Shelly came flying down the stairs and into the kitchen, blonde hair fanning out behind her and eyes glittering like angry sapphires.

"I want a lock on my door."

"Well, you aren't going to get one, what happened?" Emma asked.

"I have spent the last few days working tirelessly to get my room fixed up just the way I want it. I go for a little walk around the neighborhood and come home, and one of those little A-holes has been in my room and moved all the stuff around in my drawers, and the stuff I had on top of my nightstand and windowsill. They touched my personal things, Mom."

"First off, watch your mouth, secondly, the boys have been gone for several hours, so they couldn't have touched your stuff."

"Well, someone did," she said bitterly, giving her mother a suspicious look. "I want a lock."

"No lock," Emma said firmly. "And don't be giving me the hairy eyeball, I haven't been in your room all day. Let's go take a look."

The three of them made their way up the back staircase and Emma recognized what a problem this staircase might pose if Shelly decided she wanted to sneak out unnoticed some night. Well, that was a problem to worry about another day.

"See." Once they got to her room, Shelly pointed out the various knickknacks and stuffed animals placed around it in disarray. "And look in my drawers, I had everything just the way they should be and it's all been moved."

She looked like she was about to cry. Shelly had always been very particular about her things and both of her parents knew how important it was to her that they were kept in just the right place, and that this was a very big deal to her.

Jeremy and Emma looked at each other and Jeremy shrugged.

"I don't have any explanation for this, Shelly, but I'll help you get it back together the right way."

"No, just get out and leave me alone!" Shelly threw herself on her bed in a very dramatic fashion and buried her head under the pillow.

\*       \*       \*

Jeremy left for the city a short while later. He took the van instead of the Lexus so that he could bring all of the pets back with him.

Emma continued with her cleaning and unpacking until mid-afternoon when she was interrupted by a knock on the door. A handsome woman, who looked to be somewhere in her early forties, just a few years older than Emma, stood on the porch. She was very petite and the loaded picnic basket that filled her arms looked like it was threatening to tip her right over.

"Hi, I'm Lynne McVee, your next door neighbor across the street." She spoke quickly and angled her head back to indicate the cute Cape down the road a short distance. "I brought food, can I come in?"

"Of course, I'm Emma Draper, it's nice to meet you." Emma knew that she must look a fright since she'd been cleaning and unpacking all day, she felt at a bit of a disadvantage in her dirty old tank top and cut off shorts. Lynne was dressed in a smart looking pants suit and her chestnut brown hair and bright red nails were perfectly done.

"I'm so happy that you're here, it's nice to have someone living in this place, finally."

Emma opened the double doors into the dining room, which was just off the foyer, and then followed Lynne in.

"I'm sorry the house is such a mess, we weren't expecting company and haven't had time to get everything in its place yet. Other than dumping boxes in this room, I've barely been in it yet."

"Beautiful woodwork." Lynne commented as they both looked around the room.

Lovely mahogany cupboards were built along the inner wall with a large, ornate mirror in the center of it. The upper cabinet doors were made of glass and stained glass designs were interspersed along the woodwork. Even though there were deep scratches in some of the cupboards, and the floor, also mahogany, was badly stained in several places, neither of them had ever seen a room quite so stylish and elegant.

There were several oversized windows spaced along the outer wall which allowed for a great view of the yard and the fields beyond it. You could even make out a corner of the barn towards the back of the house.

Lynne began unpacking the basket, laying out a veritable feast on the long dining room table. She seemed to do everything almost as fast as she talked and, in no time at all, had the basket emptied and the goodies spread out on the dining room table. The table was suddenly littered with all kinds of little sandwiches, cookies, cakes, cheese and crackers, cut up veggies and fruits. She'd even brought over paper plates to put everything on.

Emma stood and watched quietly, a little unsure of what to do or how to take their new neighbor.

"Ta – Da!" Lynne exclaimed, holding up a bottle of Pinot Grigio. "Do you have your glasses unpacked? If not, I can run home and get some, I didn't have room for them in my basket. I figured you might need a little destresser."

"I think I can find some," Emma replied with a smile, as she headed towards the kitchen.

When she returned, they sipped wine and nibbled on the goodies as they got to know each other.

"Before we go any further, please realize that I have no filter and sometimes I do not think before I speak. So, if I offer information that you're uncomfortable with, or if I ask questions that I shouldn't, just tell me. I don't get insulted, it happens all the time."

Emma smiled again, appreciating Lynne's honesty and starting to believe that they might become good friends. She had slowly drifted away from her friends back home as the children had gotten older and she no longer shared much in common with them, so she was very pleased to have the opportunity to get to know her new neighbor.

"I was beginning to think no one would ever buy this place," Lynne said, glancing around the room. "It's been empty since we moved in a couple of years ago. The only time they do any maintenance is when they lower the price again and renew their sales efforts. I offered to try and sell it myself, I'm in Real Estate by the way, but got shot down. It was really bringing down the value of the other houses on the road, although it is a nice looking place. Actually, the inside is very impressive."

"Thanks," Emma replied with a frown. "So, what was the problem, why wouldn't anyone buy it?"

"I've heard rumors, but I don't know what's true and what isn't."

"What kind of rumors?"

"That it's haunted."

Emma couldn't tell from the mischievous sparkle in Lynne's eye if she was yanking her chain or not.

"No, really."

"Oh, I'm serious. Apparently, over the years there have been all kinds of stories about the goings on in this house."

"Like what?"

"People dying, people moving out in the middle of the night and never returning, you know Amityville Horror stuff."

"Well, the ghosts must have gotten bored and moved along then, we haven't had any problems at all."

Emma shuddered suddenly, recalling the hair being moved off the back of her neck when she was alone in the kitchen.

"What is it?" Lynne asked. "Something has happened, hasn't it?"

"No, nothing, I guess someone just walked over my grave." Emma shook her head to lose the unwelcome memory and changed the subject.

"Do you and your husband have any children?"

"Interesting question. Just so you know, for my Facebook status, I don't use 'Married' any more, I use 'It's Complicated'. We have two children, my daughter, Lucy, is twenty-two and lives with her fiancée. My son, Mike, Jr., or Mikey, as he so hates to be called, is nineteen, he's in the Marines stationed out in California. Mike, Sr. currently lives with his girlfriend, with whom he recently had another daughter, Cecelia."

Emma looked at her curiously. "And he's still your husband?"

"He probably always will be. I'm not giving the little prick a divorce, I need his health care coverage. I can't afford it on my own."

Emma laughed so hard that she choked on her last sip of wine and started coughing uncontrollably.

Lynne got up and started around the table to pat Emma on the back when she suddenly shivered.

"My goodness, it's freezing right here. You must have a draft, can't you feel it?"

Emma went to stand by her, still wiping away the tears from the laughter/choking incident.

"Wow, where could that be coming from?"

Both women looked around in confusion, the windows were all closed and there were no vents in the area.

"Lynne, look at the napkins on the table, they aren't moving at all, it can't be a draft. What could be causing it?"

The air suddenly became much warmer and they both rubbed away the goosebumps on their arms.

"That was very weird," Lynne said, still looking around for an answer. But, when none came to her, she decided to ignore it all and poured them both some more wine.

"Tell me about your family."

"What?" Emma answered absently, still trying to find an explanation for the strange cold spot.

"Don't dwell on it, Emma. If I worried about every draft or piece of weirdness in my life, I'd have no time for anything else. I asked about your family. What brought you here?"

"Oh, um, same old story, so much crime in the big city, we started to get really worried about the kid's safety. Even at school things seemed to be spiraling out of control. So, we found this place and fell in love with it. It was a virtual tour online. However, I'm thinking it was done a few years ago because the place seemed much more well-kept than what we found when we got here."

"It's still gorgeous though."

"It is, isn't it?" Emma responded, starting to feel proud of her new home.

"How many children?

"Shelly is seventeen, going on twenty-five. She's not happy about the move, particularly just before her senior year."

"Ooh, that's gotta be tough on all of you. There is nothing uglier than an angry teenager."

"Don't I know it?" Emma replied with a smile. "Collin is thirteen and James is almost twelve. They are handling it much better. But they have each other and Shelly has no friends here yet."

"Do you work?"

Emma sighed. "Well, I know I'm supposed to be indignant and make it perfectly clear that being a housewife and mother is a job all in itself, but, other than that, I do not work outside of my home. I once aspired to be an Interior Decorator, even went to college for it and did work at it for a few years, but, I quit when we had Shelly."

"I always wished that I could stay home when my kids were little, but we couldn't afford it. It's not easy trying to handle a job and still have time for your family and your life. I envy you."

Emma smiled wistfully. "I certainly don't regret it, I wouldn't trade a minute of being with the kids while they were growing up. But, especially lately, they seem to have outgrown me. Between the cell phones, the video games and the computers, they make no secret of the fact that they would rather be alone with their electronic gadgets or doing things with their friends. I'm pretty much invisible unless it's chow time. Maybe once I get the house settled and the kids start school, I'll see what jobs are out there, even if it's just part time. I think I'm ready to start spending time with grown-ups again."

"I think that's a great idea and I can help you out. I know pretty much everything that goes on in this town. What does your husband do?"

"He's an attorney. Unfortunately, it's a long commute to his office and he works such long hours that he'll be staying in an apartment in the city during the week."

Lynne heard the edginess in her voice and watched as Emma twisted her beautiful wedding ring around and around her finger. Lynne wasn't even sure if Emma realized that she was doing it and decided that it would be best to not delve into this particular situation any further, for now anyway.

"That ring is gorgeous, may I see it?"

"Sure," Emma replied, handing it over and immediately feeling naked with just the plain gold band left on her finger.

"It must have cost a pretty penny," Lynne said, admiring the design and workmanship. There were three ribbons, one gold, one white-gold and one diamond studded, that twisted together and met at the large round diamond at the center of the ring. "Is this a full carat?"

"I think it's a carat and a quarter," Emma replied, trying not to sound like she was bragging. "Jeremy upgraded my original engagement ring with this one as a surprise for our fifteenth wedding anniversary."

"What a sweetheart he must be, I think Mike got me a vacuum for our fifteenth, a car vacuum no less, not even a nice expensive one for the house. How long have you been married?"

"We've been together almost twenty years and married a little over eighteen."

Lynne reluctantly handed the ring back to Emma. "Anyway, it's good to have you here and with both the hubbies gone, at least during the week, it leaves more time for you, me and Pinot."

"Yes, indeed," Emma replied, lifting her glass in acknowledgement. "By the way, we also have a little menagerie of pets, cats, dogs, horses, the whole shebang. I thought I should give you a heads up about it. I'm so excited about having the horses here, right out the back door, so I don't have to trudge over to the stable when I want to ride. And the dogs will be able to play and run loose and won't have to be on a leash all the time. It was one of the reasons this place really stood out."

"I have a porky myself."

"A what?" Emma asked.

"A porky, got her at the pound, no clue what breed, or breeds, she is, but she's a terrible beggar. I give her so many treats to keep her out of my hair that she's about ten pounds overweight. The Vet reprimands me about her being so porky every time he sees her, so that's what I call her."

Emma giggled again just as the boys abruptly burst through the front door.

"Collin, James," Emma called. "Please come in the dining room, I'd like you to meet our new neighbor, Mrs. McVee."

They shuffled into the room and briefly introduced themselves before escaping up the staircase.

"Handsome lads, but not very talkative," Lynne noted.

"It's like pulling teeth to get anything out of them lately, please don't take it personally."

"Me, don't be silly," she replied, checking her watch. "Well, I'd better get going, let me help you clean up first. It was lovely finally getting to meet you."

"You too, and thanks so much for the basket of goodies, you really made my day. Please don't worry about cleaning up though, you've done enough, I can handle it. Let me just wrap up these leftovers for you to take back."

"No way," Lynne replied, "this is the best that I could do for a house-warming present and you are keeping whatever is still here."

"That's sweet, thank you."

Lynne left a couple of minutes later and, with a pleasant buzz from the wine, Emma put together a light dinner, mostly out of the leftovers from the goodie basket. She went to bed early that night and slept so hard that she never heard her closet door creaking open, or the boys whispering as they huddled together on James' bed.

"Do you think it's true?" he asked his brother.

"Of course not," Collin whispered back. "There's no such thing as ghosts. We've been here for days and nothing's happened, right?"

James just nodded, his eyes wide as he scanned the shadows of their room.

"Don't be scared, you sissy. Those kids were just busting on us." But they continued whispering together until late into the night.

# CHAPTER 3

Callie was the first to burst out of the van as soon as the door opened. She was a big, black German Shepherd who looked very intimidating, but she didn't have a mean bone in her body.

Her son, Chance, was right behind her, no one was sure who, or what, his father was, or when exactly the tryst occurred. Presumably, it occurred in a dark corner somewhere in one the dog parks that they frequented. Chance was a bit goofy and, although he was going on six years old, it didn't appear that he would ever outgrow his puppy stage.

The dogs ran back and forth to all the kids and Emma, over excited from finally being released from their kennel prison and throwing sloppy kisses at everyone.

"Get down, you big gallute." Emma laughed, as Chance put both front paws on her shoulders, covering her entire face with his doggy saliva. She was pleased to see Shelly laughing and finally looking happy. It had been a while since she had even seen her daughter smile.

Jeremy grabbed the cat boxes and headed into the house. Callie stopped short at the threshold, the hair on her neck bristled and a deep, low growl rumbled from her chest. It was very uncharacteristic of her and a bit unnerving. It took several minutes, but Emma was finally able to coax her inside the house.

Shelly had already released Smoky from her carrier by then and was hugging her enthusiastically. Smoky was a beautiful Siamese with a bit of a Queen of Sheba complex and she purred deeply and loudly while Shelly carried her upstairs to their room.

Banshee was another story altogether. He was a stray that they took in and, although probably grateful, he preferred to be left alone. He may choose to jump up on someone's lap occasionally for a nap, but other than that, he wouldn't tolerate any touching. They all tended to let him have his own way with things because he had a howl that was worse than chalk on a blackboard when he was not pleased.

Banshee quietly looked around and then skulked off to explore on his own. Jeremy wrapped his arms around Emma and kissed her forehead.

"All the kids are home now," he murmured.

"Yes, feels good, doesn't it?"

"It does. The place is coming together, you've been hard at it, I see."

"There's still so much to do," she said with a sigh, "but it is starting to feel like home. It's just so darn big. And, of course, none of the boxes were even on the right floor, let alone in the right room. But, come see what I found."

She grabbed his hand and dragged him into the kitchen.

"Look at this." Emma slid open a small door in the wall. It was in the far corner of the kitchen and partially hidden by the refrigerator. Inside were a shelf and a series of pulleys and cables. She maneuvered the cables and the box began to rise.

Emma smiled like a child with a new gift. "It's a dumb waiter, can you believe it? It goes up to every floor and I've been sending all kinds of things up in it so I don't have to lug it all up the stairs."

"Well, you are in high cotton now, Mrs. Draper," Jeremy said with an exaggerated southern drawl.

"That I am, Mr. Draper," she replied with a smile.

"Oh, before I forget, I talked to Maggie at the stable and they'll be bringing the horses out mid-week. She'll call you first. Is the barn ready?"

Emma's face fell. Although she was excited about having the horses here, she still hadn't even gotten the house in order, let alone checked the barn to see if it was even usable.

With another heavy sigh, she replied, "I guess that I'll get to work on that tomorrow."

"Em, I'm here and I'll help you, you don't have to take all of this on yourself and you have plenty of time."

Emma knew he meant well, but she also knew that his idea of helping out was to play catch with the boys so they would be out from under foot.

*     *     *

Later that afternoon, after they had finished their game of catch, Jeremy and the boys got busy weed whacking, mowing the lawn and getting the outside of the house in order. Emma knew there were still quite a few boxes that hadn't been unpacked, but couldn't locate them until she remembered the library.

"Oh, damn," she said, opening the double doors. The library was the first room on the right side of the foyer. Although there were not a lot of rooms in the house, each of them were very large and the library was no exception. And it was filled with dozens of boxes that still had to be unpacked and which were marked with the dreaded 'miscellaneous' tag, so they could belong in any room of the house.

Emma found her cleaning supplies, brought them into the library and stood there for a few minutes, trying to get some inspiration as to where she should start.

The room had a very high ceiling, just like the others in the house, but this one was made of tin with elegant designs throughout it, very Victorian looking. Stained glass lights dangled every few feet along the ceiling, which made no sense because, although they were beautiful, they didn't give off hardly any light.

Along the far wall there were two large bay windows with built in window seats under them. The windows let in a great deal of sunshine, which also emphasized the dirty streaks on them and the substantial amount of dust floating through the air.

Two of the walls were covered from floor to ceiling with exquisitely handcrafted bookcases. There was a track that ran along the top of the two of them, and a ladder hung from it which could be moved along the tracks and locked into place so books could be removed or replaced on the upper shelves.

There was another large bay window at the end of the room that looked out onto the front yard, where she could see James grimacing as he struggled to push the lawnmower through the high, overgrown grass. Callie, who preferred to be outside rather than in the house, was following along behind him.

There no window seat under this window, just a large open space, and Emma wondered if this part of the Library might have been used to greet and entertain guests. In her mind's eye, she could see the old-fashioned furniture that would have been placed around the area and even a little table where tea could be served. She smiled at the image and made a note to search out some local antique shops, hoping she might be able to decorate the room like she envisioned it was originally.

Emma grabbed the bottle of window cleaner and some paper towels and started with the windows, but hadn't gotten far when she realized that she was going to need at least a step stool to reach the upper parts of the windows. She walked out of the room into the foyer, intending to track down Jeremy to see if he might know where they had put it, but stopped suddenly before she got to the front door.

She could hear giggling and what sounded like a small child running along the hardwood floors but, even listening closely, she couldn't pinpoint where it was coming from. Emma headed down the hallway on the right side of the staircase and looked around in the capacious living room, but there was no one there.

Treading quietly in her sneakers, Emma next headed back towards the foyer. The giggling was getting louder and seemed to come from upstairs.

"Shelly, is that you?" There was no answer. She knew it couldn't be the boys because they were outside with Jeremy. "Shelly, if that is you, please answer me right now."

Still nothing, but then the giggling and footsteps started again, heading down the hall, away from her.

Thinking that a neighborhood child must have gotten into the house without them realizing it, she knew she needed to find the child and return it home before its parents became frantic with worry.

Emma took the stairs two at a time and headed down the hall to the right, which seemed to be the direction the noises had been going. She searched each and every room on that floor but could not find any child. As a last resort, she even went upstairs to Shelly's floor.

"Shelly, Shelly." There was no response to her knock on the door and Emma realized it was because she had the volume so loud on her music that the floor was vibrating in response to the bass. Emma opened the door and stepped into the room.

Shelly gave her mother an impatient look. "What?"

"Have you seen or heard any children up here?" Emma shouted, as she walked over to turn the volume down.

"What are you talking about? What children?"

"I thought I heard a kid running around and giggling, but I couldn't find anyone."

"I haven't heard or seen anything."

"How could you with your music blasting like that? Keep it down a little, okay?"

Shelly just shrugged, got up and turned the volume up, almost, but not quite, as loud as it had been, and laid back down on her bed.

Emma did a quick check of Shelly's bathroom and the back staircase but there was no one there and she was beginning to think that she had imagined the whole thing. She went back to the second floor and checked that one more time, but there was still nothing.

Heading back towards the main staircase, she suddenly got chilled to the bone. She was rubbing her arms, trying to warm up when something hit her in the middle of the back. It didn't hurt, but Emma was so surprised that she almost fell down the stairs and had to grab ahold of the banister.

Once she got her balance back, she turned and saw one of the boy's baseballs in the hallway and knew that was what had hit her.

"But, how?" Emma wondered, feeling a little shaky and a little scared. She had just checked the floor for the second time and no one was there. That ball had not been there either, and there was no feasible explanation for how it had flung itself into the air and hit her in the middle of the back.

Emma stared at the baseball for a moment, trying to understand what could have happened. She finally picked it up, tossed it into the boys' room and headed downstairs, grasping the banister hard. She couldn't shake the feeling that something was going to hit her again and she was taking no chances of it knocking her down the stairs.

She headed outside to find Jeremy, meaning to tell him about the incident, but he was busy in the garage with Collin. Emma didn't want to scare the children, so she didn't mention it, but she did find the step ladder while in the garage and got back to work in the Library. She still felt uneasy, but it took a lot of energy to clean the windows and get all those shelves dusted, so by the time she finished cleaning the library, the memory of it seemed more like dream than something that had actually happened. Emma never did end up mentioning it to Jeremy.

\*         \*         \*

By the time the horses arrived later that week, the barn was ready and the house was completely livable, although it would still be awhile before all the necessary repairs were done and everything was in its place.

The horses were acting a little spooky, but that was to be expected after their long trip and with the new surroundings.

Emma was exhausted, but happy. It had been difficult saying good-bye to Jeremy on Sunday evening, knowing that she wouldn't see him again all week. But, here it was, Friday already, and she'd been so busy that she crashed early every night and had hardly noticed that he wasn't there.

The boys were gone most of the day with their new friends and Shelly rarely left her room, where she was still able to keep in touch with her old friends by computer or cell phone, so Emma had plenty of time to get things cleaned up and put away.

Shortly before Jeremy was due home on Friday, the boys were outside playing and Shelly had gone out for a little fresh air herself so Emma decided to take advantage of the empty house and collected all their dirty laundry from where ever they had dropped it. She shook her head in exasperation as she picked some clothes up from the floor right next to the hamper and, of course, when she had to get on her hands and knees to find what was hiding under their beds.

The laundry basket was filled to the brim and Emma struggled to hold it while she opened the basement door and turned on the light switch. She hesitated in the doorway as a cold breeze blew up the stairs towards her, which was impossible because there were no doors or windows in the basement. Jeremy had checked for any broken windows before he left but, obviously there weren't any and he had no explanation for the cold breeze. Jeremy hadn't found the source of the odor either, but at least the horrid smell seemed to have faded. There was still a little tinge of rottenness in the air, but it was not nearly as overpowering as it had been.

The cold wind chilled Emma to the core and she shivered violently. Callie stood beside her, staring down into the gloom, and her low, deep growl did nothing to help settle Emma's nerves.

"It's just a basement, stupid," she said, not sure if she was talking to Callie or to herself. "Seriously, get a grip or we'll never have clean clothes again."

She took a deep breath, straightened her spine and headed down the stairs with Callie right behind her.

The washer and dryer were on the far side of the room, of course. Emma made sure to pull every single chain to turn on the bulbs along the way. Just a little extra light seemed to help settle her down and ease her fears. But it didn't help Callie, because she was still periodically letting out that deep, low growl and the hair along her back was standing up.

"What it is, girl? It's just you and me down here."

Nevertheless, Emma hurried over to the washer and threw as many of the clothes in as it would hold. Panic started to creep up on her as she tossed in some detergent and fabric softener while Callie's growl was getting deeper and louder. Emma turned the machine on and sprinted back to the stairs.

28

Halfway up, the door at the top slammed shut, the noise startling a little scream out of her. Callie escalated from the low growl to a sharp bark as she stared down into the oppressive darkness below them. Emma's heart did a little hop-skip as she ran up the rest of the stairs and she almost wept in relief when the doorknob opened easily in her hands.

"Oh, Callie," she said, hugging the dog hard once they were safely in the kitchen and the door to the basement was securely closed. "I'm so glad that I have you, but why is this place so damned creepy?"

# CHAPTER 4

When Jeremy arrived a short while later, Emma gave him an exuberant greeting and followed him upstairs to help him unpack. Realizing that she probably over-reacted in the basement, she didn't mention her panic attack, but she did appreciate having him home again and didn't want to get too far from his side.

"So, how did you make out on your own this week?" she asked, wrapping her arms around his waist.

"It was different, to say the least. Unfortunately, I think I'll probably gain a ton of weight on my own. All I did was takeout and it wasn't exactly health food."

She stepped back and eyed his tall, slim physique critically. "You still look pretty good to me."

"Later, tiger," he whispered in her ear, throwing his suit coat onto the bed and heading into the bathroom to clean up before dinner.

"Who's Lori?" Emma asked, when Jeremy returned to the bedroom a few minutes later.

He stopped abruptly. "Who?"

"Lori, there's a note on the bed next to your suit jacket and it says 'Lori 7pm, don't be late'."

"What are you doing going through my things?" Jeremy's jaw was set and his face flushed in anger.

"I wasn't, it was lying on the bed, next to your jacket. Why are you being like that?"

"Like what? Don't expect me to believe that note just fell out of the inside pocket of my jacket. If you have a question, just ask, don't go snooping through my things."

He grabbed the note out of her hand and left the room.

Emma stood rooted to spot, twisting her ring around her finger and wondering what the devil had just happened. When she found the note lying on the bed, she'd assumed that it was something to do with work and was just being curious. His reaction indicated something else, and she suddenly felt like she'd been punched in the stomach and had to sit down on the bed for a few moments.

"He couldn't possibly have something going on with this person, could he?" she wondered, her stomach now doing flip-flops.

"Of course not," Emma assured herself. "He would never do that. It's just been a long, stressful week for both of us and he overreacted."

But she didn't believe a word of it. Jeremy had never acted like that before and she knew it wasn't because he was tired or because he over-reacted. And yet, she couldn't bring herself to accept the alternative, so she decided to let it go for now and walked downstairs to finish preparing their special reunion dinner.

They enjoyed their dinner together, spaghetti and meatballs with cheesy garlic bread had always been a family favorite. After just a short period of time, Jeremy's mood improved and he was his usual charming self, teasing the kids and making them laugh with silly stories about what had happened at Court that week. Even Shelly smiled a couple of times and joined in the conversation.

Emma was noticeably quieter than usual and later, as she was cleaning up, Jeremy came over to help.

"I'm sorry, Em. I'm just a little frazzled with everything going on this week, work's been a bear and being away from all of you took quite a toll on me. Forgive me, please?"

He was so damned handsome and those sparkling blue eyes were completely mesmerizing when he caught you with them. Jeremy also knew that every time he gave her that sad, puppy dog look with his baby blues all wide and angelic, that she would inevitably give in to him.

"Of course, we're all a little edgy," Emma replied. She sounded sincere, but Jeremy could tell that her heart wasn't really in it and was surprised that he hadn't been able to bring her around.

Emma knew this man well and she loved him with all her heart. Deep down, she knew that he would never do anything to hurt her, or their family, but, for some reason, the icy pit in her belly just wouldn't melt away.

*     *     *

"Jeremy, Jeremy, wake up. Did you hear that?" It was about three am on Sunday morning and a loud, banging noise startled Emma awake.

"Humpf, what?"

"Jeremy, wake up, something just made a huge crashing noise. I think it came from upstairs."

"Couldn't have been anything serious, I never heard it." He rolled over and went back to sleep.

"Asshole," she whispered, then shrugged on her bathrobe and slipped out into the hall. She didn't hear anything else, but her heart was still beating erratically and the house was freezing again. Callie was at Emma's side, she was never more than a few steps away ever since she'd finally been coaxed into the house.

Emma looked in the boys' room and they were both sound asleep. She wondered if maybe it had just been a dream after all, since no one else seemed to have heard it. But it had sounded real enough to her and when she woke up, Callie's hair was standing on end and she was staring intently out the bedroom door, so Callie obviously heard something, too.

She turned the light on in the hall and made her way to the third floor where she could vaguely hear a rustling sound. Callie let out a low growl but Emma shushed her.

From the doorway, Emma could see that Shelly was lying on her bed. She blinked hard as she realized the blankets and top sheet over Shelly were slowly sliding towards the end of the bed, making the same rustling sound that she'd heard on the stairway. Shelly remained perfectly still, sound asleep and not moving a muscle.

Emma was frozen, unable to move, not even sure of what she was seeing. Callie suddenly let out a sharp bark, startling Emma and waking Shelly.

"Mom, what are doing?" Shelly grumbled. "Turn off the light, it's blinding me. Why did you take the blankets off me? It's cold in here."

Shelly shivered and reached down to pull the sheet and blankets back up under her chin. Then she suddenly sat up straight.

"Where's Smoky?"

Emma finally found her voice. "I don't know, honey. I haven't seen her. Maybe that loud bang scared her and she ran away, didn't you hear anything?"

"There was no noise up here, I have to find her though."

Shelly got out of bed and walked towards Emma, who gasped loudly just as Callie began to whine.

A dark shadow rose up just behind Shelly. It was difficult to identify, or to describe, it was darker than the normal shadows in the room and seemed to move of its own volition. It hovered over Shelly, wavered, and then faded away.

"What is it, Mom? You look like you've seen a ghost. Will you help me find Smoky?"

"Um," Emma was speechless. When her heart finally started to beat again, it felt like a jackhammer tearing at her chest. She was unable to process what she had just seen and had to take a deep breath and try to get herself under control.

"Sure, you go on downstairs, I'll be right there." After Shelly left, she turned all the lights on in the room, looking under the bed, in the closet, anywhere someone, or something, could be hiding. There was nothing other than an indescribable chill in the air and the faint odor of something rotting.

They scoured the house until they found Smoky curled into a frightened little ball under one of the chairs in the living room. She scratched Shelly when she tried to drag the cat out from underneath it, and began to hiss and struggle violently to get out of her arms when Shelly carried her towards the stairs.

"Mom, why is she acting like this?" Shelly finally gave up the fight and dropped the cat, who scurried back to safety in the living room.

"I don't know, honey, something must have scared her." Emma felt her heart trip again, she couldn't get the picture of that eerie, dark shadow hovering over Shelly out of her head. Emma was as frightened as the cat, but she didn't know what to do. She couldn't let her daughter go back up into that bedroom, but the whole thing sounded crazy, even to herself. She'd talk it over with Jeremy in the morning and they'd find out what was going on, but she still had to figure out what to do right now.

"Why don't I grab some blankets and pillows and we'll sleep on the couches tonight. Smoky will know we're here for her when she gets over her fright."

"Okay, that would be good," Shelly conceded. Emma was relieved that, at least for tonight, she could watch over her daughter and keep her safe.

It helped having Callie resting on the floor nearby. She paced the living room occasionally, patrolling, but never seemed to find anything to concern her. Even so, Emma slept very little the rest of that night.

\*     \*     \*

Emma waited until after the kids had eaten breakfast the next morning and she and Jeremy were left alone to sip their coffee before broaching the subject.

"Honey, do you remember me waking up in the middle of the night?"

"Sure, you were dreaming about some sort of loud noise."

"I don't think it was a dream, Callie heard it too. It's weird, though, no one but she and I did hear it, and it got even stranger when I went upstairs to check on Shelly."

"What do you mean?"

"Well, it's hard to explain, but I swear that I saw her sheet and bedspread being pulled down to the bottom of her bed, while she was still sound asleep. And I didn't see anything that could be doing it until Shelly got up and came towards me, then I saw this dark, strange shadow thing right behind her for a moment, and then it just disappeared.

"What the hell are you talking about?"

"I don't really know," Emma stated with exasperation, not getting the reaction that she had expected. "Something bad was in that room."

"Something bad? A loud noise that no one else heard, a weird shadow, how very unexpected with the hall light shining into a dark room. Come on, Emma, enough with the histrionics, that's just silly."

"What about the sheets and bedspread?"

"Again, it was shadowy in the room, how do you know Shelly wasn't kicking them off herself? There's no boogeyman here, Em. What's really going on with you?"

In the light of day her fears did seem a little foolish, but they were very real the night before, and Callie had experienced it, too. That made Emma feel a little more sure of herself, but it wasn't a good enough argument to use on her husband, the lawyer.

"Forget about it, I guess it was my imagination."

"Seriously, Em. What's going on? You don't seem like yourself lately. Have you been drinking?"

"What? You think I got tanked last night after you went to sleep and then hallucinated all this?"

"There is no 'all this', Emma. That's the problem."

"Okay, I really don't need this from you right now. Maybe you'd better leave for the city early today."

"Fine, is my laundry done?"

Emma gave him a smoldering look. "Do your own damn laundry."

She turned and walked out the back door with Callie on her heels. Jeremy was gone by the time they returned.

*       *       *

Emma didn't sleep well again that night and was up frequently to check on the boys and Shelly. There were no more strange or unusual occurrences, but she was pretty logy the next morning.

"Mom, you burnt my bacon," Collin complained when she put his plate down in front of him.

"I'm sorry, honey, but I think it's still edible, right?"

"I suppose," he grumbled.

"What are you two up to today?" Emma asked, sipping a nice, strong cup of coffee.

"There's gonna be a baseball game this morning."

"Nice, at the park down the street?"

"Yup," James replied, wolfing down his breakfast. "We're going to be late too, Collin, so hurry up. If we're late, we won't get picked for the good team, come on."

"Okay, okay." Collin cleaned up the rest of his plate, grabbed his glove and ran out the door after his brother.

"Have fun," Emma called after them, then added quietly, "Nice talking to you."

Shelly had been down for a glass of juice and piece of toast and was already back in her room tweeting or Facebooking, or whatever it was that she did all day. Emma didn't plan on seeing her again until lunchtime. She was still unnerved about what had happened in Shelly's room the other night but, apparently, Shelly wasn't noticing anything unusual, so Emma tried not to worry about it.

She finished her coffee and headed upstairs for a long, hot shower, hoping that would help her wake up.

Emma let the hot water pulse over her for a long time, thinking about nothing but how good it felt. That feeling left her immediately when she pulled back the shower curtain and stepped out of the claw-footed tub. She literally felt her heart stop beating in her chest and was unable to draw a full breath, as she stared mindlessly at the word "DIE" written childishly in the steam of the medicine cabinet mirror, and then she began to tremble uncontrollably. Wrapping herself in a towel, she ran to her bedroom and crawled under the quilt, sobbing quietly until she was completely drained and finally able to stop shaking.

Once she had herself back under control, Emma forced herself to walk back into the bathroom. The steam had cleared and there was no longer evidence of any words written on the mirror. She knew she had seen it, but now began to question herself. Was that word really written there? She had only glanced at it quickly before running out of the room in a panic, and she had pretty much been sleep walking most of the morning as it was, so now she wasn't sure what she had seen. She wasn't sure of anything at all, for that matter.

She wanted to call Jeremy and tell him what had happened but, after the way they'd left things yesterday, Emma didn't believe he would be very receptive to hearing about this and might even think that she'd made it up.

Things only got worse when she went out to take care of the horses.

"What the devil happened here?" Emma asked, staring around the barn. There were five stalls and the three horses were always in the same ones. First Charlie, then Sam, and then Prince, right down the line. But, they were all in the wrong place, not even in the stalls they used for them.

Prince, the little Shetland pony they'd gotten for the kids when they were younger, was in the farthest stall, where there was no bedding, no water, and the tack was piled up in one corner. The poor thing was just cowering behind the tack with his head and tail hanging down.

All of the horses were nervous. Charlie was a high-strung thoroughbred, a large bay who was strikingly handsome and very high energy. He was a handful and only Emma was able to ride him. Charlie's neck was covered in foamy sweat and he was snorting and striking the floorboards repeatedly with his front hoof.

Sam was a chestnut quarter horse, quiet, patient and easy to handle. They bought him for Shelly a couple of years ago, when she outgrew Prince. Right now, Sam was pacing in small circles around and around the stall he'd been put into.

"Poor babies," Emma murmured, as she went and stroked them one at a time, trying to calm them down. She fed and watered each of them and then took them out to the paddock. Once outside they seemed more like themselves and Emma sighed in relief.

She stood there watching them for the longest time, her concern fading and her anger growing. Each stall door was latched with a bolt, there was no way the horses could open the stalls themselves. She never locked the barn door, why should they need to? But, now she was furious, someone had come into her barn and intentionally tormented her animals.

Emma had no idea how she could find out who had done it, but she strode back into the house with purpose, left a brief note for the kids, grabbed her car keys and headed to the local hardware store.

At the store, she picked up a heavy duty padlock for the barn door. As she was walking down one of the aisles towards the checkout, she spotted a motion-activated camera. Jeremy would have a fit at how much it cost, but she bought it anyway.

When Emma got home, she spent the rest of the morning figuring out how to use the camera and getting it situated in a nearby tree at approximately the right distance away. She'd find out who the little bastards were that were messing with her horses, and they would be sorry they ever stepped foot on her property.

# CHAPTER 5

Nothing unusual happened over the next few days. Everything was quiet, the boys were busy with their new friends and Shelly was still spending most of her time in her room. Emma was somewhat encouraged by the fact that Shelly was at least getting outside occasionally and enjoying the beautiful weather by taking a walk around the neighborhood. She hated to see Shelly waste her entire summer locked up in her room, but whenever Emma tried to get her to come and do something, Shelly always refused and she said was too busy.

Emma made sure all of the stalls were properly bolted and the padlock secured on the door when she put the horses in their stalls every night.

There were no further disturbances in the barn until Friday morning, when Emma was shocked to find each of the horses in the wrong stall, again. She'd unlocked the padlock herself, it hadn't been tampered with and the door was securely locked. She walked around the barn, but could find no holes or loose boards that would have allowed someone access.

The lights in the barn flickered momentarily and Emma suddenly felt a deep chill in the air. The horses started snorting, their nostrils flared and their eyes rolled until the whites showed. Emma felt unaccountably frightened, although there was nothing there to be afraid of.

The feeling was so intense that she wanted to run back into the house and hide in bed with the covers pulled over her head, but she couldn't leave her babies out here like this.

Taking a deep, steadying breath, Emma brought some grain and water to each of the horses, but they wouldn't touch either of them. Trying to calm them down, she led them to the paddock one at a time. She saved Charlie for last, since he was the most agitated. She had just clipped the lead to his halter and was walking him toward the open door when the air became so cold that she could see her own breath and she suddenly felt a tremendous push in the middle of her back.

With an 'umph' she fell forward to the ground. Charlie whinnied and rose on his hind legs. Emma froze as she saw those huge hooves coming down towards her face. They thumped to the floor, raising clouds of dust and missing her head by mere inches, then he thundered through the barn door and down the driveway.

"Oh, Charlie, no," Emma screamed, as he ran straight towards the road. She jumped up and ran after him, yelling his name, praying he would respond to her voice. But he continued to run blindly with the long lead trailing behind him. Emma could only be grateful that they lived on a dead end street and that there was very little traffic at this time of the day.

Charlie continued running down the road a short distance and then veered right into a field. Her other horses were whinnying in the paddock and, when he heard them, Charlie whirled back in the direction of the house, running at top speed through the field.

Emma slowed down, there was no way she could catch him and it looked like he was coming back towards their paddock, so she waited where she was and watched him make his way back to them.

Charlie had almost reached the paddock when he suddenly stumbled forward and went down in a patch of long weeds. His screams of pain were bone-chilling and Emma sprinted over to him, ignoring the stitch in her side and her labored breathing. Charlie was on the ground when she got to him, his right front leg had gone into a hole of some sort and looked like it might be broken. He kept trying to get up and, at first, she tried to keep him down, but then realized that she couldn't just leave him here in the middle of the field.

Eventually, she was able to help him up and they slowly made their way back to the barn. Charlie balked at being led in, but she had no choice and locked him in a stall while she ran to the house to call the local veterinary.

He arrived a short time later, a frail, elderly man with kind eyes and steady hands.

"Oh, my," Dr. Ferrell said, as he gently ran his hand over Charlie's leg, "I'm pretty sure it's broken."

Emma's breath caught in her throat and she fought back tears as the doctor continued to examine Charlie.

He finally stood and shook his head sadly. "There's no easy way to say this to you, but he's going to have to have surgery or else we'll have to put him down. I can get you some information on the costs, but a decision will have to be made rather quickly."

"No, that's okay." Emma didn't hesitate. "Will you be able to transport him to your facility for the surgery?"

Dr. Ferrell nodded. "I'll get my crew out here and we'll get him all padded up for the trip. It'll be expensive, you know, I can get you an estimate."

"I don't care how much it costs, please just do what you have to for him."

"Okay, we'll be back shortly to get him."

Emma stayed in the barn, comforting Charlie as best she could. The sedative he'd been given helped keep him fairly calm, but he was obviously still in a great deal of pain.

After Dr. Ferrell and his staff returned, gently loaded Charlie and drove off to the clinic, Emma leaned back and slid slowly down to the floor. Bringing her hands up over her eyes, she began to weep, with sadness, with fear and with confusion, unable to stop until she had no tears left and her voice was completely hoarse.

\*　　　\*　　　\*

"Calm down, Emma," Jeremy said. He had just arrived home from the city and was exhausted. She was still teary-eyed as she tried to explain what had happened, and it was making no sense at all to Jeremy.

"What do you mean someone pushed you? Was there someone in the barn?"

"No, that's the bizarre part. No one was there, but something hit me in the back and made me fall and lose the line. Otherwise, Charlie would never have gotten away. Something weird is going on in this place. It's not the first odd thing, there are cold spots, doors opening and closing, sometimes I swear I feel someone watching me or touching me when no one else is in the room."

Her voice was rising as she spoke. Emma realized it and took a deep breath, trying to get herself back under control before she became completely hysterical.

"Emma, it's just your imagination. Have you been drinking a lot?" he asked, nodding his head toward the glass of wine in her hand.

"Are you kidding, is that going to be your pat response to everything? No, I have not been drinking a lot. I opened that bottle," she nodded to the open bottle on the counter, "about a half an hour ago because it's been a really shit day and I feel confused and sad, and now, really angry on top of everything else. Why won't you take me seriously about these things? They really are happening, you know, I'm not going crazy and I'm not drunk."

"Em, please try to understand where I'm coming from." God, she hated it when he got all lawyerly with her. "You are talking about seeing things that aren't there, being pushed, being touched, by someone or something that isn't there. You tell me, how can I take that seriously? Nothing has happened to the rest of us, so how do you explain why these things are only happening to you? I'm just asking you to put it in perspective, could it have anything to do with the stress of moving here, starting all over? Or are you just trying to punish me because of the apartment?"

As if it was happening to someone else, Emma felt her mouth drop open and her eyes widen in disbelief, she could not believe the words that had come out of his mouth. She had loved this man with her whole being for twenty years and she was just now realizing that she didn't even know who he was. The fact that he was not just completely discounting what she was going through but, somehow, was able to turn it around and make it about him, just boggled her mind.

"Em?"

"Jeremy, I am not making any of this up and it has absolutely nothing to do with you. It is happening and, if you can't give me the benefit of the doubt and help me find some answers, then I do not want to discuss it with you anymore. But, if anything bad happens to my children, that lands on you and I will never forgive you for it."

She grabbed Callie's leash and walked out the back door. They wandered for a bit while Emma tried to straighten things out in her own mind.

"Hey, Emma."

She looked up from her musings to see Lynne sitting on her porch swing, waving crazily at her.

Emma smiled and made her way up the sidewalk.

"It's so good to see you. Come on in and bring your scary-looking doggie, too."

Lynne was as vivacious as ever, but she could see that something was troubling Emma.

"What's going on, you look like someone just fired your favorite hairdresser."

It would crush Emma if Lynne also thought she was crazy, but she decided to take a chance and unburden herself anyway.

"You'll probably think I'm out of mind, too," she began hesitantly.

"Ergo, someone has already determined that and told you as much, correct?" Lynne interrupted.

"Yes, Jeremy thinks I am either bona fide crazy or have turned into the town drunk."

"What's going on?" Lynne asked with genuine concern.

They were interrupted by several sharp, little yaps as Lynne's, Porky, discovered that Callie was in the house. The little dog was a wide as it was tall and full of bravado. Thankfully, Callie was polite and, once the two dogs got a good sniff of one another, they were fine together and the little one waddled along behind Callie as she went to explore the rest of the house.

Emma was going to call Callie back, but Lynne waved her down onto the sofa. "She's fine, there's nothing she can get into and she'll keep my little Porky out of our hair. Now, what's going on?"

"Well, where do I start?" Emma asked with a harsh little laugh. "It's just crazy, there have been all of these strange things happening at the house, and I just don't know what to do or what to think anymore. Maybe I am just losing my mind."

"Strange things, like what?"

"Loud banging in the night, cold spots, feeling like someone is touching me when no one is there, pictures falling or being turned upside down on the wall, I could go on and on. Just small things at first, but then today something actually knocked me down when I was in the barn, my horse got loose and ended up breaking his leg. It was horrible."

"I'm so sorry about your horse, are you okay?"

Emma just nodded, afraid that she would start crying again if she spoke.

"Well," Lynne said, "I'm thinking that maybe those stories about your place being haunted aren't so crazy right now. Let me see," she said, her brow creased in concentration as she tried to figure out a solution. "I know that in all the movies I've seen about haunted houses, the first thing they do is look up the history of the home. I'm doing an open house all day tomorrow and the library isn't open on Sunday, so let's make a date for Monday morning and we'll start our research."

"So, you believe me?"

"Of course, why wouldn't I?"

"Thank you for that. Now, I've never been much for scary movies, so how will learning the history of the house help us?"

"I don't know exactly, but knowledge is power, right? At the least, it's some place to start. Have you talked to your kids about these weird occurrences?"

"No, I don't want to scare them."

"How do you know that things haven't been happening to them, too? I know your boys kind of keep things to themselves and your daughter is very anti-parent right now. You might want to talk to them and find out. If things have happened to them too, then your husband won't have any choice but to be more open-minded about all of this."

"Fat chance of that," Emma replied with a smile. "But it's a good idea. I just don't want to worry them unnecessarily."

Her cell phone rang at that moment.

"Jeremy," she said quietly, staring down at the screen.

"Answer it, hon. He's probably worried about you. We'll talk Monday morning."

Emma answered the phone as she and Callie walked down the path to the sidewalk. "Yes."

"Where are you? I was starting to get concerned. Are you alright?"

"I'm fine, I'll be home in a couple of minutes."

"Good, I do want you to talk to me about this, maybe I was being a bit too judgmental."

"Ya think?" she wanted to respond, but didn't, knowing that it would ruin any chance they had to work this out together.

*    *    *

"So, talk to me."

Jeremy led Emma over to the loveseat in the living room and put his arm around her. Lifting her chin towards him, he kissed her gently and then sat back, giving her his full attention.

Emma just wanted to cry, again, but she had no tears left. This time it was because Jeremy had been acting like such a jerk, but now he was back to being his old self, loving, tender and supportive. It was exactly what she needed, but it was also throwing her completely off balance.

The boys had gone to bed and Shelly was in her room, so they had the house to themselves. Emma tried to pull herself together so that she could try to explain, rationally, what she had been experiencing. She had to get him to accept that these things were actually happening.

"Jeremy, I just need you to listen, maybe some of this can be explained, but I don't think all of it can. I'm scared, Jeremy, and I need you."

"I'm here, Em, and I'm sorry I was being such an ass, but you know me, if I don't see it, it isn't there."

"I know, but you also know I'm not an alcoholic, I don't have a flighty imagination and I do not make up things just to punish you."

"I do know all of that," he conceded, brushing a lock of her thick blonde hair off of her face. "and I apologize, I didn't handle any of this well. I guess that I've just been trying to come up with an explanation that I can understand. I've been under a lot of stress myself and that's my only excuse. So, tell me everything again and, this time, I really will listen and try to help."

Emma started going through all of the odd things that had been happening when Callie, who had been lying at her feet, suddenly sat up and began that low growl deep in her chest. The hair all along her spine was standing erect and she was staring at one of the living room walls. Chance suddenly jumped up out of a sound sleep and looked towards the same wall. He began to bark frantically and then started turning in a slow circle, almost as if he was watching something that was moving around the room.

Both Emma and Jeremy stopped talking and watched Chance. He started to run around the room, barking loudly at something they could not see. Callie never moved from Emma's side, but she turned her body, her eyes following the same thing that Chance seemed to be chasing after, her deep growl continuing the entire time.

Chance ran around the room, zig-zagging, circling the furniture, he looked absolutely insane. His speed increased and he ran straight at the wall and slammed into it. Chance hit it so hard that he stopped barking and sagged to the ground, slowly shaking his head. At the same time, the hair on Callie's neck and back went down, she stopped growling and the strange charge in the air disappeared.

Emma ran over to Chance, petted him gently and ran her hands over him to be sure he wasn't hurt anywhere. He never whined or cried and seemed okay, apparently his head was harder than you might imagine, since he didn't appear to have any significant injury.

"Was that something you could consider seeing with your own eyes?" Emma's voice was trembling as she turned to Jeremy, tears shimmering in her eyes.

He just sat silently on the couch, watching her and Chance, trying to process what had just happened.

"It's almost as if whatever he was chasing disappeared through the wall," Jeremy finally stated. "I don't get it. There are no such things as ghosts."

"Well, maybe there are. What do we do now?"

"I don't know, honey. I don't know. This is crazy."

"I know it is, but I'm starting to get really scared, Jeremy."

"Have the kids noticed anything?"

"None of them have said anything, and I haven't brought it up because I didn't want to scare them."

"Let's talk to them tomorrow, we won't say anything about this, we'll just try to find out if they've been experiencing anything out of the ordinary."

## CHAPTER 6

"Pancakes for breakfast, boys. One of you run upstairs and get your sister down here before the kitchen closes."

Jeremy was having fun, flipping pancakes and trying to avoid a serious grease burn from the bacon at the same time.

Emma giggled as she sat at the table, watching him and sipping her coffee. The red checkered apron he had on was several sizes too small and looked positively silly over his golf shirt and chinos.

For the briefest of moments, Emma allowed herself to forget all the craziness and just relax and enjoy herself.

"Collin," Jeremy asked, as he placed a plate of pancakes and bacon down in front of him with a flourish, "does this meet with your approval?"

"Looks great, Dad," Collin replied, pouring what looked like about a half a bottle of syrup onto the stack.

James and Shelly came stomping down the back staircase and Jeremy served them just as theatrically. Emma waved away the proffered plate and just continued to sip at her coffee.

Jeremy sat down and started to dig into his own short stack, looking around the table, enjoying seeing his family all together like this.

Emma felt at peace for the first time in a long time, but then Jeremy started asking the kids questions and her heart skipped a beat, her stomach clenched, and reality came screaming back.

"So, James, tell me, what's going on? What do you like here? What don't you like?"

James finished chewing his mouthful of pancake, then replied, "I like the kids we met. I don't like the baseball team we got on."

"What about the house, everything okay here?"

"Yeah." He reached for the syrup and concentrated on saturating the rest of his pancakes, apparently having nothing further to add.

"And you, Collin? Likes? Dislikes?"

"Same as James."

"Interesting," Jeremy responded, and Emma could hear the frustration seeping into his voice. "Do you like the house?"

"Sure."

"No problems with your room or anything?"

"No, it's a lotta lawn to mow though."

"Shelly, what about you?" Jeremy's voice was definitely getting edgy.

"Well, the room is nice, but as I've told Mom several times, I need the walls painted, I need new curtains, new bedding and I should have a complete new bedroom set to go in such a big room. It just looks so bare like it is now."

Jeremy couldn't help but smile. "We'll see what we can do about that, Shelly, but money's a little tight right now, we've had a lot of unexpected expenses."

After the kids finished eating and headed off to do their own things, Jeremy started to complain.

"It's impossible to have a conversation with either of those boys, since they are apparently only able to converse in words with no more than one syllable. As for Shelly, I should have seen that coming before I even opened my mouth."

"Maybe it's good thing," Emma replied. "Maybe that means nothing has happened to any of them."

"Or they are too scared to talk about it."

"Don't say that," Emma responded, her voice uncharacteristically shaky.

"So what now, Em? Even considering what happened with Chance last night, I'm hard pressed to accept the fact that we are being haunted."

"I know, it seems silly in the middle of the day, but these things are really happening."

"I believe you. I'm just at a loss as far as what we do about it."

"Let's see what Lynne and I come up with at the library on Monday, then we can figure it out from there."

"I still don't understand why you had to share our business with the neighbors."

"I only talked to Lynne and, if you recall, I had no one else that would listen to me."

Jeremy's eyes hardened and he just stared at Emma for a moment.

"Are you alright with me going to the apartment tomorrow night?"

Emma didn't answer for a moment. She desperately wanted to ask him to stay at the house with them, but was afraid he would just get angry and leave anyway.

"Em?"

"Yes, you can go, but if anything happens and I call to ask to you to come home, you have to promise me that you will."

"I promise." Jeremy relented and pulled her close against him, kissing the top of her head. "I will be here as quickly as I can if anything happens and you need me."

*     *     *

As much as Emma dreaded the thought of going into the basement again, the laundry needed to be done so, shortly after Jeremy left for the apartment on Sunday afternoon, Emma began to collect all of their dirty clothes.

"Ugh," she exclaimed, when she reached into the boys' hamper and grabbed a handful of wet sheet. She tossed it into the basket and delicately reached for the wet pajama bottoms right under it. They belonged to James and he hadn't wet to bed since he was four years old.

Emma didn't want to embarrass him in front of the other children so, after dinner was done, she asked if he would walk out to the barn with her to take care of the horses. James grumbled and groaned, but did come out with her and Callie.

They watered and fed the horses and were doing a final check on them when she broached the bed-wetting subject.

"So, honey, did you have an accident last night? Why didn't you tell me?"

He remained quiet, staring at the ground with his cheeks blossoming pink. Emma was afraid that he wasn't going to talk to her about it at all.

"I felt stupid, I haven't peed to bed since I was a baby."

"Accidents happen sometimes, it's nothing to be embarrassed about."

James still wouldn't look her in the eye, his head hung down and he continually kicked at one of the bales of hay.

"Not to me," he said in a very small voice.

"Can you tell me what happened? A bad dream, maybe?"

He sighed. "I woke up because I had to pee. I heard something, but I couldn't see anything. The bulb must have burned out in the nightlight and it was just so dark and there was this noise."

"What kind of noise?"

"I don't know exactly, not loud or banging, but like a swooshing or slithering sound. Made me think of snakes, so I didn't want to get out of my bed."

Emma wanted so badly to comfort him, he was still her baby, after all. It broke her heart to think of him being so afraid to get up and go to the bathroom, that he allowed himself to do it in his bed. But, James was still very embarrassed and wouldn't even look at her, so she fought her motherly instincts and stayed back away from him.

"Have you heard that noise before?"

"Not that noise."

"What kind noises have you heard?"

"Sometimes a bang, sometimes it sounds like something scratching on the inside of the walls. Sometimes I hear a monkey, but I never see it. Collin and me looked, but we couldn't find it."

"You've both heard something that sounds like a monkey?"

He nodded his head.

"Has anything else happened, besides the noises?"

"Little things, sometimes my stuff isn't where I put it, and once my ball came bouncing down the hall at me, but I don't know who threw it. There was no one there."

Little fingers of fear crept up Emma's spine. "How come you didn't tell me?"

He just shrugged. "Mom, are ghosts mean?"

"I, I don't know. Why do you ask? Do you think that ghosts are doing those things?"

"Robbie and Jeff told us that there are ghosts in our house. They said the ghosts are mad because they're dead, so they're mean to people that are still alive."

"And how do Robbie and Jeff know all that?"

"They said they knew a boy that used to live in our house that died. They said the ghosts killed him."

"Oh, James." Emma couldn't hold back any further and folded him into her arms. He gripped her tightly around the waist and her heart clenched when she realized just how frightened he was.

"Please don't listen to those silly boys. Nothing is going to hurt you. I won't let them, and neither will Callie," Emma added uneasily, watching as the hair stood up on Callie's back and she began that low, deep, growl again. The horses started snorting and stomping their feet and the air suddenly felt strange, heavy, and very, very cold.

"Come on, Hon, let's go back in the house."

*       *       *

Emma went out to take care of the horses the next morning and found them once again in the wrong stalls. This time they were exhausted, completely worn out, and she couldn't begin to imagine what they'd been through. Their coats were dull, their heads hung low and their tails drooped.

Both of them became a little livelier when they got to the paddock, but Emma decided then and there, that she would not let them spend another night in that barn. Charlie's surgery was successful and he would be staying at the vet clinic until the break in his leg was completely healed, so Emma only had to find another place for Prince and Sam.

She hurried inside and turned on her computer. There was a small stable which wasn't too far away, and Emma was relieved to learn that they had openings and could pick up the horses that afternoon. Normally, she would have spent more time looking into the quality of the stable, but she didn't have time to be picky and doubted that it could be any worse than what they'd been through in this barn. Once that decision was made, it relieved some of her anxiety, but now she had to figure out how to keep the rest of the family safe.

*       *       *

"Aren't you a little overdressed for the library?" Emma asked, as Lynne jumped into passenger seat of her van.

"Of course not," she replied. "I'm a Real Estate agent. I have to be ready for that emergency call to come in and ready to make that sale, any time, night or day."

"Wow, you sound like some kind of superhero, but you do look great, the colors in that scarf are amazing. It really makes the outfit."

"You're no slouch yourself," Lynne replied. "You've got that casual, sexy thing going on with your tight little jeans and that pretty silk blouse."

"Unfortunately, pretty much all I own are jeans. It's been so long since I've gotten dressed up and gone out, that I can't even remember when the last time was."

"Sounds like you and the hubby need a date night."

"You know, that's a great idea, I really think that is what we need, especially with all this crazy stuff going on."

"I'd be happy to watch the kids, as long as it's at my house, not yours."

"Thanks, I may take you up on that."

"Here's the library, on the right, just past the Town Hall."

"It's silent as a tomb in here." Emma whispered to Lynne a few minutes later, as they entered the antiquated library.

"Well, silly, what did you expect? No one actually reads books any more. But, we need local history, actual pen to paper information. Hopefully, we'll be able to find something here that will help."

The Librarian, Mrs. McGillicuddy, was tall, slim and bespectacled, and extremely helpful. She showed them where the archives for local history were located and then helped them begin their search.

"Okay, I think this is it." Lynne looked over at Emma excitedly. "The Creeghan House, located at, your address, was built in 1894 by Joshua Creeghan, a Colonel in the Confederate army. Their family plantation was lost in the war and he decided it was time to move north, where he felt it would be easier to earn a living and to live in the manner to which he had been accustomed."

"That explains the old plantation manor feel to the house. Is there anything else?"

"He lived there with his wife, Jocelyn, who gave him three children, one girl and two boys." Lynne hesitated. "Just like your family Emma."

"Don't get crazy on me, that's just a coincidence."

"Apparently, Joshua got a bit eccentric as he got older. He would invite most of the town over to some very extravagant balls, just like the good old days back at the plantation. Oh, my!"

"What?"

"In 1918, he threw a very exclusive party for only the elite in the community. There were some circus acts brought in for entertainment and some of the animals got loose and killed and or maimed numerous guests."

"Oh, my God."

"Then," Lynne's eyes were scanning the article furiously, "a mysterious fire broke out at Creeghan House a few days later. No one knows what happened but they suspected arson, possibly from a relative of someone who was injured or killed at the party. No suspect was ever apprehended."

"The house burnt almost to the ground and the entire family, except the oldest son, Jonathan, died in the fire."

"Wow, I guess there could be quite a few ghosts in the house then."

"Sounds like it. There's just one more paragraph, Jonathan rebuilt the house and lived there until he died in 1938."

"So, how did Joshua, or even Jonathan for that matter, earn a living?"

"It doesn't say anything about that."

"Okay, it's creepy and sad, but how does this help us?"

"I have no clue," Lynne replied with the utmost sincerity. Emma thought about it for a few minutes as she browsed over the article again.

"Let's go over to the County Clerk's office and get the records on who has owned the house since Jonathan died and we can try to find some articles on them. I don't know what else to try."

"Let's do it. Can't hurt, right?"

The next couple of hours flew by as they gathered information on the previous owners.

"Darn," Emma stated, checking her wristwatch. "I forgot all about the people from the new stable coming to pick up the horses. They'll be there in just a little bit, so I guess we'd better get going. We have their names and the dates they lived there, so I'll have to see what else I can find online tonight."

# CHAPTER 7

After taking care of the horses, the kids and dinner, Emma curled up on the couch with her laptop and the list of previous owners.

It was odd, dozens of families had owned the house over the almost eighty years since Jonathan died, yet none of them lived in it over a year, and many moved out within just a few months of purchasing it. The house stood vacant more years than it was occupied.

Emma started googling the prior owner's names but had no hits until 1973, when the Lord family owned the house. They apparently moved out and sold it after six months when their youngest child, Susan, age four, climbed onto the roof from a third floor window and fell to her death.

In 1987, the Martin Johnson family resided in the house for three months, until their youngest child, Matthew, age seven, fell down the back staircase, broke his neck and died.

In 1996, the house was owned by Jan and Caleb Rogers. The Rogers' were arrested and convicted of child neglect and abuse after their six-year-old daughter, Stephanie, was found battered, beaten and near death in the locked basement.

Both parents insisted they were innocent and that someone, or something, was in the basement with Stephanie, that the door was bolted from the basement side and they couldn't get to her. The arresting officer testified that there was no bolt or lock from the basement side of the door and that it had opened easily when he turned the knob.

In 2009, the Marvin Walters family bought the house. They moved out later that same year, after their son, Marvin, Jr., age six, fell down the main staircase, broke his neck and died.

Emma shuddered. That must be the boy that James' and Collin's friends told them about.

The house had stood empty since then. Emma's chest was tight and her hand trembled as she read the articles. Callie whined nervously, sensing her fear.

"Oh Callie, what do we do? Whatever it is, it's going after the children."

*　　　*　　　*

They met at Lynne's house for coffee the next morning and Emma told her about the articles that she'd found. Lynne couldn't help but notice that Emma's brilliant green eyes looked huge in her gaunt, pale face.

"Emma, there's no need to panic. You are obviously getting yourself way too worked up about this. You look like hell, aren't you sleeping at all?"

Before she could respond, the shrill cry of a baby came piercing through the monitor sitting on the end table. Emma hadn't even noticed it and looked at Lynne curiously.

"It's Cecilia, my husband's daughter."

"What's she doing here?"

"Well," Lynne hesitated, and looked a little embarrassed, "the girlfriend kicked him out and he didn't have anywhere to go, so I'm letting him stay here with us."

"Why?"

"Actually, he's a big help, with the lawn and things like that. And, to tell you the truth, Emma, with all this creepy stuff going on lately, I kind of like the company."

"Is Cecilia staying here, too?"

"No, she's just visiting. Don't get me wrong, she's a smart, cute kid, but my baby days are done. Mike ran to the store for me. Let me run up and check on Cecelia, she probably just dropped her binky, yet again."

Emma smiled for the first time in several days, but sobered quickly as she got back to the subject at hand.

"So, where were we?" Lynne asked, as she returned a few minutes later and sat down across from Emma.

"Nowhere. I really just don't know what to do next. I think I'm going to see if I can track down the girl that got locked in the basement, Stephanie Rogers. She's the only child that was attacked and lived to tell about it."

"But, even if she confirms something supernatural happened, what then?"

57

Emma shrugged her shoulders. "I don't know, but wasn't it you that told me that knowledge is power?"

"Yes, but, I meant from books, not firsthand accounts from the victims of these creatures." She sighed heavily. "Let me know what you find out about where she is, I'm not letting you go do this yourself."

Emma smiled. "Thanks, I appreciate it. I'll keep you posted."

*     *     *

"Shelly," Emma asked over dinner that night, "how do you like the house, now that you're settled in?"

"I already told you so many times that my room needs to be painted and I need new curtains, bedding, everything. Once I get those, I'd like my friends to come over for the weekend. I miss them."

"I know, Shelly, and we'll try to make arrangements for that as soon as we can." Emma tried to reassure her, but had no intention of allowing any other children into the house until she was confident that nothing would happen to them.

"Right." Shelly turned back to her meatloaf and mashed potatoes with an ugly scowl on her face.

"But," Emma wasn't sure quite how to broach the subject, "other than needing to redecorate, have you had any specific issues or problems with the house?"

"Like what?"

"I don't know, odd things happening or strange sounds."

Now she had Shelly's full attention. "Are we haunted, Mom?"

Both boys stopped eating and stared at Emma with wide eyes.

"Of course not, I think it's just this big, old house and was wondering if any of you noticed anything strange, that's all."

They all shook their heads, but their eyes remained fixed on Emma. Suddenly, a horrible shrieking noise started from inside the kitchen wall and startled them all.

"What the hell is that?" Shelly asked in a wavering voice.

"Watch your mouth," Emma responded automatically, her heart hammering against her chest as she fought the urge to run screaming from the house as fast as she could.

"Damn you, Jeremy," she thought to herself, "for not being here."

"Mom, make it stop," whispered James, his hands covering his ears as the howling continued and seemed to echo within the walls.

Emma's stomach clenched when she realized that the noise had to be made by Banshee, no other creature on earth could sound like that. She moved slowly around the kitchen, trying to find the source of the noise, but it was starting to die down to a whimper and was difficult to pinpoint.

"Banshee, is that you? Where are you, kitty?"

Callie barked sharply, drawing Emma's attention.

"Good girl, Callie." Emma's voice was shaky as she walked over to Callie, who had positioned herself under the dumb waiter, her eyes going back and forth from its door to Emma.

She held her breath as she opened it, and screamed like a little girl when Banshee jumped out at her.

Emma caught the cat in her arms and turned to the kids who were huddled together in the middle of the room.

"He's okay guys, he just got himself stuck in the dumb waiter, the silly thing." Banshee was still shaking like a leaf and meowing pitifully. He was acting as if she was hurting him, although Emma was just gently cradling him in her arms.

"I think we should take him to the Animal Hospital and get him checked out though. I would like all of you to come with me." There was no way she was leaving any of them alone in the house again, ever.

They returned home a few hours later without the cat. The Vet had to put him under anesthesia so they could x-ray him and would have to keep him overnight.

Shelly immediately ran to her room to make sure Smoky was alright.

"Are you okay, boys?"

"Yeah," Collin replied, "but that was pretty weird."

"It was, wasn't it? Let's hit the sack now, okay? Banshee will be all right, we should be able to pick him up tomorrow."

But she was very mistaken. The Vet called the next morning to tell her that Banshee had never come out from under the anesthesia. The x-rays showed that he had sustained massive internal damage and there was nothing they could have done to save him anyway, so it was probably for the best.

Emma sat all alone at the kitchen table and sobbed like a baby.

*     *     *

"But, Jeremy, you promised." Emma's voice was sharp, and he could feel her anger and despair over the telephone line.

"I know, but I just can't come home today. I have too much to do here."

"What about tonight?"

Jeremy hesitated. "I have a breakfast meeting tomorrow that I can't miss. I'll come home right after that, okay?"

"No, it's not okay, I'm losing it, Jeremy, and I need you. Now I have to go and tell our children about Banshee."

"I'm sorry you have to deal with that by yourself, Em."

She couldn't think of an appropriate reply that she wouldn't regret later, so she just hung up the phone.

They were all very subdued that day, the boys were uncharacteristically quiet and Shelly wouldn't venture out of her room without Smoky held tightly in her arms.

Emma was a mess, sad, angry and more frightened than she'd ever been before. And, for the life of her, she could not figure out what to do next.

Lynne came over that afternoon and, for the first time ever, had nothing to say.

"I just don't know what to do," Emma said, running her hand through her hair, trying to get it back off of her face. "I located the Rogers girl, she's at a Sanitarium called The Good Neighbor Mental Health Institute. I called there, but they won't allow anyone other than family to see her, so that's a dead end."

"Look at this." She showed Lynne the handful of hair that came out when she ran her fingers through it. "I think it's just stress, but I'm going to be bald soon if something doesn't change."

"Get your computer out," Lynne said suddenly. "I might have an idea."

Once it was powered up, they sat down at the kitchen table and began to search for Paranormal Societies in the area. Most of the websites were really out there, but they did find some that might be for real, and Emma was able to write down the names and contact information for a few of them before the power went out.

"What now?" Emma asked.

"A fuse maybe?"

"Shit, the box is in the basement." Their gaze shifted to the basement door, but neither of them moved.

"Can't you wait until Jeremy gets home?"

"He'd think I was an idiot if I let the kids stay in the dark with no power overnight, just because I'm afraid to go into the basement." But, still she just stared at the door without moving.

"Shall I go with you?"

Emma took a deep breath and exhaled loudly. She got up, found two flashlights in the utility drawer and handed one to Lynne, her hand shaking badly as she did so.

"No, thanks, stay here at the top of the stairs and, if anything happens,"

"Come on, Emma, let me go with you," Lynne interrupted.

"No," she responded forcefully, "if anything happens, you grab my kids and get them out of this house, promise?"

"I promise."

Emma walked slowly down the creaky, wooden stairs. The hammering in her chest quieted a little as she realized that Callie, who was coming down the stairs almost on her heels, was not growling and her hair was lying flat along her back.

She made her way across the basement to the fuse box and moved the breaker switch off and then back on. There had been no lights on in the basement and the main switch was at the top of the stairs, so she didn't know if that fixed the problem or not.

She was making her way back across the basement when Callie began to growl.

"Leave it, Callie, leave it, come on girl, upstairs quick."

Emma bolted for the stairs and Callie almost tripped her as she sprinted past. They made it upstairs and into the kitchen just as the basement door slammed itself shut. Emma could barely bolt the door because her hands were shaking so badly.

"Are you okay," Lynne asked.

"Just about scared myself to death, but I think I'll make it. Did the power come back on?" she asked.

"No."

"Damn, would you know an electrician that I could call to come check this out? I'm not going back down there."

"Let me go home and make some calls for you. Want me to call a couple of these too?" she asked, grabbing the list of Paranormal Societies.

"Sure, that would be great. I don't want to use up all the juice in my cell phone in case I need it."

"Alright, I'll touch base with you later. You're welcome to bring the kids over and stay at my place if you'd like." The murkiness of the house was getting under Lynne's skin, and she didn't understand how they could stay in it at all, let alone at night with no power.

"Thanks, but I think we'll be okay. If anything changes, we'll just show up at your doorstep."

"That wouldn't be a problem. I'll call you after I get ahold of someone about the power," she said, hurrying out into the warm sunshine.

Lynne phoned Emma an hour or so later. "I finally found an electrician that can come out for you. Bad news is that it's too late today, so he won't be there until about mid-day tomorrow. Are you sure you don't want to stay here?"

"No, we'll be fine, thank you though. I appreciate your help with all of this." Emma knew that Lynne's husband was living with her again, and that he also had his baby there right now. Unless something really horrible happened, she couldn't envision the four of them, plus two dogs and a cat invading Lynne's home. So, they would make the best of a bad situation right here.

Emma gathered up all of the flashlights, batteries, candles and matches that she could locate. Then she had the kids grab their comforters and pillows from their beds and bring them down to the living room.

"We'll have a little camp out in the house tonight since there's no power. How about we go into town and load up on junk food and board games to keep us busy?"

"Sure," Collin responded and James nodded his agreement. Shelly seemed unsure as she hugged Smoky tightly to her chest.

"You can bring Smoky, Shelly, and either wait with her in the car, or leave her in it when we get to the store."

"Okay, I'll go then."

They spent a quiet night eating pizza, chips and dip and cookies and playing Chinese Checkers and occasionally sinking each other's battleship. Then they all crashed early, except Emma. She dozed fitfully, waking at every little noise. Only after seeing the dogs resting and remaining calm was she able to doze off again for a little while longer.

## CHAPTER 8

They were all a bit logy the next morning, no one had slept well and they were all on edge. Breakfast was just cold cereal with milk, but not even Shelly complained about it.

Emma was relieved to see the electrician's van pull up in the driveway later that morning and went out to greet him.

"Ron Waters, Ma'am," he said extending his hand. He was a rather large fellow who seemed pleasant enough.

"Thanks for coming out so quickly. I don't know what happened, the power just went out and I don't think it was a fuse."

"These old houses can be pretty quirky," he replied, looking up towards the top floor window. "You folks been here long?"

"Not really."

"Any other electrical problems?"

"Well, now that you mention it, lights do occasionally flicker off and on. But it never lasts more than a few seconds, and it happens in all different rooms of the house."

"Could be a short somewhere causing that and might be what blew the whole system." He went to the back of his van to get his tools and then followed Emma into the house.

"I think I'd best start in the basement."

Emma led him to the basement door in the kitchen, feeling a little guilty sending him down there when she was so frightened of it herself. But he was a big, solid man and didn't seem the least bit bothered by going into a cold, damp basement. He pulled out a huge industrial flashlight and headed down into the darkness.

*       *       *

Jeremy arrived home a few minutes later.

64

"Is everyone okay?" he asked, as he dropped his briefcase and suit coat onto a chair in the foyer.

"Yes, I'm glad that you're home." Emma hugged him tightly.

"What's with the van in the driveway?"

"We haven't had power since yesterday afternoon. He just got here and is in the basement checking things out."

"Emma, the vet bills are outrageous and now we're paying to board the horses again, these expenses are getting out of hand, there was no need to call in an electrician."

"Excuse me, but since you couldn't be bothered to answer my calls yesterday afternoon or last night, I had to make a judgment call. What exactly would have been appropriate for me to do?"

"First off, I don't appreciate your tone of voice, and I'm pretty sure I could have figured out what the problem was myself, without costing us an arm and a leg in the process."

"Well, first off," Emma replied mockingly, "I don't give a damn what you think of my tone. Secondly, how can I count on you to take care of anything, if you are never here when we need you?"

"That was completely uncalled for, Emma."

"Jeremy, this week has been hell for us, and I have neither the energy nor the desire to try and soft-soap any of it so that your poor ego doesn't get bruised."

Jeremy's dark blue eyes stared hard at her and she refused to look away. "Well, don't I feel foolish, leaving a desk load of work to rush home for you, only to be ridiculed and mocked as soon as I walk through the door?"

"You can take care of Mr. Waters when he comes up from the basement. I'm taking a walk." Emma took both dogs with her so they didn't get curious and go down into the basement.

As for Jeremy, she didn't know if it was the house or not, but something had significantly changed in their relationship. They had always been able to talk to each other and work out any problems, but things felt different now. There was bitterness and disrespect, and Emma didn't know why or what to do about it. And, worst of all, she didn't know if she even wanted to bother trying to fix it.

Emma and the dogs had just rounded the corner at the end of the street a little while later when the silence was shattered by the wailing of approaching sirens. Emma held tight to the dogs' leashes as they all watched rescue vehicles and police cars go screeching past. Emma stared, watching to see where they would stop, but they kept going and kept going, until the only place left to stop was the house at the end of the road, her house.

"Oh, my God, no," she screamed. Emma began to run and the dogs pulled her forward even faster, seeming to understand the urgency.

Emma sprinted up the street to her house, barely able to draw a breath and grasping at the stitch in her side that was threatening to incapacitate her. There were rescue vehicles parked helter-skelter all over the road, the lawn and the driveway.

She tried to catch her breath, but it was difficult because her panic increased exponentially at the sight of all of the officers and emergency responders. Emma was stopped at the end of her driveway by a young police officer, but she pulled her arm out of his grasp and kept walking, almost as if she was in the middle of daydream.

"Ma'am," the officer stated firmly, grabbing her arm again, "you can't go in there."

"But, it's my house," she managed to say, breathing heavily through her mouth, her heart pounding out of control. "My family is in there, I need to get in and find out what happened. Please, you have to let me in."

"Wait here a minute." The officer walked over to an older man near the porch and whispered briefly to him. The man was wearing an old, dark suit, not a uniform, but he had the carriage of someone used to being in charge and the deference paid by the younger officer confirmed he was a superior officer.

The older man turned his cold, hard eyes towards her, he looked down at the dogs with a frown and said something quietly to the officer. Then he motioned her over.

"Are the dogs okay?"

"They're fine," she responded in confusion. Why was he worried about the dogs?

"I mean," he said with exasperation, "are they friendly? Will they bite?"

"Oh, no, they won't bite, they're very friendly. Please may I go in? My family is in there and I need to make sure everyone is okay. Please tell me what happened."

"Come with me," he said, ignoring her request and pushing his way past the cluster of uniformed officers standing on the porch. He led her into the house and then to the living room, where Jeremy and the three kids all bolted up from the sofa and ran to hug her.

"Oh, thank God you are all okay," Emma said, with a sigh of relief, as she heartily returned their group hug.

The detective gave them a few moments to collect themselves, but then had to interrupt.

"I'm Detective Bisson, your husband called us because something happened to Ron Waters."

"The electrician? Oh no, what happened? Is he okay?"

"No, he's not. Can I speak with you and your husband in the kitchen, alone?"

"Certainly, kids stay here with Callie and Chance, okay? We'll be right back." She grasped Jeremy's hand as they followed the detective out of the room.

When they got to the kitchen and sat down, Jeremy pulled out one of his business cards and handed it to him. Detective Bisson was not a fan of attorneys in general, but he did slide it into his jacket pocket, in the event he needed further information from Draper in the future.

"Mr. Draper, what can you tell me about what happened?" The detective asked, pulling out a small pad of paper and a pen.

He frowned suddenly, as one of the many officers in the room jostled him and knocked the pen out of his hand.

"Sorry, sir," the young man said, bending down quickly to retrieve it. With his pen once more in hand, the detective looked over at Jeremy.

"Not much," Jeremy stated. "Mr. Waters was down in the basement when I got home today. Our power has been out since yesterday. Anyway, he came upstairs once, introduced himself and said he thought that he had figured out what the problem was. He went out to his truck for some other tools and then back down into the cellar. It was about fifteen minutes later when the lights came on, then I heard him scream, the lights flickered again and went out."

Detective Bisson looked around curiously because all of the lights in the house seemed to be working fine.

"I went down into the basement," Jeremy continued "and found him tangled up in a pile of cables or wires on the far side of the basement. There was a pool of water around him so I didn't get very close. I came back upstairs and called 911."

"When did the power come back on?"

"Right after the police and rescue arrived. I directed them down into the basement, but stayed up here with my kids. A few minutes later, the power was back on."

The detective was scribbling notes in his pad. He looked up at Jeremy, stared at him for a moment and then suggested they go back into the living room for now. Then he made his way down into the basement.

The rescue workers and officers working down there were all fully clothed and booted in rubber, so there was just minimal concern about stepping into the water around the body.

"Who turned the power back on?"

"I did, Sir," Officer Johnny Meyers replied.

"How did you manage to do that?"

"I had a flashlight, saw the fuse box. The main breaker was off, I just flipped it and the power came on. At the time, I didn't know what had happened to the victim or I never would have messed with it. We hadn't even seen him yet."

"Did he get hit with the electrical current after you turned the power back on?" Detective Bisson was frowning at the young officer.

"No sir, he was already dead. It didn't look like any of the cables around him had any juice in them, but we stayed back just in case."

"Call John Schmegel, he's a master electrician. I want him to thoroughly check out the wiring in the house, including those cables near the victim. How did all those cables get wrapped around his body?"

"I'm not sure, sir. Maybe he slipped in the water, panicked and wrapped himself up in them."

"Where did the water on the floor come from?"

"I'm not sure, sir."

"Well, figure it out. Let me know as soon as the Coroner arrives." He headed back upstairs and got some more information from Emma about the victim's arrival and what had occurred prior to her going for a walk.

"We're going to be here for a while. You might want to take the kids out to get something to eat."

Emma knew that none of them were hungry, but she appreciated the opportunity to get the kids out of the house and away from all of the commotion.

"Okay, we'll be back in an hour or so, is that okay?"

"That would be fine."

*   *   *

"It was awful, Lynne. They were at the house for hours and we just huddled together in the living room. And, when they took the body away, it was surreal. I can't believe that happened in my house."

"I was so worried when I saw the rescue vehicles go down the street. And when I saw all of you drive away a little while later, I was relieved, yet confused. I had no clue what was going on. You could have called to let me know."

She set her coffee mug down on the table and gave Emma a withering look.

"I'm so sorry, Lynne. Honest to God, it never crossed my mind. I know that's awful and I truly am sorry. I just don't know what I'm doing any more."

Emma looked like she was on the verge of tears so Lynne relented and let it go.

"No worries, just don't leave me out like that again. How are the kids holding up?"

"A little freaked out, quieter than usual. I don't know what to say to them about all of this, and I'm scared silly something bad is going to happen to them."

"Hey, I got through to some of those people on our Paranormal list. A few were way too creepy, even over the phone, but there were a couple that I thought were possibles. Do you want to call them yourself?"

"Sure, we have to do something as soon as possible. I'm going to need to run it by Jeremy before I set anything up. I'll also have figure out what to do with the kids, I don't want them involved in any of this."

"Have them stay here, Shelly can watch the boys."

"What about you?"

"Oh, I wouldn't miss this for the world, even though it scares the bejesus out of me just thinking about it, I have to be a part of this."

"You're the best." Emma gave her a big hug and headed home to talk to Jeremy before making her calls.

Unfortunately, that conversation had to be temporarily delayed. There was an electrician's van in the driveway when she arrived back home and she found Jeremy in the kitchen, having a cup of coffee with an older, gray-haired man in overalls.

"John, this is my wife, Emma. Emma, this is John Schmegel, the police asked him to come and check out our wiring, see if he can figure out what happened to Ron Waters."

"Nice to meet you."

"You too, Mrs. Draper."

"Were you able to find anything?"

"Not a thing, the wiring is fine. I couldn't find any shorts or anything that would have caused the power to go out to begin with. The cables that he was wrapped in were not connected to any live juice, so I have no explanation for how they could have electrocuted him."

He was shaking his head slowly from side to side, his brow furrowed as he tried to come up with a reasonable explanation.

"What about the water?" Emma asked. "I do laundry down there and never noticed any puddle of water on the floor before."

Turning his tired eyes towards Emma, he just shook his head again and shrugged his shoulders.

"The puddle of water is pretty well dried up now, but I could see the water line on the floor where it was. No water came in from the outside, it didn't leak from the washer, it didn't leak from the floor above. It seems to have come from nowhere and formed a nice little pool right where Mr. Waters was walking. Detective Bisson is not going to be very happy with me, I'm afraid."

"Should we be worried about going down there?" Jeremy asked.

"I didn't find anything that would concern me about it. Again, the electrical wiring is fine, no problems with that at all. Well, thanks for the coffee, I guess I'd better get down to the station and give Detective Bisson the news."

Once Jeremy had walked the electrician out, Emma took advantage of the timing and asked him if would sit and talk with her for a few minutes.

"So, Jeremy, what do think about what he found, or didn't find? Don't you think that cements our supernatural issue?"

"I wouldn't exactly say that, but it is curious."

"I'd like to see if we can get a paranormal investigator over here to check things out." Emma didn't realize that she was holding her breath, she was so afraid that Jeremy would laugh at her and, if he did, she wasn't sure exactly how she would respond, but was bracing herself, just in case.

Jeremy stared hard at Emma and she couldn't interpret the look. It was odd, she'd always been able to read him like a book, but lately he seemed to be masking his thoughts and feelings around her. Trying to figure out what these peculiar looks meant was baffling, to say the least.

"How would you find someone?"

Emma expelled her breath and felt a deep sense of relief. "I have a few names that we found online. I have no idea if they are any good, or even if we can get them over here. I just wanted to run it by you before I started making calls."

"Thank you," he said, pulling her towards his chest and kissing the top of her head. "I can't help but think how unbelievable all of this is, but I agree that we have to do something. Why don't you see who you can find, what they charge, all that business, and we can talk it over before we give them the go ahead. Is that fair?"

"Very fair," she responded, with a smile of gratitude.

"You start making some calls and getting the information. I've called in to the office and I'm going to stay home an extra day or two. I just don't feel right leaving all of you after what happened with the electrician."

"Thank you, that means a lot." Emma hurried off to grab her list of names and start making calls, before Jeremy had a chance to change his mind.

# CHAPTER 9

Emma began to try the numbers on the list of mediums that Lynne had given her, but was only able to leave voicemail messages for the first few. She was starting to feel a little discouraged and was afraid that she might not be able to reach someone timely enough to get Jeremy completely on board.

She dialed the next number on the list and was pleasantly surprised when a human being picked up after just a couple of rings.

"Venetia Oswald," a husky voice whispered over the line.

"Good afternoon, my name is Emma Draper." Emma hesitated. "I'm sorry, I don't even know where to start. I think our house might be haunted and we need some help."

"What makes you think that?"

Emma explained some of the things that had been happening.

"You do realize that all of those things could have an explanation that is not supernatural, don't you?"

"Yes, I do, could you please just come over and see what you think. Would you be able to sense if there was a spirit here?"

"Most likely, but I'm pretty booked up right now. Where do you live?"

"It's called the old Creeghan House, we're on Lilac Avenue in Endwell. Do you know where that is?"

It was Venetia's turn to hesitate. "Yes, I do. I think I could fit you in, after all. Could I stop out tomorrow? Depending on what I find, we may want to schedule a Deliverance Ceremony shortly after that."

"Can you give me a little more information first, about what exactly this involves, how much it will cost, things like that. I need to run it by my husband before we finalize anything."

"I can't know exactly what I will need to do until I am able to do a walk-through of the house. Then I determine what I'm dealing with. I can give you some ballpark figures, but that also will have to be finalized after my first visit."

She gave a monetary range that Emma knew would make Jeremy go apoplectic, but if no one else called her back, she was going to insist on hiring this woman. Seriously, they could not let money be an issue right now.

"When might you get back to me about this?" Venetia asked rather irritably. "I will have to rearrange my schedule if you need someone there quickly."

"Of course, let me talk to my husband tonight and I'll call you back in the morning. Will that be alright?"

Her long drawn out sigh spoke volumes, but Venetia had no choice except to be agreeable. She had wanted to check out the Old Creeghan House for years, just walking along the street outside of it brought her all kinds of communications from the other world, and she was impatient to see what waited for her inside the old manor house. She would do whatever she had to in order to get inside and investigate that house.

*　　*　　*

"Hi, Lynne." Emma was speaking quietly into the phone, afraid that Jeremy might overhear. "I got ahold of one of the Mediums, but I think I'm going to need your help."

"Sure, what do you need?"

"Were you serious when you said that you'd watch the kids if Jeremy and I had a date night?"

"Of course."

"Well, if you don't mind last minute notice, I'd like to take you up on that for tonight. This medium is super expensive, and I need to get Jeremy in the right frame of mind before I give him the grim details."

"Oh, what fun, sure bring them over whenever you'd like. I can keep them busy for a few hours."

"You're a life-saver, thanks. See you in a bit."

Emma tracked Jeremy down in the back yard playing catch with the boys.

"Can I talk to you for minute?"

"Sure." He tossed the ball back to Collin, and raised his eyebrows at her as he walked over to where she stood, surprised to see that she was all dolled up with her hair and makeup done, and she was wearing a cute little sun dress that fit her very nicely.

"What's up?

Emma fingered the collar of his golf shirt and smiled up at him, trying to ignore the fact that her sexy little seduction moves were being severely diminished by the heels of her shoes sinking into the soft ground and putting her slightly off balance.

"I need you to go in the house and get cleaned up. You and I are having a date night and I won't take no for an answer."

He smiled down at her, his blue eyes glittering. "Well, you look absolutely lovely, so how could I refuse? I'll be ready in no time. What are we doing with the kids?"

"Lynne said they could stay at her house while we're gone."

He nodded his agreement and started walking towards the house, but stopped suddenly and turned towards Emma. "So, they are that ridiculously expensive, are they?"

"What are you talking about?" she asked, her cheeks flaming. He just smiled and turned back towards the house.

"Damn it," she mumbled, "I guess I must have used this ruse a time or two, too many. Oh, well, at least I'll get a nice dinner out of it."

Jeremy was ready in a much shorter time than it had taken Emma and they loaded the kids up into the van and dropped them off at Lynne's house.

It didn't take long for them to find Joey's, a nice, quiet Italian restaurant with a cozy, corner table available for them. It felt good, it had been a long time since just the two of them spent any time together.

"It's nice being here alone with you." Jeremy said, after ordering them both a nice glass of Pinot Noir and reaching across the table to grab hold of her hand.

"It really is, we should do this more often. You are looking quite dapper this evening."

"Trying to keep up with you, that's a cute little dress, where'd you pick that up?"

She laughed. "I've had it for a few years, I just didn't have an occasion to wear it."

He tenderly rubbed her hand in both of his and stared down at the table, lost in thought.

"Are you okay?" she asked.

"Yes, I am." He raised his eyes and gave her a dazzling smile. "You know I love you, don't you? And the kids?"

"Of course, why would you even ask that?"

"I don't know, everything has just been so crazy since we moved here that, I think I forget to let you know how much you all mean to me. And I'm sorry about that."

Emma could feel tears brimming in her eyes and quickly brushed them away. She squeezed his hand and then they separated as the waitress returned with their drinks and began her recitation of the evening specials.

They made small talk until their dinners arrived and, in between eating their own and sampling each other's, Emma broached the subject of the Medium.

Jeremy did choke a little on his wine when she gave him the possible costs and Emma held her breath.

He watched her closely for a moment and could see the fear and concern in her face. Jeremy knew that he would be willing to pay any amount of money to take that away, and to give her back the peace of mind she had before they moved here.

"It's not a problem, Emma, but she'd better be good. I want this taken care of once and for all."

"I think she can come over tomorrow and take a look around. Then she'll let me know when she can come back to do whatever it is she has to do. She called it a Deliverance Ceremony or something like that. If they can do it one evening this week, will you be able to join us?"

"Of course, I can't have some freaky gypsy walking around my house unattended. Just let me know for sure. I think I'll head into the office tomorrow morning and then just plan on coming home whichever night they do their ceremony, is that alright with you?"

"Yes, thank you, Jeremy, it means a lot that you'll be with me for this."

*　　*　　*

Emma and Lynne couldn't help looking at each other helplessly as they stood on the porch and watched Venetia approach. She looked like such a cliché that they had trouble restraining their giggles.

Venetia was tall and heavy-boned. Her loud, yellow-flowered caftan flowed around her and long, black hair fell mid-way down her back. Venetia paused dramatically, glancing up at the house and her face suddenly changed expression. A look of fear flitted across her features, but then she took a deep breath, looked down to the ground as if collecting herself, and then back up at Lynne and Emma. The fear was now gone from her face and she smiled broadly at them.

"Good afternoon, ladies," she stated in a breathy voice. "I am Venetia Oswald."

"It's a pleasure to meet you," Emma said. "I'm Emma Draper and this is my neighbor, Lynne McVee. Please come in."

Venetia's head seemed to almost swivel on her shoulders, as she tried to take in as much of the house as she could from the foyer.

"It's lovely," she rasped, "just as I'd imagined. Can you please take me around the entire house?"

"Certainly," Emma replied unnecessarily, as Venetia had already begun to make her way through the downstairs rooms. She walked slowly, touching items, stopping to cock her head to the side occasionally, almost as if she was listening for something.

"Yes, yes," she would whisper.

Emma and Lynne hung back, trailing behind and watching her curiously. The dogs stayed well behind the women, not sure what to make of any of this.

Once Venetia had made a round of the first floor, she looked up the staircase, grasped a large gemstone that she was wearing around her neck, and hesitated at the bottom of the stairs.

"I have no doubt," she said slowly, in her raspy voice, "that I will discover even more spirits residing in this house if I go upstairs. How many remains to be seen."

"More?" Emma repeated, goosebumps rising on her arms.

"Yes, dear," Venetia replied, swiveling her head and turning her dark gaze onto Emma. "There are multiple spirits here that have exposed themselves to me already. I'm sure there will be more, the air is heavy and I can hear murmuring from the others. You see, I am a clairaudient, not a clairvoyant."

"What exactly does that mean?"

"I can hear the spirits, but I cannot see them."

"All right, so, what now?" Emma asked, hugging herself.

Venetia smiled at her, excitement evident in every line in her face as she contemplated what was ahead of her. This would be the biggest haunting that she had ever been involved with and, even though the air was heavy with darkness and evil, she could also feel good spirits here that were ready to move on. She was up for the challenge and visions of the money she would get from the book sales from this story took away any reservations that she had about the evil vibrations pulsing over her.

"I must meditate on this and determine the right approach. It's unusual to have multiple hauntings in the same location, so I need to be sure the Deliverance Ceremony is appropriate for all of the spirits residing here. I may need to bring someone to assist for the ceremony. Is that acceptable to you?"

"Certainly, whatever you need to do to get rid of them is fine."

The words were no sooner out of her mouth when a large picture fell off the wall and crashed to the floor, scattering glass all over.

All three women jumped and Callie began to snarl.

"I'd prefer that this be done sooner rather than later. How long before you can begin?"

Venetia was still staring down at the broken picture with narrowed eyes. "I'll get working on it this afternoon and, hopefully, we can begin tomorrow evening. It may take more than one Ceremony to get them all out, particularly if some of them are not interested in moving on. Here is my preliminary bill, I'll expect payment at the end of the Ceremony. There could be additional costs if further visits are required."

Emma took the piece of paper from her and didn't even glance at it. The cost was irrelevant as far as she was concerned.

"Thank you, please let me know for sure if you'll be able to make it tomorrow, so I can let my husband know."

"Of course." She gave one more curious look around the house and headed out to her car.

*       *       *

Venetia returned the next evening with an associate, John Klaus. They came with various paraphernalia, like candles and herbs. John began walking around the house and placing items in different rooms. Venetia murmured to herself as she sifted through the items, picking up some and setting them in piles, and gently discarding others.

Jeremy had reluctantly joined them and was standing back by the wall, watching skeptically, his arms crossed tightly against his chest. He was annoyed that, although he had agreed to it, he had to drive in from the city in the middle of the week and pay such a ridiculous amount of money for this nonsense.

Once all of the items were separated and placed throughout the house, they sat down around the dining room table. Venetia and John began a chant, quietly at first and then a little louder.

They were all startled by a sudden knocking at the front door. Emma could see that Venetia was extremely irritated at being interrupted once she had already begun the Ceremony, and hoped this wouldn't affect the outcome for the evening.

"I'll see who it is." Jeremy stepped around Lynne's chair and headed into the foyer. The others weren't able to see what was going on, but could hear him conversing with someone.

He returned to the dining room a couple of moments later, looking a bit confused, and with two men in business suits following close behind him.

The men looked around curiously while everyone sat and stared at them.

The shorter one moved closer to the group and nodded. "Agent Gabriel, FBI, and this is my partner, Agent Collins."

Although he was the shorter of the two, he was by no means short, he was both taller and broader than Jeremy. But the other was a behemoth, very tall and well-muscled. Emma couldn't help noticing that they were both very handsome in their own way, with dark brown hair and intense brown eyes, the taller one's just a shade lighter than the other's.

Emma's gaze continued to be drawn to the shorter one, his hair was just beginning to show some signs of gray and, between that and the way he carried himself, she assumed he was the older of the two and, most likely, the senior officer.

They both exuded a certain manliness and seemed very intense, and not just a little intimidating. They were nothing like Detective Bisson or his men, who had been deferential and polite, these two were more like bulls in a china shop.

Agent Gabriel looked over the group. It was easy enough to figure out that the slim blonde that stood up and walked over to stand near the owner of the house was obviously his wife. He wasn't able to figure out who the petite, well-dressed woman was at the end of the table, but she looked almost shell-shocked and was just sitting back quietly observing the activities.

A large-boned woman in a caftan was sitting at the head of the table with some herbs and spices smoking in a bowl in front of her. A mousy, little man was in the seat next to her and, for some reason, Agent Gabriel assumed he must be with the caftan lady.

"What can we do for you?" Emma asked.

"We understand that there was a murder here a couple of days ago."

"There was no murder," Emma replied, starting to feel uneasy. "It was just a horrible accident. But what does the FBI have to do with it?"

"Well, Ma'am, we need to get some more details and find out what exactly did happen. Have the local police told you how they officially ruled Ron Waters' death?"

"Well, no," she replied, "but the electrician didn't find anything wrong. How could it have been a murder?"

There was a sharp intake of breath from Venetia, Emma hadn't mentioned the death of the electrician to her.

"And who are you?" Agent Gabriel asked, turning to her.

"Venetia Oswald, I'm a Medium."

"Come again?"

"A Medium, I am in contact with the spirits."

"Of course, you are." Then he looked curiously at Jeremy and Emma. "Does this have something to do with Ron Waters? Do you have some reason to believe that a ghost was behind it?"

"We aren't saying any such thing," Jeremy stated, feeling a little embarrassed about the whole Medium thing now.

"We don't know," Emma interjected, feeling slightly foolish herself, after hearing it put like that. "There have been a lot of strange things happening since we moved in and we needed help, so we called Venetia."

"And, I'm to assume that is your real name?" he asked, turning his dark gaze back to Venetia.

"It is my real name and I don't care for your attitude."

Agent Gabriel stepped forward and leaned down, his face just inches from hers. "I don't much care what you think of my attitude, we need answers, not some charlatan's mumbo jumbo."

His voice was low and calm, but sounded threatening nontheless. Emma was impressed at Venetia's courage when she responded to him.

"I'm not a charlatan, I am respected in my field and I help people. Why don't you let me get to work and come back tomorrow? We should have some answers for you then."

He tried not to smile, but the smirk was even more telling.

"Why don't we stick around and watch you *work*. Please, carry on, we'll stay out of your way."

Venetia looked directly at Emma. "I will not continue tonight if this cretin insists on following me around and mocking me. This is a serious situation and, if it is to be done correctly, then I need to feel peace and serenity. I do not anticipate that will happen as long as the two *gentlemen* are among us."

Jeremy could see Emma tensing up and knew that she would fall to pieces if they didn't get this taken care of tonight, one way or the other.

"I'm sorry, but I must ask you to leave." He turned his steely blue gaze to the two officers, challenging them to argue with him. "We'd be happy to answer any of your questions, but now is not the time."

The shorter one looked like he was about to say something, but the taller one responded first.

"I understand, here's my card." He handed it to Emma who was standing closest to him. "Please call me if there are any further problems. We'll be in touch in a few days to get some information about the incident with Mr. Waters."

"Please call, anytime, if you have further problems." He stared directly into Emma's eyes and seemed to be trying to communicate something to her. She felt a shiver go down her spine. It was almost as if he knew that Venetia was not the answer to their dilemma. She tucked the card into her jeans pocket with trembling hands and watched Jeremy walk them to the door.

# CHAPTER 10

Once they'd left and everyone was back together at the table, Venetia and John continued their chanting. Their words sounded like a request or a prayer, pleading with the spirits to find their way home, in God's name.

A few minutes later Venetia put some more herbs into a large ceramic basin in front of her and watched them catch fire and start to smolder.

"What is that?" Lynne asked.

"White sage, sweet grass and frankincense," Venetia replied absently. "Jeremy, go and open the window in the living room, that is the furthest room to the west, isn't it?"

"Yes," he replied, feeling confused and rather stupid, but obeying her wishes anyway.

"Is there an attic?" she asked, when he returned to the room.

"Yes."

"We'll begin there, please lead the way."

Only Venetia and John entered the attic, it was small and there wasn't room for all of them, so Emma wasn't able to see what they did while they were up there.

They next followed her down into the basement. Venetia cast the smoke throughout the room, all the while uttering her plea to the spirits. "Leave in the name of God, you are not welcome here."

While she walked around the entire room chanting, John would dip his finger in the holy oil and make the sign of the cross over any doorway or window.

Emma did not move far from the bottom of the stairs. The basement held a dark coldness that seeped into her bones, and which couldn't be explained away just because it was a basement. She continued to shudder uncontrollably as Venetia and John worked the room.

Jeremy stood in the center of it, watching the two of them suspiciously. He looked bored and Emma worried that he would start getting impatient and say something rude.

She suddenly heard what sounded like a low growl coming from somewhere in the room. Venetia paused at the same time, but chose to ignore the noise and kept on with her pleas and smudging.

When Venetia had finished with every nook and cranny in the basement, they moved up to the third floor, where Shelly's bedroom was, and began the smudging and anointing of the oil throughout the rooms on that floor.

Jeremy's boredom quickly diminished when the closet doors started slamming open and closed. Then, suddenly, there was terrific roar which sounded like someone, or something, was either in horrendous pain or very, very angry.

Venetia ignored the sounds and the slamming doors and continued her mantra even more forcefully. There was a slight smile on her face, she was winning and she knew it.

When they finished with that floor, they moved to the rooms on the second floor. Venetia hesitated when she entered the boys' room and the words she was about to speak were silenced. She cocked her head to the side, listening.

"What is it, little one? What do you want?"

Lynne was standing close to Emma, looking at Venetia quizzically.

"What's going on now?" she whispered.

"I don't know."

"We have the spirit of a young child in this room," Venetia stated. "She must have lost her way and can't find the light."

Venetia relaxed a bit and set down her smudging herbs.

"Please, talk to me little one. I can help you find your way."

It was almost comical to watch Venetia, in her flowing caftan, twirl around the room and cock her head from side to side, trying to hear the child's voice.

"Tell me what it is that you want and I can help you."

"Your head on a pike," came a dark, disembodied voice.

Just as Venetia's shocked face showed complete understanding, she was thrown across the room into a dresser, where she crumbled to the floor.

John ran over to her. "Are you alright?"

"I will be, it's a demon, not a child. We need to get out this room for now, quickly." Her voice was weak, but the import of her words was strong enough that Emma and Lynne sprinted down the stairs, leaving the two men behind to help Venetia.

"What just happened?" Jeremy asked, when they were all back in the dining room.

"Demons will sometimes try to get you to let your guard down, they are tricky, evil souls, and are difficult to get rid of. This one pretended to be a child to take advantage of me."

"Can you get rid of it?" Emma asked nervously.

"Of course, now that I know what I am dealing with. Let me get some additional supplies and we will go back up there and remove this evil from your home. It's possible there are not as many spirits here as I initially thought. A demon can pretend to be many things."

She and John got their things together and they all made their way back up the stairs. Lynne was holding tightly to Emma's hand, both of them were petrified. Lynne almost didn't go back up, but her curiosity was stronger than her fear, for the time being, at least.

The air was heavier now and there was a horribly, foul odor that permeated the entire floor. Suddenly a toilet flushed down the hall and they all stopped and stared in that direction.

Venetia began waving her smoke as she spoke. "We are not afraid of you. In God's name, leave this house. You are not welcome here. In God's name, leave now."

She went back into the bedroom where the demon had attacked her, the air was lighter now, but a nasty smell still hung in the air. Venetia continued her prayers and John made the sign of the cross in oil over the windows and doors.

They continued down the hall and into Emma and Jeremy's bedroom. Once again, closet doors and the drawers of the dresser started banging open and shut. Clothes started flying out of the closet, almost as if someone was having a temper tantrum and throwing them in a fit of rage.

85

Venetia's voice started to weaken and she looked as if she was having trouble breathing.

"Venetia?" John questioned in concern.

"I'm alright," she gasped. She continued with the smoke, but had to stop and retch drily in a corner at one point, reaching out to grab the wall to hold herself up.

"In God's name, leave this place, you are not welcome here." Her voice was not as strong and it sounded like she was in pain, but Venetia continued on until the entire room was smudged and anointed with holy oil. The door to the hallway slammed loudly and suddenly the air seemed lighter and less rank.

"I have him on the run," Venetia stated, that slight, triumphant smile back on her wide face. They stayed in that room for a few minutes while Venetia got her wind back and prepared herself for the rest of the battle. "It will get worse as we bless each room and leave it with nowhere to go."

The smudging of the rest of the house went fairly quietly, until they got to the last room, the living room.

The air was heaviest there, and the foul odor was so strong that they all fought the urge to retch. Lynne pulled her stylish scarf up around her face to try to block it out somewhat, but even that didn't help.

Venetia started chanting and John began to anoint the doors and windows, they made their way through the room, leaving the area around the open window for last.

Out of nowhere a strong wind developed, whipping Venetia's caftan and hair around her and tossing objects off the mantle with a loud crash. She ignored the commotion and continued her smudging and chanting, her voice was getting stronger and stronger, forcing the sprit closer and closer to the open window.

There was a horrific shriek and then silence. The air was suddenly lighter and the rank smell was gone. Emma, Jeremy and Lynne all took a deep breath and looked at each other in disbelief. John went to the window and closed it tight, then began anointing the holy oil over it in the sign of the cross. Venetia turned to them with a weary smile. "We did it."

Emma ran over and gave her a big hug. "Oh, thank you so much, I just can't believe it."

Venetia's smile widened as she returned the hug. "He was a difficult one, but you are safe now. The house is free of spirits."

*     *     *

Later that night as they lay holding each other in bed, Jeremy said, "I am still having such a hard time accepting that this is real, even though I saw some of it with my own eyes."

"I know what you mean, I'm just glad that I'm not crazy, after all," Emma replied with a giggle. "Do you really believe that it's gone and won't be back?"

"I have to believe that it's completely gone after feeling the difference in the house. Can't you feel it?"

"I do, it's strange, I never noticed it when we first moved in, but the air has always been so cold and heavy, until tonight."

He kissed her on the forehead and hugged her tight. "You have nothing more to worry about. It's going to be alright from now on."

*     *     *

It was quiet for the rest of the weekend, they all seemed to be holding their breath, waiting for something else to happen, but it never did.

"Are you sure?" Jeremy asked.

"Yes, honey, go, its fine. I really do believe that whatever was here, is gone now."

"If you're sure," he replied, relieved that she was accepting the fact that this was over, that there was nothing more to worry about.

Jeremy packed up the car a short time later and headed into the city.

Later that afternoon the doorbell rang and Emma was pleasantly surprised to find Lynne standing on her porch.

"How is everything? Is it gone?" Her nervous energy was obvious, but she spoke in a whisper, apparently afraid that "It" might hear her, if it was still there.

"It's gone, come in and see for yourself."

"It does feel different," Lynne said, as she took her first tentative steps into the house. "The air doesn't seem so oppressive."

She began to smile. "How freaky is this? Did you believe in ghosts before you moved here? I mean, I'd heard the rumors about the place, but I never took them seriously."

"I never really gave ghosts any thought at all, one way or the other. This has all been so surreal. But, I'm glad that it's finally all over and we are all safe and sound."

For no apparent reason, goosebumps suddenly rose on Emma's arms, and she wished that she could completely believe the words that she was saying.

*    *    *

That night Emma was plagued by extremely vivid dreams. She was more frightened than she had ever been before and was running through their house, she was moving in slow motion, barely covering any ground at all, and whatever was after her was getting closer and closer.

At times, she could scarcely breathe and it felt like a huge weight was pressing down on her chest. As the night wore on, Emma continued to toss and turn as she tried to escape whatever was pursuing her in the dream.

In the darkest hours of the night, she felt a sharp, piercing pain as something scraped along her chest and she woke with a gasp, her body drenched in sweat, her heart pounding erratically. Callie had her paws up on the side of the bed and was whining in concern.

"It's okay, baby, just a dream." She petted Callie's head with a shaky hand, trying to get herself back together.

"What do you think, post-traumatic stress, maybe?" Emma fought an urge to giggle hysterically, but that feeling disappeared almost immediately, and the unknown dread that had haunted her in the dream was back full force. She suddenly had an overwhelming need to check the children, to be sure they were safe.

She and Callie entered the boys' room first and found them sleeping peacefully. Emma brushed the hair off Collin's forehead and pulled his blanket back up over him. He was a restless sleeper and always kicked his covers off in the night.

Then she went over and caressed James' sleeping face. He surprised her by opening his eyes and looking straight through her.

"What is it?" she whispered. "Can't you sleep?"

"Mommy, I think it's back."

"Why do you think that, James? James," she whispered, but there was no response. He had drifted back off to sleep.

"Maybe he's just dreaming, too," she thought, trying to lose this absurd, uneasy feeling that was threatening to overwhelm her.

Shelly was sound asleep upstairs and Emma gazed at her fondly as she tucked the covers in around her. Returning to her own room, Emma noticed that the clock read a little after three am, and she wondered how she was ever going to get back to sleep, and how she would ever survive the day if she didn't.

Emma tossed and turned and slept fitfully for another couple of hours, but then gave up trying and got up and made herself a good, strong pot of coffee.

When the boys came down for breakfast, she tried to act casual as she flipped their eggs and made their toast, but she was dying of curiosity to find out why James had said that the demon was back.

"Did you boys sleep well?"

"Sure," Collin replied. James just nodded his head.

"Do you remember when I came into your room, James?"

He looked at her quizzically. "No, when did you do that?

"It was in the middle of the night, I thought you were asleep, but then you started talking to me."

"I did?"

"Yes, you don't remember?"

"No, what did I say?"

"I don't remember, nothing important."

Emma placed their plates in front of them and they started wolfing down their breakfasts.

"Do you both feel alright here now, nothing unusual has been happening any more, has it?"

James shrugged again and Collin just shook his head while stuffing food in his mouth.

"Everything should be alright from now on, but you need to tell me if anything strange happens, okay?"

They mutely nodded their acquiescence and seemed fine, but Emma still felt uneasy.

Her fear spiked a little bit later when she went upstairs to take a shower. Removing her robe and nightgown, she found three long, deep scratch marks on her chest. Her nightgown wasn't ripped and there was no reasonable explanation for how they got there. Emma trembled nervously as she traced the marks and recalled her night terrors, and the pain she felt just before she woke up in the middle of the night.

*     *     *

"Venetia, I'm not sure it's gone, can you come back over?" Emma called as soon as the boys went outside to play and Shelly was back upstairs in her room.

"That's very unlikely," Venetia rasped into the phone, "but, of course, I'll come back over. I can fit you in on Thursday."

"Isn't there any way you can come sooner? I think it scratched me last night and I'm worried about the children."

"You have scratch marks?"

"Yes."

"How many?"

"Three, across my chest, and they are quite deep."

"I see," her voice was quieter, subdued. "Okay, let me rearrange my schedule and I will stop over this afternoon."

"Thank you," Emma replied, grateful that Venetia was willing to come over so quickly, and scared to death, because Venetia was going to drop everything and come over so quickly.

# CHAPTER 11

Venetia came over about mid-afternoon and Emma led her into the kitchen where they shared a pot of freshly brewed hazelnut coffee. Emma found the situation oddly amusing, it was like two friends spending a quiet afternoon together, but in this case their conversation involved only ghosts and demons, how freaky was that?

"So, tell me what happened."

Emma told her about the nightmare she had and what James said when she went into his room. Then she unbuttoned her blouse and showed Venetia the deep scratches.

It seemed surreal to her as she rubbed the cuts, this couldn't possibly be happening again, or still.

"Demons enjoy mocking the trilogy, that's why they leave three claw marks on their victims."

"I'm a victim now?"

"Do you have a better word for it?" she asked, daintily picking up her cup and sipping the fragrant coffee. "We missed something here, but I don't know what."

Her browed furrowed as she replayed the evening of the House Cleansing Ceremony. "Is there another part of the house that we didn't go into?"

"No."

"It doesn't make sense, if that is the case, there was no place for any of them to hide. I just don't understand how we missed one. And, if there is still a demon in the house, it will be very angry now because we tried to get rid of it, and will become much more physical."

Emma shivered. "What do we do?"

"Let me think about it. If there was some place in this house that we missed, that would explain it, however, if we covered everything, there is the possibility this house holds a portal and they can come and go as they please."

"What is a portal?"

"It's an opening between our world and theirs. It can be either manmade or natural. I need to ask you some questions, have you or anyone in your family experimented with a Ouija Board?"

"No."

"Is there discontent, unrest within your family?"

"Just the normal everyday issues that every family goes through."

"Has it become worse since you've been in this house?"

"Between, my husband and me, yes, but that has to do more with all these unusual occurrences than anything else."

"Demons also enjoy causing chaos and unrest. Their most powerful weapon is psychological warfare. They are attracted to negative energy. The more stress and upheaval they cause, the stronger they become."

"So how…"

"What is that?" Venetia interrupted, pointing to the small door in the corner of the kitchen.

"It's a dumb waiter."

"How did we miss that when we were here for the cleansing?" Venetia asked, almost to herself.

"It's kind of hidden in the corner, there are no doors or windows near it, so you probably never saw it. Could it have hidden in there?"

Venetia nodded, looking satisfied and annoyed all at the same time.

"Very well, we'll come back tonight and finish this up. We'll have to do the entire house again and this time we'll include the dumb waiter. That should end this haunting once and for all."

Emma spent a nervous afternoon waiting for the time to pass until Venetia and John arrived, and prayed that nothing unnatural would happen in the meantime. She'd already spoken with Lynne, and the kids and dogs would go back to her house again tonight. Lynne waffled about coming over for the Cleansing, but when Emma told her about the claw marks on her chest, that made up her mind and she gracefully bowed out.

Emma called Jeremy to let him know what was happening, but it would be difficult for him to come home again in the middle of the week. Emma assured him that they would be fine without him and he gratefully declined to join them. Emma was crushed by his response but, to be fair, she had to admit that she was the one that gave him the out to begin with, so she really couldn't place all of the blame on him. But she was still extremely disappointed by his decision.

Venetia and John began the Cleansing Ceremony later that evening with Emma following along behind them. It went similarly to the previous Cleansing, but the Demon was much angrier and more forceful this time. Venetia became extremely sick in several of the rooms and, although able to continue, she was much weaker in those areas and Emma was concerned that she might not be able to continue on and do the entire house.

The poltergeist activities were also stepped up, toilets flushed constantly, pictures were knocked off the wall, all three of them were attacked physically, either by items being thrown at them or a mysterious wind that would come up out of nowhere and push the three of them around and into pieces of furniture. Each time, Venetia just kept on repeating that in the Name of God, the Demon must leave, it was not welcome in this home. With a loud bang, the door to the room would close and the air would lighten. Then they would move onto the next one, where similar occurrences took place.

It was a long, stressful night, but they made it through with no permanent injuries. With another wailing scream, the Demon flew through the open window and John quickly closed and locked it, then anointed it with Holy Oil.

"Well," Venetia said, "this time I think we got rid of it for good. We covered every nook and corner in this house, so there is no way anything was able to hide from us."

Something occurred to Emma right then and, although she felt bad putting an additional burden on Venetia, who looked absolutely exhausted, she knew she had to bring this up.

"Venetia, I hate to do this, but we never talked about the barn."

"The barn?"

"Yes, it slipped my mind because it hasn't been a factor since I sent the horses off to another stable, but something is in there also. Can the Demon move from the house to the barn? If so, I'm afraid it will be back again."

Venetia looked at John and took a long, exhausted breath. "We have to end this completely. Let's get more oil and herbs for the smoke and we can finish it up. Are there lights in the barn?"

"Yes."

"Alright, let's get our supplies and head out there."

The full moon lit their way to the barn, Venetia was walking slowly, her purple caftan barely swinging around her. Emma hoped that she was strong enough to finish this.

The Cleansing began quietly enough but, within a few short minutes, hay was swirling around the barn and getting into their eyes and faces. Venetia spit pieces out as she continued with her mantra and headed to the upper floor of the barn.

It was just an open hayloft that went halfway across the barn, no walls, no windows or doors, so she went alone.

Emma and John heard a sudden grunt of pain and he quickly climbed up the ladder onto the second floor.

"Venetia, are you okay?"

Emma could hear him, but they were back away from the edge so she couldn't see what was going on. John suddenly yelped in pain and Venetia appeared at the edge of the floor.

"No," she screamed. "I command you in the name of God to leave now. You are not welcome here and I am not afraid of you."

Venetia teetered on the edge of the second floor, looking for all the world like she was getting ready to leap. She continued screaming at the entity and demanding that it leave, and Emma could see the teetering stop as Venetia took a deep breath and slowly stepped back from the precipice.

Emma didn't realize that she was holding her own breath, until both Venetia and John made their way down the ladder to the safety of the first floor. They both looked dazed and a little frightened, but Venetia continued with the smudging and, after taking a few steadying breaths, John followed her with the holy oil. All three of them sighed in relief when the last window had been anointed with oil, closed and locked.

"But there was no scream like before," Emma whispered. "Is it really gone?"

Venetia looked around and cocked her head to see if she could hear any further evidence of the demon.

"There is nothing here, it is really gone this time. It was very strong, I've never had one that tried so hard to kill me before." She shuddered uncontrollably.

"What happened to you guys up there?" Emma asked.

"Nothing you need to know about. We are both fine, we were stronger than the demon and that is what matters. I do need to go home though, this has taken quite a physical toll on me."

Venetia took Emma's hand in both of hers. "You will be safe now."

Her raspy voice was weak and she looked like she might tip right over out of fatigue.

"I don't know how to thank you. I am forever in your debt."

"I left an invoice for the additional services on your kitchen table. You can mail me the check." Venetia smiled weakly at her and headed out the barn door.

*    *    *

Emma went through her daily chores with healthy optimism for the next few days. No more nightmares or mysterious scratches, no unusual activity at all.

Jeremy came home for the weekend, but he was subdued and not very talkative. He listened patiently as Emma told him about the second Cleansing, but other than expressing his relief that it was over and that everyone was now safe, he didn't have much to add.

"Is everything, okay, Jeremy? You seem a little distracted."

He shifted his gaze to her and, once again, Emma found herself unable to interpret the look on his face. Sadness maybe, or regret?

"What is it, Jeremy? You're scaring me. Is something going on?"

"Of course not, honey." He traced his finger along her jaw line, wrapped a long, blonde lock of her hair behind her ear and bent down to nuzzle her neck. "Everything's fine, I'm just swamped at work and can't seem to get it out of my head."

That didn't ring true to Emma, the look he gave her was something completely different from anything that she'd seen before. He was not feeling overwhelmed at work, it was about her, it was personal and, somehow, she just knew that was the truth.

Emma was about to press the matter when the sudden shrieks that she heard coming from Shelly's room tore any other thoughts out of her head.

She and Jeremy raced up the stairs to find Shelly standing on her bed, screaming as if she was being tortured and clasping Smoky tightly against her chest.

"Over there." Shelly pointed to the closet.

Jeremy tentatively headed over to the closet, the door was partially closed so he swung it wide, almost dislocating his shoulder in the process.

"What?" he asked, seeing nothing but clothes inside.

"A rat," she screeched. "It ran into the closet."

"Oh, for God's sake," Jeremy muttered. He pushed the clothes aside but found no rodent in the closet.

"There's nothing there, are you sure you weren't dreaming?"

"No, I saw it out of the corner of my eye, it was huge, it had to be a rat."

"Isn't that stupid cat good for anything?"

Emma noticed that the cat was purring contently in Shelly's arms. That was a little surprising, since Smoky obviously hadn't noticed the rat or mouse, or whatever, and gone after it. The cat was a great hunter and never hesitated to pounce on any varmint that she came across, so it was all very odd, to say the least.

"It was there, really. You have to do something."

"Fine, I'll go to the hardware store and get a trap, okay?"

"Can't you shoot it?"

Jeremy gave her a withering look. "First, I'd have to actually see it, then, somehow, I would have to try to shoot its little body without shooting up the house as well. Use your head, Shelly."

He stomped out of the room and left the house a few minutes later to go to the hardware store.

The rest of the weekend was quiet, very quiet. Everyone seemed a bit edgy, although there was no particular reason for it. Emma suspected that the children realized their father was not in the best frame of mind and were trying to stay off his radar. They all breathed a bit easier when he left for his apartment early Sunday afternoon.

*     *     *

"What the?" Emma mumbled as she walked across the living room. She stared curiously at the painting they had hung behind the couch.  It was a landscape, with muted colors that matched their tan and brown furniture, and it was hanging upside down.

"How could that happen?" she wondered aloud. The wire hanger was at the top of the picture, so it couldn't possibly be hung upside down by mistake.

Emma started to feel a little uneasy, but reassured herself that it could have been done by the demon before they got rid of it, and she just hadn't noticed it before now.

"Anything is possible, I suppose."

Emma struggled to get the large painting off the wall. "Ugh, what is that?"

The back of it was covered in a dark, black goo, which had somehow kept the heavy painting stuck to the wall. The slimy goo now coated the entire wall where the painting had hung.

Emma took the painting out to the garage, idly wondering how pissed off Jeremy was going to be when he found out how much it would cost to repair it. She put on some long rubber gloves and scrubbed down the wall until every bit of the creepy goo was gone.

After dinner and the dishes were done, the family decided to settle down with a good movie for the rest of the evening. As Emma approached the living room, her steps faltered and she was afraid that she might actually pass out. The wall behind the couch was completely covered in the black goo again.

"Yuck, mom, what is that?" Shelly asked, her face twisted in disgust. "I am not going anywhere near it, that's for sure."

"I don't know, honey, I saw it earlier and thought I had cleaned it all up, but I guess not."

She was at a loss as to what to do. None of them wanted to sit in the room with the creepy goo and she didn't want to even stay in the house, but where would they go? Shelly wouldn't go anywhere without Smoky, so they were pretty limited because Emma certainly wasn't going to let her stay in the house alone.

They decided to play some board games in the kitchen. Emma could tell they weren't too thrilled about it, but they all felt a little more comfortable staying together as a group.

A few hours later the kids went up to their bedrooms and Emma immediately called Venetia.

"Goo?" she questioned in her raspy voice. "I don't understand, we got rid of all of the entities in your house."

"I know," Emma replied. "There haven't been any other incidents, but what else could have caused this?"

"I'm sure there is a logical explanation, not everything is related to spirits, you know."

Emma did not appreciate the condescending tone of her voice, but couldn't afford to alienate Venetia right now, so she ignored it.

"Can you come back over tomorrow, just to check things out?"

Venetia hesitated, the experience in the barn was still fresh in her mind. She had never been filled with such terror before, not like she'd felt that night. She shuddered uncontrollably, grateful that Emma couldn't see her over the phone line.

"I'm sorry, Emma, I've done what I can for you. I have other clients that need my help and I don't think I'll have time to get back over to your house."

"So, what do I do?" Emma was desperate, filled with fear and despair, and she had no idea which way to turn now.

"I really don't know, you may want to call in a priest."

"A priest, why?"

"If there is still something in your house, it is stronger than anything that I've ever encountered. Maybe a priest could help, I don't really know what to tell you at this point. Look, I have to run, good luck."

Emma sat with the phone against her ear, listening to the dial tone and wondering what in the hell she should do now. Tears bubbled up in her eyes and she just sat sobbing hoarsely at the kitchen table for what seemed like hours. Then, completely drained, she tried in vain to once again to reach Jeremy.

"Please call me as soon as you get this message, it doesn't matter what time it is. Something's happened again. We need you."

She and Callie made their way up to her bedroom, but Emma slept very little that night.

# CHAPTER 12

"Relax, honey, I'm sure it's nothing. Venetia took care of everything."

Emma was still edgy the next morning when Jeremy finally returned her call. "Then how do you explain it?"

"Well, obviously, I can't without seeing it. The goo doesn't sound dangerous and, as long as you are all okay, I don't see why it can't wait until I come home on Friday."

"Jeremy, I can't keep living in this house if these things are going to continue. I am a nervous wreck and I'm petrified that something is going to happen to the children."

Jeremy's voice had a hard edge when he finally responded.

"You wanted to move, you wanted that house, we cannot afford to just walk away from it. Are all five of us going to live in this damned one bedroom apartment? Use some common sense, Emma, I know this has been a strange time, and it's still a little hard to believe there was a demon in the house, but it's gone now. I think you might be making a bigger issue out of this than it actually is, because you like being able to make me run home every time there's a crisis, regardless of how inconvenient it is for me."

"Are you fucking kidding me?" The words were out of Emma's mouth before she even realized what she was saying, but she had no intention of apologizing for them.

"Emma." Jeremy stated harshly.

"I am so sorry that your children and I are such an inconvenience to you," she interrupted. "Please, don't rush home on our account. I'll handle it, like usual, and with any luck no one will get hurt in the meantime."

She hung up the phone and stood in the kitchen, trembling with anger. As the children made their way down to the kitchen, Emma did her best to swallow her feelings and put on a happy, confident face while she made their breakfast. They were nervous enough, there was no need to make it worse for them.

Emma cleaned up the goo again and it was back a few hours later. Other than that, nothing more happened until late afternoon.

Shelly had been reading in the window seat and saw the boys returning from their baseball game. Once she was sure that they were in the house, she slid the window up a little further and scooched out so that her butt was on the window frame and her feet on the siding. It was pretty steep, but she was able to keep her balance by holding onto the window frame with one hand. She'd been out here quite a few times before and hadn't had any trouble.

She ducked her head back inside and grabbed the half pack of cigarettes lying on the window seat along with a cheap disposable lighter. She lit a cigarette and took a deep drag, planning to practice her smoke rings. Her friend, Jenny, could do them perfectly, but Shelly was pretty sure that she'd never get the hang of it.

That first drag made her feel a little dizzy, like it usually did, because she didn't have the courage to sneak a cigarette very often.

Today she was a little edgy and thought having one might help her calm down. The whole ghost thing was pretty freaky, but it really was the only interesting thing that had happened since they moved here.

Shelly knew that her mom was really freaked about everything and actually started to hope that they might be able to move back to the city because of it. But, now that they'd had that creepy Medium come over, everything was normal again and her hopes for that were dashed.

It wouldn't be too long before school would start and she was dreading it already. She had no interest in meeting new friends or trying to fit in at a new school, it was all so unfair and absolutely infuriating.

Shelly let go of the window frame and leaned forward to flick the ash off the end of her cigarette, just as she did so, it felt as if someone pushed her and she almost tumbled down the side of the house. Shelly frantically tried to grab the frame again, as she felt her sneakers slipping forward.

Shelly was just barely able to grab ahold of it and stop herself from sliding any further when the window slammed shut on her fingers. She screamed and used her feet to try and scramble back up so that she was even with the window. It took at least a minute or two because the rubber soles of her sneakers kept slipping, and by then the pain in her fingers was excruciating.

Once she was able to get her body back up to the window's level, she gently used her left hand to raise it few inches and remove her other hand. She wanted to scream and yell, but knew that she had to stay calm until she got back inside, so that she wouldn't lose her balance altogether and fall to the ground.

Very slowly, she inched her way back through the opening, holding her breath, afraid that at any moment the window would come smashing down on her. She made it through, but had barely brought her feet in when the window slammed shut hard enough that the glass vibrated. The noise it made was so loud that it sounded like a gunshot and it startled Shelly badly.

She looked around for Smoky and found her cowering under the vanity chair. Shelly shoved the chair out of the way and grabbed Smoky, ignoring the scratches and snarling as she ran out of her room and down the main staircase.

Emma was getting vegetables out of the refrigerator so she could begin making dinner when she heard Shelly scream. She dropped everything and ran towards the foyer, with Callie and the boys right behind her.

"Mom," Shelly yelled from the top of the main staircase. "Something's in my room."

She had Smoky in her arms and was about to take her first step down the stairs, when her stomach extended forward and her shoulders and upper body jerked backwards, as if someone had kicked her in the middle of her back. With her arms full, she couldn't regain her balance and fell forward, falling head over heels down the steps. Smoky leapt out of her arms and raced down ahead of Shelly's rolling body.

Emma screamed as she listened to the loud thumping of Shelly's body hitting each step and heard her grunts of pain. She ran up the stairs, hoping she could somehow stop Shelly's momentum. Instead, Shelly bounced into her and they fell down the rest of the stairs together.

"Are you okay?" Emma asked, as they tried to disentangle their limbs and get up off the floor.

"Ooh, I don't know." Emma helped Shelly up. Her face was badly bruised, she had a nasty cut on her left arm which had apparently hit the railing, hard, and the fingers on her right hand were swollen and bruised.

"Move your hands, your arms, are your legs okay, nothing's broken?"

"I don't think so," Shelly responded, and then burst out crying.

Emma hugged her tightly until Shelly jerked out of her arms.

"Where's Smoky?"

"Boys, go find Smoky. When you do, please bring her to the kitchen. Come on, Shelly, let me get your cut cleaned up."

Emma washed off the gash on Shelly's arm and then handed her a couple of bags of frozen peas, one for her swollen face and the other for her fingers, and had her sit down at the kitchen table.

"Shelly, keep Callie and Chance here with you." Emma ran up to her room to find her purse and car keys.

"Where the hell are they?" She threw items around in her purse, then searched her dresser and the rest of the room, but the keys were nowhere to be found.

Frustrated, Emma was about to return downstairs to look for them when she gasped and stopped short. The keys were suspended in mid-air in the doorway. She stared for a moment, mesmerized by the key chain dangling back and forth, being held in place by some invisible hand, and she was not prepared when they suddenly flew straight at her and hit her in the left cheekbone.

She cried out, bent down to grab the keys, snatched her purse off the bed and ran out of the room. Every door on that floor began to slam shut, open and then slam shut again; the toilet was flushing, little knickknacks and pictures were falling to the floor. Emma ignored it all and sprinted back down to the kitchen.

The boys were already there and Smoky was wrapped tightly in Shelly's arms.

"Come on, kids, let's go."

"Mom, your face is bleeding."

"Its fine, James, come on, quickly." She herded them towards the front door, her heart pounding furiously.

"Mom!" Collin screamed and stopped short, just as the huge chandelier in the foyer came crashing down to the floor right in front of them and shattered glass flew everywhere.

They huddled together in a tight circle, trying to protect their faces from the pieces of flying glass.

"Is everybody okay?" Emma asked, when the horrendous crashing sound stopped reverberating throughout the room.

They all nodded their heads or mumbled, no one seemed hurt so they ran across the foyer, glass crunching under their feet as they approached the door.

Emma prayed frantically, and was relieved that the door opened easily when she turned the knob. She jumped in the van, turned the key and fired up the engine, then waited for the kids and dogs to get settled in.

She stared for a minute at the monstrosity in front of her and could swear that she heard muffled laughter coming from the house.

Emma shook off the feeling and headed out of the driveway.

\*      \*      \*

Emma was surprised to find that her hands were still shaking as she dug through her purse to find the keys to Jeremy's apartment building. She took a deep breath, steadied herself, and managed to insert the key into the outer door.

She hadn't been back to the apartment since Jeremy moved in, but it was easy enough to find on the second floor. She stood outside his door, feeling awkward, not sure what to do when he didn't respond to their knocking.

"For goodness sake," Emma thought to herself, "your husband lives here, you don't have to knock, just let yourself in."

She fumbled with the key again, but managed to get the door unlocked and let the kids in first. After their last conversation, she was not at all sure how Jeremy was going to react to their showing up unexpectedly like this.

Everyone stood around, not sure where to go or what to do, Jeremy was nowhere to be seen.

"Go on into the living room, kids, maybe your father's still at work."

But Emma was wrong, very wrong as it turned out, and which she discovered a few short moments later when a slim, pretty blonde, wearing nothing but her husband's dress shirt, came down the long hall and into the living room. The woman stopped in her tracks, her mouth dropping open in surprise as she stared at them.

"Callie," Emma called, as the hair on the dog's back bristled and she snarled at the girl.

"Jeremy," the girl yelled out in a loud voice. "Get out here, now."

Jeremy came down the hall a minute later, his brow furrowed as he tied his robe together, too late to hide the fact that he had nothing on underneath it.

With the bedroom door wide open, Emma could hear the loud music and understood now why they hadn't been heard when they first arrived. Other than that observation, she felt nothing, no emotion, no feelings, just stunned numbness as she stared at the man that she had loved for most of her adult life.

They stood in awkward silence for what seemed like hours, but was, in reality, just seconds.

"Emma, kids," Jeremy regained his composure, put on his barrister face and started damage control. "What's going on, why are you here? Is everyone okay?"

Emma just continued to stare at him, twisting her wedding ring around and around her finger. Shelly began to cry and the boys looked down at the floor, Emma couldn't tell if they were embarrassed or just very, very angry.

"Get her out of here, now."

"Emma."

"I said now."

"Lori, why don't you run along and I'll talk to you later and explain everything."

"Sure," she replied, and returned to the bedroom. She left a few minutes later after putting on her own clothes. Jeremy walked her to the door and whispered something to her. Emma could feel her nails digging hard enough into the palms of her hands to make them bleed, but she said nothing.

Jeremy looked at the group of them standing around his living room. He felt a little unsure of himself, which was a completely foreign emotion and made him angry. Emma's face was inscrutable, but he couldn't escape the looks on his children faces, their anger and sense of betrayal was obvious.

"Emma, first off, what are you all doing here?"

She simply stared at him, unable to fathom how those could be the first words he uttered.

"Well?"

"Take a look at your daughter's face."

"What?" He turned to Shelly and saw her bruised and swollen face. "What happened, are you okay, Shelly?"

He went over to her and tried to touch her face.

"Get away from me." Her voice was as brittle as ice, a tone Emma had never heard before.

"So, what happened, what's going on?" he asked, turning back to Emma.

"Are you seriously going to pretend that we did not walk in on what we walked in on?" she asked incredulously.

"There is an explanation for that, but it's nothing we need to discuss in front of the children."

"As a matter of fact, there is nothing we need to discuss at all. The kids and Chance will be staying with you until I can find a place for the four of us. Make sure to get Shelly to a hospital to get checked out, today. I'm afraid that one or more of her fingers might be broken."

"Kids," she turned to them, fighting the tears that were threatening. "I'm going to go now. Once I get things squared away with that damned house and get us a place to stay, I'll be back for you. For now, stay here with your dad and call me if you need anything, okay?"

They all nodded hesitantly and gave her a hug.

"But when will you be back?" Connor asked.

"I don't know, hon, but it won't be long."

"Look, Emma," Jeremy began in his sternest attorney voice, grabbing her arm to stop her.

"Don't talk to me and do not touch me. I need to get away from here, right now. Get out of my way."

"But we need to talk about all of this."

"Right now, we have nothing to say to each other. I'll give you a call once I get my head wrapped around whatever this is."

Emma grabbed her purse and walked slowly to the door, knowing that once she walked out of it, her life would be changed forever. She turned the knob, didn't look back at any of them, and left the apartment with Callie at her side.

# CHAPTER 13

Emma drove around aimlessly for hours and finally found a small motel that would let her bring Callie into the room. It wasn't until the wee hours of the morning that Emma finally cried herself to sleep and she didn't wake until late the next day.

She left Callie in the room while she went out to find a diner where she could saturate herself with coffee. But, even after several cups, her head remained foggy, verging on numbness, and no amount of caffeine seemed to help.

Emma had no clue what to do next or where to go. She couldn't go back to that house and she wouldn't go back to the apartment.

Her cell phone rang and she hesitated when she saw Jeremy's name come up.

With a deep sigh, she relented and answered it. "Yes?"

"Emma, finally, where are you?"

"I don't even know."

"Come back, we need to talk. Please."

She successfully fought the tears that threatened, but her voice was shaky and small when she responded.

"Jeremy, do you have any idea how deeply you've hurt me? I can't see you right now because I would either fall into a heap of weepy nothingness, or say something so hurtful that I would never be able to take it back."

She took a deep breath, steadying herself. "I don't know where we go from here or what happens next, but I need you to leave me alone for a little while. Don't call me unless the kids need something."

Emma hung up the phone before he could try to wheedle his way into her head and convince her to come back and talk to him. They both knew that he was much better at arguing a position, and she wasn't strong enough right now to do that kind of battle with him.

She finished her coffee and pulled out her wallet. As she did, a business card flitted out and landed on the table. Emma picked it up and saw that it was the one Agent Collins' had given her after Ron Waters died in their basement.

They hadn't really seemed like FBI agents and she got the impression from Agent Collins that he knew something that he wasn't sharing.

"What the hell," she thought, as she pulled out her phone and entered the number.

"Agent Collins," he answered, moments later.

"Good morning," she said, suddenly unsure of herself, wondering why she had called. "I'm Emma Draper, you came to my house last week. We've had some more problems and, I just thought I'd talk to you about them, if you have time."

"Draper," he sounded like he was trying to place the name, "oh, you had a medium at your house when we came, right? At the old Creeghan place?"

"Yes."

"So, what's going on?"

"It's gotten worse, we've moved out and I don't know what to do anymore. I'm not even sure why I called, but I found your card and thought maybe you could help. I'm sorry I bothered you, I'll let you go."

"No, wait, wait, are you there?"

"Yes."

"We can help, where are you now?"

"I'm in a little town called Fayette, about a half an hour away from the house."

"Is the rest of your family with you?"

"No," she hesitated, "they're with my husband at his apartment. I'm by myself, well, with my dog."

"Okay, we're a few hours away, but we can be there by late afternoon. Can you meet us at the house?"

She didn't answer immediately because the thought of going back inside, particularly by herself, was paralyzing.

"I can't go in there alone."

"No, of course not. Is there some place we could meet first?"

"At my friend, Lynne's, house. She has the blue cape, it's on the left before you get to our house at the end of the street. I'll go over there this afternoon and you can stop in whenever you get there. And, thanks, Agent Collins, I really appreciate your help."

"It's no problem, stay safe, we'll be there as soon as we can."

*     *     *

"Seriously, Emma, who are those guys?"

Lynne and Emma, hidden on either side of the large picture window behind the heavy, mauve drapes were peering out at the sporty coupe that had pulled into the driveway.

"I'm not sure any more. I've never seen an FBI agent that drove a car like that. Do you even know what it is?"

"Clueless," Lynne muttered, "looks old and cool though."

"It does, doesn't it? Oh crap, they're getting out of the car." Emma pulled back and hid further behind the drapes.

"And again, I say, who are those guys? No suits, but damn, they look good." Lynne was starting to whisper as she peeked out the window, although the men were still out in the driveway and couldn't hear anything inside the house. "I particularly like the tall one in the long, suede jacket, smoking hot, isn't he?"

Emma giggled. "I prefer the one in the leather coat, he looks like a badass, much more my type."

The men knocked on the front door and Emma tried to swallow back her amusement. After all, she had just caught her husband cheating on her with a beautiful, younger woman and her freaking house was haunted. This was not a funny situation, or maybe it was, she acknowledged with a last little burst of the giggles before she pulled herself together.

"Gentlemen," Lynne graciously invited the men in, the whisper of a silly smile lingering on her lips as she did so.

"Ma'am," the taller one nodded at her and then turned towards Emma. "Are you okay?"

"I'll be fine," she said, although she was still feeling pretty sore after her fall down the stairs with Shelly.

"What happened to your face?" he asked.

"Damned ghost threw my keys at me just before we got out of there," she replied, subconsciously running her finger along the little cut on her cheek. "So, what happens now, agents?"

The other one started talking, watching Emma closely as he did so. His dark brown eyes were intense, mesmerizing, and she couldn't seem to break the connection and look away while he spoke.

"We need to know everything that has happened in the house since you've been there, to who,"

"To whom." Lynne corrected him without thinking, but when she saw the scathing look he gave her, she vowed to keep her mouth shut and say nothing further. He looked positively frightening, and she did not want to find out what could happen if she made him really angry.

"To whom it happened. It would also be helpful if you could show us where it happened, do you think you could do that?"

"I don't know if I can go back into that house."

"We'll be there and won't let anything happen to you."

"How the hell do you protect me from a ghost or a demon?"

"It's what we do, Ma'am."

"You can call me Emma. And, you aren't in some special ghost division of the FBI, so please be honest with me. Who are you and how can you really help?"

The men looked at the two women, then at each other and the younger, taller one explained as best he could.

"You're right, we do not work for the FBI, this is my brother, Scott, and my name is Tim Devereaux. We help people in situations like yours. We figure out what the problem is and get rid of it."

"Get rid of it how? And how do you figure out what the problem is to begin with?"

"First, we have to get into the house and find out exactly what we're up against," said the older brother, Scott. "I'm not going to go through the whole process with you. You're just going to have to trust us. And, if you want to help us get this taken care of even quicker, you can sack up, come to the house with us and show us what we need to see. Otherwise, just step back out of the way and let us do what we've got to do."

He was an unusual man, brusque, verging on rude, and very difficult to read. Emma could see that he didn't really care if she believed them or not. He was going to do what he felt he had to do, regardless of what she thought and, for some reason that, more than anything else, led her to trust him and, by extension, his brother.

"Let's go then."

Scott was pleasantly surprised at her bravado, particularly since he could see how frightened she was at the thought of going back inside that house. He was impressed and gave her a slight smile and a quick nod, then looked questioningly at Lynne.

"Hell no, I'm never setting foot in that house again, I don't even want to be in the vicinity of it. Well, no closer than I am right now, anyway, and sometimes I think that's actually too close."

Another quick smile and Scott started to lead the three of them out of the house.

"Wait," Emma said, as Callie stood and started following them out. "Do we need Callie to come? She can sense when something is around but, no matter what, we can't let anything happen to her."

Scott stared thoughtfully at the dog, trying to figure out if she would be more of an asset or a hindrance.

"Would you be less scared if she was with you in the house?"

Emma hesitated and then nodded her assent. Even though she was very frightened for Callie, she realized that she, herself, would be much more comfortable with Callie at her side.

"Okay, bring her along."

"How much more selfish could I be?" Emma wondered, as she grabbed the leash and hooked it to Callie's collar.

She hugged Lynne briefly. "Thank you, for everything, I'm not sure what happens next, but I'll check in with you to let you know what's going on when I can, okay?"

"Alright, please stay safe."

"I will." With another quick hug, she led Callie outside and was surprised to see that Scott was getting into his car.

"Why are we driving there, it's just up the road?"

"Our weapons are in the trunk, we'll want the car there in case we need them."

"What kind of weapons? I really don't understand what's going on."

Tim took pity on her and tried to set her mind at rest. "Go ahead and drive up, Scott. We'll meet you there."

The short walk helped calm Emma's nerves a little, but as Tim tried to explain, she became even more confused.

"We have to figure out exactly what is haunting your home and we will get rid of it, but until we get all of the information that we need, we have various weapons that we can use to protect ourselves from ghosts and demons. It doesn't get rid of them, it just neutralizes them temporarily, giving us more time to do what we have to. Understand?"

"Not really, this is all way too much for me to comprehend."

They were at the house in just minutes and Emma felt every bone in her body turn into weak, terrified jelly as she stared at the monstrosity in front of her.

She took a deep breath and tried to steady her trembling hands, but pure terror at the thought of going back inside threatened to overwhelm her. Callie started a low growl which unnerved Emma even more.

Scott got a couple of shotguns from the trunk of his car and casually threw one to Tim, who caught it effortlessly. Then he retrieved two strange looking pistols and threw one of them to Tim, as well.

"How will guns help?"

"The shotgun shells are loaded with rock salt and the handguns have holy water in them." Scott explained. "Neither will kill them, but it will slow them down a little. I need you to stay close to me, okay? We don't want anything to happen to you."

He paused as they started towards the house. "Pretty creepy looking place, even in the daylight."

"Why do you say that?" Emma asked, wringing her hands together in an effort to get some control over herself.

Scott just shrugged and strode towards the house. "Just calling it like I see it."

Emma took another deep breath and hurried up the porch steps behind him, not wanting to be left behind. Once inside the house, she immediately felt the cold heaviness of the air and shivered.

"I'd better clean up this glass first," she said, as they tried to find a clean spot on the foyer floor. "The chandelier falling was the last thing that happened to us before we took off."

"Probably a good idea, no need for us to get all cut up on that before the real fun begins."

Tim went with her to get the broom, dustpan and garbage bags and they had the floor pretty well cleaned up in no time, at least the main areas where they would be walking.

Tim pulled a strange little gadget out of his coat pocket and turned it on.

"Anything?" Scott asked.

"Not yet."

"What's that?" Emma asked.

Scott let out an exasperated sigh and rolled his eyes. "Man, you are just full of questions. It's an EMF machine, it'll let us know if there are any spirits nearby. I appreciate that this is all new to you and that you're curious, but if you could hold your questions until we have some downtime, it would really help us out."

Emma flushed and looked away. Tim caught her eye and gave her an encouraging smile.

"Don't worry about him, Emma. He's always lacked some rather important people skills."

The hair along Callie's back suddenly stood up and she began a low, deep growl at the exact same time that the lights began flashing on the EMF machine and it started making strange loud noises.

Both men came over to Emma, sandwiching her between them. Emma held tight to Callie's leash as she began to bark frantically at something on the stairway that only she could see.

Scott blasted off a round from the shotgun in that direction and Callie stopped barking.

"Okay, take us on a little tour of your house and let us know what happened, when and to who, excuse me, whom, okay, Emma?"

"Sure," she replied, although the shotgun blast was still echoing in her eardrums and she still hadn't quite processed the fact that he had just shot a ghost on the staircase of her home.

She led them into the kitchen. "I was in here our first night when something brushed the hair off my neck, I thought it was Jeremy, but no one else was in the room. And it was a couple of weeks later when Banshee, our cat, had something happen to him in the dumb waiter. I don't even know how he got in there or what exactly happened, but he screamed and cried and according to the vet he sustained massive internal damage."

Emma's voice caught in her throat and she felt like she was going to start sobbing. She refused to do that in front of these two men and had to stop for a minute and get herself back under control before continuing.

Neither of them approached her or offered any sympathy. She was grateful for that, because it would only have opened the flood gates and all of her emotions would have tumbled out unchecked.

CHAPTER 14

"Where does this staircase go?" Scott asked.

"Directly up to the third floor where my daughter's room is."

"No issues there?"

"On that staircase, no." Emma led them down the hall and into the dining room. "In here, all I've ever noticed are cold spots, and sometimes things were moved around and I would find them in the oddest places."

"Poltergeist?" Tim asked, looking at his brother.

"Could be."

Emma bit her tongue when she started to ask what a poltergeist was and, as requested, decided to wait until they had some 'downtime' to get all of her questions answered.

Then she led them to the library. "We really haven't spent much time in this room, I'm not aware of anything happening here."

"The living room though, is a different story. It's the last room down this hallway, and it's where the black goo appeared under my upside down picture and keeps reappearing even after I clean it up."

"Ectoplasm, most likely," Tim stated, as they entered the room and he stared curiously at the goo still smeared on the wall. "Usually, you don't see it, especially this much of it, unless you have an extremely pissed off spirit."

He took a sample with a Q-tip and put that into a small jar which he threw into his backpack. "Anything else happen in this room?"

Emma thought for a moment and then remembered the episode with Chance. "My other dog went a little crazy in here, he chased something around the room that we couldn't see, and ended up running right into that wall over there."

"That wall adjoins the kitchen, doesn't it?"

"Yes, it does."

Tim pursed his lips and his brows drew together as he looked around the room, trying to work something out. "I'm going to take a walk outside, get a better picture of the whole house. You guys keep going in here."

Emma led Scott up the main staircase. They hadn't even gotten halfway up before Scott's EMF and Callie simultaneously let out their warnings about the entity that had joined them.

Scott took a moment to see where Callie was looking and then fired off his shotgun again. She barked a couple more times and then the hair on her back smoothed and she quieted down.

"She's a great help," Scott said, nodding at the dog.

"Yes, she is, I just really can't have anything happen to her. It would kill me."

"She'll be fine, don't worry. Any problems on these stairs?"

"This is where something pushed my daughter. I swear you could see her chest and stomach bow forward, as if something shoved her in the middle of the back."

They made their way through the second and third floors and Emma pointed out the other incidents that had occurred. The EMF and Callie remained quiet as they finished their tour of the upstairs.

"Anything else that you can think of?" Scott asked, as they made their way back to the kitchen.

Emma hesitated as she looked over at the basement door, just the thought of it gave her the heebie-jeebies.

"The basement is about the creepiest place in the house. It just feels bad down there and its where Ron Waters died. I don't think it's safe."

Scott walked over and opened the door wide, turned on the light and took the first step down into the dank, murky cellar.

"Please, don't."

Scott was not afraid to head down into the basement alone, but hesitated when he looked over at Emma. He was pleasantly surprised that she had found the courage to come back into the house at all, but suddenly her face became extremely pale and her whole body tensed. Obviously, the basement was a trigger for her terror and her courage was fading fast. He relented and stepped back into the kitchen, turned off the light and closed and locked the door.

"We can check that out some other time. So, is that it then?"

"Well, there were quite a few incidents in the barn."

"The barn? That's odd, usually a haunting will stick inside one building, although there is the rare case where it occurs on the entire premises. Let's get Tim and check it out."

They found Tim right outside the back of the house, pacing off the length of it.

"What's up?" Scott asked.

"The numbers don't add up," Tim replied. "I got the measurements inside and out, and I think there might be another room separating the living room and the kitchen."

Both men looked curiously at the back of the house and it was the first time that Emma had really paid any attention to it. There was a long section where there were absolutely no windows or doors at all, between the kitchen door and the nice big living room window at the other end of the house.

"Interesting," Scott said. "Emma, are you going to have a problem with us breaking down the wall in your living room?"

"Not particularly," she replied with a smile. "You can tear the whole damn house down, as far as I'm concerned."

"Well, let's just start with the wall. We can hit the hardware store tonight and work on that tomorrow. Come on, Tim, we're going to go check out the barn."

"Multiple location haunting?" Tim asked, as he followed them out to the barn. "That's pretty unusual."

Since the horses were no longer in there, the barn door wasn't padlocked. Emma opened the door and showed the men where the horses had been stalled, and how she found them those mornings when they were mysteriously moved around.

"I was right here when something shoved me in the middle of my back so hard that I fell to the ground and thought Charlie was going to stomp on me. He barely missed my head with his hooves and then took off down the road. He ended up breaking his leg and is still at the Veterinary Hospital."

Emma surprised herself by how calm she was able to remain while talking about it, even though it had been extremely traumatic at the time. Either she was beginning to toughen up or so many painful things had happened, that talking about them just wasn't having the same impact on her anymore.

Emma jumped as the EMF machine began to go haywire and Callie started barking frantically at the exact same time. She almost pulled herself free from Emma's grasp, but Emma held tight to the leash as Callie strained to get loose and go after whatever it was that only she could see.

Emma watched in disbelief as Tim was suddenly lifted into the air and flung across the room into one of the stall doors. He sank to the ground with an 'oompf', shook his head to clear it and tried to stand up. He was deftly thrown back into the door again and this time did not recover as quickly.

"Timmy," Scott called. "Timmy, you okay?"

Scott had the shotgun up and was prepared to shoot, but the way Callie was barking it looked like the entity was right above Tim. The salt pellets wouldn't kill him, but they would sting a lot, so Scott waited.

"Tim, answer me, you okay?"

"Yeah," he said, taking a deep breath and getting ready to try to stand up again.

"Hold off," Scott said, watching Callie closely, her head turned to the right, followed something along the timbers in the ceiling of the barn and then circled back towards Tim.

Before her gaze got all the way back to him on the ground, Scott took a shot above Tim, off to his right, and swore he could hear some type of animal scream. The coldness and dank air seemed to give way and Callie's barking became just a low whine as her hair smoothed out again.

After everything quieted down, Tim said, "Okay, believe it or not, I think I was just attacked by a monkey."

"Seriously, dude, a monkey? How'd you come up with that?"

"I felt it and it could not have been anything else. I can't believe it was strong enough to throw me around like that, but I swear that's what it was."

Scott just looked at him in disbelief.

"Um, my boys thought they heard a monkey in their room. I forgot all about them mentioning it, but now it seems rather important."

Scott gave her a withering look but kept his thoughts to himself.

"Okay, enough fun for one day. Let's hit the hardware store, find a motel and come up with a game plan for tomorrow."

\*     \*     \*

They found a decent motel on the outskirts of town and got two rooms, one for the two of them and one for Emma and Callie.

Emma had hastily packed a bag back at the house and Scott even carried it to her room for her. He was an odd duck. He could be gentlemanly and thoughtful and then, like quicksilver, he was cold and rude, almost frightening in his intensity. Emma didn't quite know what to make of him or how to act around him.

"Timmy and I are going to run over to the hardware store before it closes. We won't be gone long and we can grab something to eat once we get back, okay?"

"Sure, I'll just get Callie squared away."

He looked thoughtfully at the black beast sitting patiently at her side.

"That dog is freakin' awesome," he said with a smile, and then left the room.

Emma laughed and rubbed Callie's head. "I already knew you were awesome. Ready for some dinner?"

Callie wagged her tail and rubbed affectionately up against Emma's leg. After she ate, Emma took her for a short walk around the neighborhood and they arrived back just as the men pulled into the parking lot.

The Little Gem Diner was kitty-corner from the hotel, with a big neon sign advertising the best flapjacks in the tri-state area. It was clean and bright and all the young waitresses wore matching pink dresses with name tags. They grabbed a booth in the back, away from the other patrons, and settled in.

In between mouthfuls of greasy burgers and gravy covered fries, Emma was finally able to get answers to some of the questions that had been burning in her brain all day.

After a few questions, it became a kind of game, Scott and Tim vying over who could answer first. They were both relaxed and eager to educate her and she enjoyed their company. When they weren't being all scary and intense, they were actually pretty fun to be around.

"Okay, the funny little doo-hickey with the lights and funny noises?"

"EMF, electromagnetic field detector." Tim jumped in before Scott could swallow his last bite of burger. "It indicates the presence a physical field produced by electrically charged objects."

"I don't understand." Emma stated honestly.

"The spirits, ghosts, demons, whatever, radiate energy that can be picked up by an EMF. It's how we know when they are around. The louder the do-hickey is, the closer they are."

"But, what was really amazing," Scott interrupted, his dark brown eyes flashing with excitement, "was that dog. I didn't know they could sense spirits like that. We are going to have to get us one of those, bro. No batteries needed."

Tim just looked at him and laughed.

"What?"

"Seriously, dude, it's a living, breathing creature. You can't even take care of yourself, how are you going to take care of a dog, on the road no less?"

"How hard can it be?"

"Oh, it's piece of cake," Emma added. "You'll definitely need a lot of these though, particularly for a big shepherd like Callie."

She slid a few clean, unused and brightly colored refuse bags across the table to him with a giggle.

"Right." He gave a half laugh, obviously not finding it the least bit funny, and shrugged his shoulders. "The EMF works fine anyway."

And just like that the subject was done and Scott was moving on to more gastronomical issues.

"Excuse me, Tammy, is it?" The young brunette nodded her head and hurried over, flashing him a bright smile.

"Yes, can I do something for you?"

"Boy, could you," he said, bringing a blush to her cheeks, "but, for now I think I just need a piece of cheesecake, what kind do you have?"

She rattled off several different flavors, her eyes never leaving Scott's face.

"Strawberry sounds excellent. What about you two?" he asked, since Tammy had apparently forgotten there was anyone else at the table.

Both of them declined and Emma couldn't help but wonder how the two of them managed to keep in such great shape with a daily diet of greasy burgers and cheesecake.

"Little young for you, isn't she?" Tim asked, as Tammy sashayed away, her little pink skirt flitting from side to side.

"Never," Scott replied with a devilish smile.

Tim rolled his eyes and turned to Emma. "So, did we answer all your questions?"

"Not quite, I still don't understand exactly what a demon is."

"They are inhumans, they've never been alive in human form, not like a ghost or spirit was."

"Spiritual parasites that feed off of people's energy and create havoc. They can hurt people physically, emotionally and mentally," Scott added.

"But why are they here? How can they be here?"

Tim tried to explain. "There are lots of different reasons, for instance they can be summoned."

"Think Ouija board," Scott interjected, then thanked the waitress for his strawberry cheesecake and was quiet while he dug into it.

"Like I said," Tim gave Scott a baleful look and continued with his explanation, "they can be summoned, and sometimes they come in through open portals. Once they're here, they can be very tough to get rid of."

"Venetia mentioned portals, what exactly are they?"

"They are like doorways to the other side, they allow demons to enter our dimension."

"And how are those portals created?"

"Again, different ways, sometimes by people dabbling in the occult and opening the portal without even realizing it."

"And how do you tell if there is a portal?"

Tim looked at Scott who nodded affirmatively and then continued with his dessert.

"We have a crystal, a special crystal, and it if gets anywhere near a portal, it begins to vibrate intensely."

"And then what?" Emma asked, her mind spinning with all of this information.

"We figure out how to close it."

"But how?"

"Emma," Scott interrupted. "It's been fun playing twenty questions with you, but sometimes we can't figure out the answer until we know exactly what the problem is first."

He called the waitress back over, told her how great the cheesecake was and asked for the check.

Tammy blushed again as she pulled out their ticket and handed it to Scott, then she smiled prettily and walked away. Emma found it amusing that Scott did not take his eyes off her swaying hips until she reached the other end of the diner.

Then he turned his attention back to Emma. "We don't know what we're dealing with at your house yet. It could be just a vengeful spirit, it could be multiple spirits, or it could be one or more demons. We just don't have enough information and we don't have all the answers that you want. So, we're done playing 'What If' for now, you just have to give us a little time to figure out what's what first, okay?"

Emma just nodded, taken aback at his sudden change in attitude.

Tim rolled his eyes and gave a brief shake of his head. "Emma, your questions are fine, ask whatever you want. We understand that this is all new and strange for you, so just ignore him, he can be such a dick sometimes."

"It's okay," she replied. "I appreciate the honesty, but it really is helpful to me if you can explain things as they happen. If I can understand some of what is going on, regardless of how unbelievable and crazy it seems, it might help keep me grounded and I won't feel quite so much like I'm losing my mind."

She looked directly at Scott. "And I really don't need to be talked to like I'm a twelve-year-old, okay?"

"I'll see what I can do about that," Scott replied, his dark brown eyes positively sparkling, and his face suddenly lit up with a smile so charming that it was almost criminal.

# CHAPTER 15

Emma wasn't sure what the correct protocol was the next morning. She was up early and planned on taking Callie for a nice long walk before the day got all crazy on them, but she wasn't sure what Scott and Tim's plans were.

She knocked tentatively on their door and was relieved that it was answered quickly, so she hadn't woken them up. Tim stepped back to let them into the room and Emma could see Scott on the floor behind him doing pushups.

He looked up, smiled, grunted and did a few more. Emma had to consciously tear her eyes away from his broad, bare, muscular back when she realized that Tim was talking to her.

"Um, I'm sorry, what did you say?"

He looked at her curiously, with a little half smile on his face. "Just asked what's up."

"I, um, plan on taking Callie for a walk," Emma replied, feeling the blush in her cheeks and getting angry at her reaction. "I just wanted to make sure that you two wouldn't go to the house without me, we'll be back in just a little bit, okay?"

"Of course, we'll wait. We can meet you across the street at the Little Gem when you get back, we'll have breakfast and head out."

"That sounds good," she replied, and turned back towards the door.

"Hold up," Scott said, jumping up from the floor and wiping the sweat off his brow with a towel. "Give me two minutes and I'll meet you out front. I'll walk with you for a little bit and then run back. I can be all showered and changed by the time you two finish your walk."

"Alright," Emma replied hesitantly, not sure exactly how she felt about his intrusion into her morning routine. "We'll be outside then."

He met up with them just moments later and they started walking down the street. For a few minutes, they just walked along in silence, stopping to let Callie sniff when she found something interesting.

The birds were starting to get busy and were chirping away. It was still a little too early for there to be much traffic, so it was fairly quiet and peaceful.

"This is nice," Scott said. "I'm usually up early to take a run, but this is different, relaxing."

"Yes, it is, it's Callie and my quality time, I try to do this with her as much as I can, but I've kind of neglected her with all the craziness going on."

"She seems fine. I wouldn't worry about it, if I were you."

"Callie's a good girl, I don't know what I'd do without her."

Emma glanced sideways at him. "If you don't mind my asking, why did you and your brother pretend to be FBI agents when you first came to the house?"

"Well, we aren't always welcomed with open arms when we show up and tell people we can get rid of their ghosts for them. I mean, sometimes people ask for that help, like you did, and then we can be up front about what we do. But, most people have a hard time believing ghosts are real to begin with and think we're just trying to scam them. So, we use whatever ruse we have to in order to get our foot in the door, so we can try to help."

"How did you and your brother get started in such a lucrative business as ghost hunting?"

He gave her a charming half-smile, then looked straight ahead as he explained.

"We just followed in our dad's footsteps. It wasn't even really a choice, what little kid wouldn't want to do the same thing, once they found out their dad hunted ghosts?"

"But, how many little boys even know that ghosts are real?"

"Good point," he replied, "but we learned about a lot of things at a young age, for our own protection."

"What kind of things?"

He turned and raised a brow at her. "You already know more than you should about certain things, so I think we can drop that subject for now."

"Fine, can I know more about your family?"

"Maybe, what do you want to know?"

"Where are your parents now?"

Scott was quiet for a moment and there was the briefest flash of sadness on his face.

"My dad died a few years ago, and my mom still lives in the house that Timmy and I grew up in."

"I'm so sorry about your father." Emma hesitated for a moment.

"No," Scott responded to her silent question, "he did not get killed on a hunt, it was a massive heart attack that snuck up and killed him one quiet Sunday afternoon. He never saw it coming."

"And your mother?"

Scott's eyes positively glowed with affection and his face lit up. "She is an amazing woman, spry and healthy and smarter than anyone I've ever met. We call and check in on her at least once a week, and stop to see her whenever we're in that area. As a matter of fact, I think I owe her a call."

"She doesn't have a problem with you doing this for a living?"

"If she did, she wouldn't say so. She lived the life with my dad for so many years that she's used to it, but she does worry a lot, which is why we check in with her so often, just to let her know we're okay. She pretty much raised us alone with my dad gone so much of the time."

"I don't imagine that was very easy."

"You can take that to the bank."

"And, are you married, do the two of you have families waiting for you back home?"

"Tim was engaged once, but it fell through. This is a tough life and it's hard to make a relationship work when you're on the road all the time, and pretty much on call every day of the year. Frankly, I'm surprised that my parents stayed together all those years. I think he was just lucky and found a very special woman."

"That could happen for you, too."

"Not likely, I'm not sure if you've noticed, but I can be a little rough around the edges."

"You don't say," she replied with a smile.

"And what about you? It's kind of curious that you're the one taking the initiative to get that house cleaned up and not your husband. It's not something for the faint of heart."

Tears unexpectedly bubbled up in Emma's eyes. She tried to wipe them away quickly, but wasn't able to do so before Scott noticed.

"I think I left him."

"You think? Usually, people are pretty sure one way or the other about that kind of thing."

Emma laughed harshly. "I am definitely not sure about anything anymore. Between living in a haunted house and catching my husband cheating on me, I'm not even sure who the hell I am or what I'm doing."

Scott watched her curiously as her lashes lowered over those brilliant green eyes and she subconsciously began to twist her wedding ring around and around her finger.

"But, I really do miss my kids," she added, almost in a whisper, afraid to admit it out loud because then she might actually crumble and break.

Emma gave Scott a brave smile but couldn't keep her lips from trembling, so she took a deep breath and looked away, trying to get her emotions back under control.

He reached over and grabbed her hand, squeezed it gently and gave her a tender smile.

"You're a strong woman and you are very brave. You know what's important, to yourself and to your family. We'll do everything we can to take care of the ghost problem, the rest you'll sort out yourself when it's time. I know you will. Take however much time you need with the dog, we'll meet you back at the diner when you're ready, okay?"

"All right, and thanks." She watched as he jogged off down a side street and did feel a little stronger, a little more capable, kind of rejuvenated. For being such a brusque, arrogant person, he certainly had found the right things to snap her out of her little pity party and get her ready to take on the day.

*     *     *

"And what do we have here?" Scott asked with relief.

They'd been working on the living room wall for almost an hour and both of them were covered in a sheen of sweat after taking turns swinging the heavy sledge hammer time and again. The wall didn't budge for the longest time and then suddenly, with a heaving groan, a huge section of it fell in.

Scott dropped the hammer and they both dug through their duffel bags, grabbing their guns and some other items, and then gingerly stepped through the opening.

Emma followed them, trying not to trip on the pieces of the rubble strewn all over the room or choke on the thick plaster dust floating through the air. She was glad that she'd decided to leave Callie back at the hotel this time.

The room was small, about the size of a pantry, which made sense since the wall on the opposite side abutted the kitchen.

Mid way across the room, there was a set of spiral stairs heading downward. The men shined their flashlights down into the gloom and looked at each other.

"Listen, Emma, I told you this morning that you should stay back at the motel." Tim's tone, and the look that he gave her, were very stern. "We agreed to let you come this far, but now we're headed into unchartered territory and you need to go out to the car where its safe."

"I am not doing that, Timmy."

"No one gets to call me Timmy, except my brother, and that's just because I can't make him stop doing it. And you need to stop being so freakin' stubborn about this."

"I'm not being stubborn, Tim, this is my house. Are you afraid that I'll get in your way, that I can't take care of myself because I'm a woman?"

"You're being a woman has nothing to do with it," Scott said. "We do these jobs ourselves, we don't bring any guests along for the ride."

"You wanted me here yesterday."

"Yes, to give us an idea of what we're dealing with. Now, we have to do our job and you will just get in the way." Scott's brow was furrowed in a menacing scowl.

"You don't scare me," Emma said, her voice wavering a little more than she anticipated. "Please understand that I have to see this through. I have to know that whatever is here, is taken care of, or I can never feel safe again, for myself or for my children. Please?"

"Fine, stay close, but stay out of the way."

Scott headed down the steps and Tim was dumbfounded, unable to believe that Scott had given up the fight that easy. It was not like him to let a civilian be this involved in their work, and it was starting to concern Tim that Scott was making up new rules when it came to the attractive Mrs. Draper.

He reluctantly motioned Emma down and then followed her, shining his light over her shoulder to help her see where she was going.

Scott stepped off the last stair and flashed his light around the room.

"Tim, you have any matches on you?"

"Yeah, why?"

"Because my lighter died and there are oil lamps down here that might actually still work."

Between the two of them, they found several and, once they were lit, the room brightened with an eerie yellow glow. The three of them stood and stared around in amazement.

"What the hell are we looking at Timmy?"

"Well, I think I can say with a great deal of certainty that someone used this room for a little black magic. Those are some kind of warding symbols on the floor and walls."

"What's with the spice jars?" Emma asked, checking out one of the walls that were covered with shelves containing jars labeled myrrh, cloves, periwinkle, sage and many, many others.

"Different spices are used in different rituals. Most are to help protect the person conjuring the spirit. Anything with preservative qualities are loathed by demons or evil spirits, that's why the salt pellets help to get rid of them, at least temporarily."

"Excuse me, Professor." Scott broke in from over in a dark corner of the room. "Would you like to try to explain this?"

Emma swallowed a scream as she and Tim walked over and saw the skeleton lying on the floor at Scott's feet.

"Oh, shit." Tim was almost as surprised as Emma. "Who do you suppose that was?"

"Seriously? There is a human skeleton in my basement and your only issue is its identity?" Her voice was rising as she spoke and they both looked at her with concern.

"Calm down," Scott said, "he's been dead a long time. There is nothing for you to be scared about."

"Don't tell me to calm down," she replied in a steely tone as she glared at him.

"Fine, be what you gotta be." He turned back to Tim. "What's that on his head?"

Tim squatted down beside the body to get a better look.

"Looks like a wreath of Vervain. Conjurers would wear them for protection when summoning demons. It doesn't look like it worked too well for this guy, though."

"So, what do we do?" Emma asked. "Should I go upstairs and call the police?"

"No." They both shouted it at the same time.

"Why not? It's a person, we have to report it."

"We need to figure out who he is and then we need to burn the bones."

"We need to what?" she asked incredulously.

Scott looked at her impatiently. "This guy's spirit could be one of the ones causing you trouble. The only way to release him from here for good, if that's the case, is to salt and burn his bones. The cops might frown on our doing that."

Then he turned back to Tim. "What's with those symbols on his robe?"

"They could be an indication of the demon that he was trying to summon. They did that sometimes, to invoke more mojo, which they would need for a heavy-duty, bad ass demon. If we can figure out what the demon's name is from these symbols, it might help us get rid of it."

"And what about the bones? How do we figure out who he was?"

"He must be connected with the house somehow and there are a lot of books and paperwork down here. We should be able to figure it out."

"Okay, then," Scott stated. "Let's get started."

To Emma's horror, they started by removing the robe from the skeleton and laying it out on the floor so they could get photos of all of the symbols and writing on it. Then they folded it up and carefully set it on one of the shelves.

Then they wrapped the bones in an old blanket they found and carried them up the stairs. Emma hurried over to lead the way, supposedly to light the steps with the flashlight for them, but more so because she had no intention of staying down in that creepy room without them.

They carried their bundle out to the backside of the barn, then they all returned to the basement room to carry up as many of the papers and books as they could get their hands on.

After those were safely stored in the trunk, Scott slammed it down and just stood quietly, staring at the house with a thoughtful look on his handsome face, running his fingers absently through his thick hair.

"Something doesn't feel right."

"What?"

"I'm not sure, but with so much activity in this house, why hasn't anything bothered us while were trying to get to that room?"

Both of the men stared up at the house as if they would find the answer there. Emma followed their gaze and shivered uncontrollably.

# CHAPTER 16

The men decided that the area was secluded enough that they could burn the bones during the day without anyone seeing them and took turns digging a huge hole out near the barn. One would dig and the other kept watch to be sure they weren't being observed. They threw the bundle with the bones into the hole, Scott poured a container of salt over it and Tim poured gasoline on that and then threw a match in.

There was a terrific burst of flames and Emma was relieved that there were no disembodied wails or screams coming out of the hole, along with the smoke and flames. But, she still had to fight to stay upright and not pass out as she tried to wrap her head around what was happening. It was a little hard to accept the fact that she was not only abetting these men in what was probably a felony, but that a skeleton was being burned on her property. No matter what happened as far as the house was concerned, as long as she lived here, she would always know what they did in this spot, and would somehow have to learn to live with it.

"Okay," Tim said, once the hole was filled back in. "I'm going to head over to the library and see what else I can dig up about this house and its owners. Emma, can I have the paperwork that you put together on it already? No sense duplicating what you've already done."

"Sure, if you'll come in the house with me to get it." She wasn't setting foot inside that house without at least one of them with her.

Once they'd collected the paperwork and dropped Tim off at the library, they went back to the motel and lugged all the books up to Scott's room and started to go through them to see what answers they might reveal.

"Oh, my God," Emma exclaimed, "the things they use in some of these spells is so gross, pigeon's blood or human blood, the eyes of a bull and dried head of frogs, the powdered brains of a black cat. I'm at a loss to see how these things could be useful for anything. Did they really collect them?"

"Yes, they did, and probably still do. You must have gotten your hands on his Grimoire," Scott said, smiling at the disgusted look on her face. "A Grimoire is a book of spells and incantations, every self-respecting witch or wizard has one. It's like a recipe book for the dark side."

"I can't believe he would have actually used these." Emma threw the Grimoire over onto the pile of books on the floor that they had already gone through, then she flopped back against the headboard of Tim's empty bed.

"So, Tim's the brain and you're the brawn, is that how this works?"

"No, why would you think that?"

He almost sounded upset and Emma was worried that she had offended him.

"I'm sorry, you just seem to be the one out in front with guns ablazing and Tim spends a lot of time researching, so I just assumed."

"Well, to give credit where it's due, Tim is much better at research than I am. He's like an idiot savant, he never forgets anything he reads, and he reads a lot."

Scott got up, tossed the book he'd been looking through onto his bed and walked over to the mini-fridge. He grabbed both of them a beer and then sat back on Tim's bed next to her.

Emma was a little surprised that he joined her, but had to admit that she didn't mind his closeness at all, in fact she enjoyed the little tingle that she felt whenever his arm brushed against hers.

"Your family is very tightknit, isn't it?"

"Yes, it is," Scott replied. "We sort of have to be."

"What do you mean?"

"Well, even growing up, Tim and I were pretty much the only friends we had. We couldn't tell anyone about the things that we knew, so it was hard to be close with anyone else."

"That's so sad," Emma replied.

"Not really, we're only a couple of years apart and he isn't so bad once you get to know him."

"I know that, and neither are you, so you both should have been very popular with the boys your age, and the girls."

"Don't get me wrong,' he said, with a mischievous look in his eye, "I had no problem getting friendly with the girls."

"I don't imagine that you did," she replied. "I saw how you were with our cute little waitress, Tammy. I can tell you aren't too shy around the ladies."

He had a smirk on his face, but wisely decided not to respond.

"What about school, I assume you did go to school, didn't you?"

"Oh, yeah, but we missed a lot of it. Dad started taking me on hunting trips when I was twelve. Mom fought him tooth and nail, but he won that fight."

"That's so young, though."

"Not really, I learned how to shoot a gun when I was nine, I was ready."

"But, you never got to be a kid." Emma tried to envision her own sons carrying weapons and going off for extended periods of time to fight ghosts and demons, but she couldn't imagine how any mother would allow it, regardless of how old they were.

"Sure I did, just a different kind of kid. Tim didn't join us until he was fifteen. He was chomping at the bit by then, but Mom was not backing down that time. It was funny though, no matter how much school Tim missed, he still did great, me, not so much. I was not exactly an A student and couldn't wait to be done with it and get down to some real work."

Emma was quiet for a few moments. "You know, that really helps explain you."

"Meaning?"

"You have a great sense of humor, but you are the type of person that can't stand nonsense, that always wants to get down to business, get it done and then you can relax and have some fun, is that correct?"

"Pretty much, I guess."

"Like I said then, it helps to explain you. You get a little impatient, a little brusque, when things are slowing you down, but then your charming personality comes shining through once you've taken care of what needs to be done. Now, I know to just stay out of your way until the hard stuff is taken care of and wait for, what did you call it, 'downtime'?"

"Well, aren't you the clever one?" he asked, his eyes caught and held hers and although Emma's heart skipped a beat or two, he was the first to his turn his gaze away. They sat side by side, staring straight ahead for a few minutes, each dealing with their own thoughts.

Emma realized that she was a feeling a little too comfortable being snuggled up next to him with their arms and legs brushing up against each other's. She also knew that this was probably not something that she should let happen again, especially in her fragile mental state. Nevertheless, she stayed there for a little bit longer.

"I'll tell you what," Scott said, getting up off the bed, "I have to go pick up Timmy, so why don't you go back to your room and check in with your family. You need everything you've got to deal with this situation, so forget about the dried frog heads and the ghosts and ghoulies, and have a normal conversation with someone. You'll feel stronger once you've checked in with them and better prepared to start in again tomorrow."

Emma smiled, happy at the thought of talking to her kids, even if it was just for a few minutes, but curious as to why he suggested it, especially right now. She wondered if he had come to the same conclusion about the two of them getting too close, and was trying to rectify that situation before it became more complicated.

"I heard about a little pub in town called Hooligans, we'll catch dinner there and I'll kick your butt at pool, darts, anything else they have, just to help you get your mind off everything."

Her smile widened. "You are so on, and you'd better bring some cash, I never lose at the dartboard. But, honestly, that is a great idea. I'll call the kids and touch base with Lynne too, so she doesn't actually die of curiosity about what's been going on."

Scott walked her to the door, but gently grabbed hold of her arm before she left.

"Just be careful how much you share, okay? And, just to be on the safe side, you might not want to mention the burning of the bones at all. I'm pretty sure that's a jailable offense. We don't usually bring people along with us when we work, and you know a lot more than you should about what we've been doing."

"Why did you bring me?"

Scott looked at her intently, his dark eyes holding her gaze so that she couldn't look away.

He shrugged his shoulders, released her arm, and said, "Damned if I know."

Then he closed the door, leaving Emma standing alone in the hallway, feeling flushed and confused.

Just talking to the kids helped ease her mind about everything that was going on. They were okay and that was really the only thing that mattered. Emma spoke with each of them for several minutes. The boys were a little bored and frustrated, but were doing alright. Shelly was in her glory being back in town and able to spend time with her friends, and was bubbling with excitement when she told Emma about all she had been doing.

Jeremy wasn't there, so Emma escaped having to be interrogated by him. According to the kids, he was pretty upset about her leaving and not letting him know where she was, but Emma really didn't care about that at this point. She knew the whole situation would eventually have to be dealt with, but not tonight, so she put it out of her mind as best she could.

She also checked in with Lynne, but was so nervous about saying something that she shouldn't, that she kept it very brief, much to Lynne's chagrin.

Scott knocked on her door a few minutes after she got off the phone with Lynne. His face was tense and he seemed distracted.

"Hey, I'm sorry, but we're going to have to bail on dinner tonight."

"Is everything alright, you don't look so good."

"Not sure, to tell you the truth," he said, running his fingers through his hair. "I called my mom and she's not answering the phone or calling back. That's not like her at all, so Tim and I are going to head over and see what's going on."

Scott hesitated and looked at Emma curiously. "Did you want to come with us or would you rather wait here?"

"Where are we going?"

"It's about a two hour ride from here."

"Would I be able to bring Callie?"

"As long as she doesn't stink up my car, she can come. You should pack an overnight bag, just in case."

"Alright, I'll meet you out front in a few minutes."

"Okay," Scott replied, not at all sure why he had just invited her.

*     *     *

"Seriously, Scott, what the hell is going on with you?" Tim threw his duffel bag into the trunk on top of Scott's.

"What?"

"You have no idea what we're going to find at Mom's. Why would you ask Emma to come along?"

"What difference does it make?"

"Look, Scott, you're obviously getting too close to her. I'll give you the fact that she is a very attractive woman, and she seems like a legitimately good person. But, in case you forgot, she's married and has a family and, when this job is done, we're moving on and she's staying here with them."

"You think I don't know that?"

"I think you need a reality check. She's not your girlfriend and we aren't on vacation here. Get your head back in the game, bro, or you're going to end up getting hurt, bad."

"Go to hell." Scott had his hands balled into fists and was fighting the urge to smack his little brother upside the head. "I know what the score is and I have no delusions about how this is going to end, so save your breath. For now, she's a nice distraction from having to listen to all your bullshit, so shut up and get in the car."

Emma joined them a few minutes later and, as she and Callie got settled in the backseat, she could feel a definite tension in the air. She wasn't sure what was causing it, but assumed they were both just worried about their mother.

*     *     *

"Wake up, Emma, we're here."

"What?" she asked, trying to shake the cobwebs out of her head.

"We're here. You need to stay in the car a couple more minutes while we check things out, okay?"

"Sure," she replied, rubbing Callie's head and staring out into the darkness. "Are you sure she's home, there aren't any lights on."

"She's home," Scott replied brusquely, checking his pistol. Emma was pretty sure that gun did not contain Holy Water and she woke up completely at that point. She doubted that she would ever fully understand the extent of the danger that was a part of their lives, but she suddenly felt alone and afraid.

They were somewhere out in the country where there were no street lights, but the moon was bright and Emma watched the two of them walk slowly up towards the front porch with their pistols drawn.

They stood on either side of the door and Tim used his own key to unlock it. Scott turned the handle and shoved it inward and they both hurried through the doorway. Emma sat in the car and watched nervously. For several interminable minutes, she saw nothing, then lights started coming on throughout the first floor. She waited as long as she could and was about to get out of the car when Scott walked out the front door and motioned her in.

With a sigh of relief, Emma took Callie for a quick little walk so she could do her business and then headed over to Scott, who was waiting for her on the porch. "Is your mom alright?"

"She will be," Scott replied, his face was more relaxed now and he seemed like himself again. "Come on in."

"Callie, too?"

"Sure."

Emma followed him into the rustic log cabin and instantly felt at home. It was comfortable and well-kept, and you could feel the love in the house. The first thing Emma noticed were the pictures of Tim and Scott, at all different ages, scattered throughout the house. Their mother would be able to see them constantly, no matter which way she turned.

Mrs. Devereaux was lying on the couch and Tim was tucking an afghan around her. She was a petite woman, with short silver hair that framed her delicate face. Still attractive at this point in her life, Emma imagined that she must have been quite a beauty when she was younger.

"I'm fine, Tim, quit fussing." Her voice was weak, but Tim relented and stepped back. "Please honey, go get me a glass of orange juice, okay?"

"Sure," he replied, and headed off to the kitchen.

"Mom," Scott went over and sat on the ottoman next to the couch. "This is Emma, we're helping her out with a haunting in her house and that's her dog, Callie. They're both friendly enough, no need to worry about them. Emma, this is my mother, Doris Devereaux."

"It's a pleasure to meet you."

"You, too," Doris looked confused. "Excuse me for being a little befuddled, but my boys don't usually bring their clients home with them."

Emma smiled at her use of 'my boys' since both of them had to be in their late thirties or early forties.

"I think they find me a little needy, so they brought me along to keep me out of trouble. I hope you don't mind. Callie, stop it."

Callie had wandered over to Doris and after checking her out had given her a nice big doggie kiss.

"Aren't you a beautiful girl," Doris said, running her hand tenderly over Callie's head.

"Come here, Callie, leave her alone." Callie responded just as Tim returned with a big glass of orange juice.

"Thank you, darling." Doris sat up on the couch, with a little assistance from Scott, and started sipping the juice. Her color was better now and she seemed stronger.

"What else do you need?"

"Nothing, Scott. I'm fine now and I'm sorry that I scared you." She turned to Emma. "I have diabetes and had a very busy day and didn't eat properly. I was a little faint."

"She wasn't just a little faint," Scott added, "she was so weak that she couldn't even get up off the couch. And why didn't you have your phone with you?"

"Like I said, I'd been busy and, truth be told, I'm not sure where I left it."

"Seriously, Mom? What are we going to do with you?"

Doris reached over and grabbed his hand. "Scott, I know that I promised to be more careful, and I will. You don't have to worry so much."

Scott just shook his head and gave her a frustrated smile. "Let's just get you to bed and worry about that tomorrow."

"I am not a child and I don't need help getting to bed. Please get Emma situated in the extra bedroom, and don't either of you wake me up before seven in the morning or you will not get any breakfast."

"We know, we know. It's not our first sleep over, you know."

"Smart ass," she whispered in Scott's ear, before giving him a kiss on his cheek. "Good night, darling."

"Tim, give your old mom a helping hand."

Tim took her arm and gently helped her up. He dwarfed Doris when she leaned back against him for support as they made their way up the stairs.

"That woman is going to be the death of me," Scott said quietly.

"Why?"

"She takes care of everyone except herself, and I don't know how I'm going to handle it if something does happen to her. Anyway, let's get you situated and, whatever you do, don't wake her up too early tomorrow."

CHAPTER 17


Emma and Callie quietly made their way outside the next morning. It was very early and she didn't want to disturb any of them. They arrived after dark the night before and Emma hadn't been able to see much, so now she just stood quietly on the lawn, listening to the birds chirp their morning songs and admiring the scenery.

The driveway twisted its way down through a thicket of evergreen trees in front of her, off to the right side of the house she saw a small barn and could hear a rooster crowing impatiently inside of it. To the left was a large fenced in vegetable garden and along the front of the house were beautiful, lush rose bushes. The blossoms were fragrant and hardy and, in the early morning light, Emma could see bees beginning their work for the day, flitting back and forth between them.

She and Callie made their way down into the evergreens to do some exploring. They hadn't gotten far when Callie let out a sharp little bark and took off down the path. Emma started running after her, afraid to call out and wake everyone in the house. She sprinted down around a sharp turn and stopped short with an 'umpf' as Scott grabbed her around the waist to catch her before she barreled into him.

"What are you doing?"

"Just taking a walk," she said, trying to catch her breath. "We didn't know anyone else was up."

"Pretty fast walk, you almost knocked me on my ass."

"Sorry about that, Callie must have known you were here and took off on me. What are you doing out here, anyway?"

"I went for a run and now I'm just checking out my old hiding spot."

"You needed a hiding spot? What did you have to hide from?" Emma asked, looking around the little enclosure. Pine trees surrounded the little alcove and needles lined the ground, several inches thick in some spots. It was very quiet, other than the birds chirping high in the treetops, and very peaceful.

"Depending on the day, either from my bratty little brother or from my dad, or mom, who always seemed to be able to find chores for me."

Emma sat down on a high, flat rock and was surprised when Scott sat down close beside her. She couldn't help noticing his muscular leg rubbing up against hers and started twisting her ring around her finger.

"How often do you come home?"

"We try to make it every couple of months at least, but we travel so far that sometimes it's not always easy."

"And do you sneak away to your secret spot every time?"

"Not every time," he replied, staring straight out ahead, "just when I have things on my mind and need a little quiet time. I love my brother, and I would die for him if necessary, but we are together pretty much twenty-four hours a day and sometimes I just need a little time by myself."

"I'm sorry," Emma mumbled and started to stand up. "I didn't mean to intrude."

"No," he replied, grabbing her wrist to keep her from moving away, "please stay."

"But, I thought you wanted to be alone." His dark brown eyes were mesmerizing and she couldn't look away, he continued to hold her wrist and began to pull her closer.

"I was alone, now you're here, and I don't mind if you want to stick around for a little while."

Emma hesitated and then sat back down beside him, her heart was hammering in her chest as she felt her leg slide back into place against his, and she stared straight ahead, wanting to avoid being caught up in his gaze again.

"Why were you so worried yesterday? And why did you and Tim pull guns before you went into your mother's house. What did you think might be going on?"

Scott ran his fingers though his hair, which was still wet from his run, and looked like he was trying to make his mind up about something.

"Emma, there are things in this world that it's best you never know about. We've had a lot of experiences and not all of them have been pleasant. We just know enough to always be prepared, because you can never know what you might be walking in to. That's the only reason we had our guns out, there were no bad expectations, we were just being cautious. And, as you saw, there was nothing to worry about, she's fine, just wasn't taking as good care of herself as she should have."

Emma couldn't even begin to imagine what unpleasant experiences they'd had and decided that she didn't want to know anything about them, so she changed the subject as smoothly as she could. "Your mother does seem very nice."

"Yes, she has a great big heart, but don't let her suck you in, she can be extremely firm and set in her ways. Don't be offended by anything she says."

"Like what?"

"She'll probably have more to say about the fact that you are here. We don't generally bring people along with us for visits, particularly women."

"It sounds like you include me in a lot more things than you normally would. Why is that?"

Their eyes caught again and Emma had to force herself to look away, trying avoid getting lost in those intense brown eyes or staring at his soft, full lips. He hadn't showered or shaved yet, and she couldn't help noticing that the stubbly growth on his face just added to his rugged handsomeness.

"I don't know." He reached up and brushed a strand of thick blonde hair back off of her cheek and Emma's face tingled along the trail that his fingers made. "I think I just really like your dog."

It took Emma a few seconds to comprehend what he said and realize that he was joking, but she also knew that he had not actually given her any answer at all.

"Come on, Mom should be up soon, so we can start heading back. You can't get her up too early, but God forbid if you are late for a meal."

They arrived back at the house a few minutes later and the smells of freshly brewed coffee and sizzling bacon greeted them as soon as they entered the front door.

Both Doris and Tim looked at them curiously when they walked into the kitchen.

"Where have you two been?" Doris asked.

"I went for a run and, literally, ran into Emma when she and Callie were out for a walk, why?"

"No reason," Doris replied, setting a plate of eggs and bacon onto the table in front of him.

"My boys like their eggs sunnyside up, is that acceptable to you?"

"Of course, that's fine," Emma replied, unable to miss the frostiness in Doris' voice, although for the life of her, she did not know what she could have done to upset the woman.

"Sit down then, I'll be right over with it."

"Can I help?"

"No, I'm fine, you can help yourself to coffee though. Take care with the pot, it's hot."

Doris continued to follow Emma's movements out of the corner of her eye as she cooked the eggs. Her lips tightened when Emma handed over a steaming cup of coffee to Scott before pouring her own.

"Would you like to help me in the garden after we eat?" Doris asked, setting Emma's plate down in front of her.

"Sure, I was admiring your roses earlier, they are so beautiful and the fragrance is amazing."

"Thank you. Eat up, everyone, I have to go clean up a few things, so help yourself if you need anything else."

"Mom," Tim said in very stern voice, "you promised."

"I had a piece of toast and orange juice. I am fine, Tim. Quit your worrying."

When she left the kitchen, Scott asked, "What's up with her, is she mad about something?"

Tim shrugged his shoulders. "I don't think so, but she probably will be when we head out of here later this morning."

"She'll be okay about that, she knows we have work to do."

"Maybe, but we haven't been home in a quite awhile, and there is definitely a bee in her bonnet today. I'd hate to be the one she takes it out on," he added, looking pointedly at Emma.

Emma and Doris made their way out to garden a little while later and Doris pointed out the items that they needed to pick, lettuce, carrots and tomatoes being the primary targets.

"What exactly are your plans for my son?" Doris asked, as soon as they had settled in to their harvesting.

"Excuse me?"

"I believe you heard me, what are your plans as far as my son is concerned? Tim tells me that you are married and have children of your own, so what exactly is going on?"

Emma just looked at her for a moment, not sure how to respond. She was very angry at the insinuation, but tried to tamp down her ire because she realized that Doris was only concerned about her son, and that was something that Emma could understand.

"Both of your sons are helping me out with a situation that I cannot handle on my own. There is nothing going on between either of them and me, so I guess I'm not sure what you are implying."

Doris had been on her knees digging in the soil, she stopped and sat back on the balls of her feet and wiped the sweat off her forehead with a dirty glove, leaving a streak of soil in the deep grooves of her skin.

"That's nonsense, I see the way that you and Scott are together, the way you look at each other, the way you react to each other. I'm not so old that I can't remember the days when his father and I were just like that, so don't pretend with me. I don't want him hurt, so you just take care that you respect who he is, and don't take advantage of his feelings, that's all I'm asking."

"I appreciate your concern, but you have nothing to worry about, there is nothing going on between Scott and me."

Doris had Scott's dark brown eyes and, although it felt like she was using them to burn a hole right through Emma's skull, she said nothing more.

Both women continued their harvesting in angry silence and a little while later they headed back into the house.

Scott couldn't miss the tension between the two of them and knew that his mother had said something that upset Emma, but now was not the time to get into it.

"Mom." He walked over and threw his arms around her, hugging her small frame close. "We have to get back to work. Are you going to be okay? We should be done in a few days and can come back once everything's taken care of, if nothing else comes up in the meantime, okay?"

"No rush, darling, I am always happy to see you, but I will be fine. You go do what you have to do and we'll spend time together soon." She smiled tenderly at him, praying quietly for God to keep both of her boys safe.

"Good-bye, love," she said to Tim, as he enveloped her in his gargantuan frame. "You watch out for each other."

"We will, Mom, call if you need anything."

"It was nice to meet you, Emma, you take care that you stay safe until you can be with all of your family again."

Emma thought that was a curious turn of phrase, but she was not under any illusion that Doris was her friend, or that she wanted Emma anywhere near her 'boys'.

"Thank you for all of your hospitality. I appreciate it."

Emma grabbed Callie and headed out the front door. Scott and Tim joined her a few moments later and they made the long drive back to the motel.

It was late afternoon by the time they got back into town, too late to do anything as far as her situation, so they decided to clean up and meet for dinner in an hour or so.

Emma wanted to get Callie out for a nice long walk before she left her alone in the room while she went to dinner. The two of them headed out through the lobby, but stopped when Emma heard someone call her name.

She turned and smiled as she saw Scott walking towards them.

"Where are you going, I thought we had a date tonight?"

"A date, really?"

"Sure, with Tim as a chaperone, nothing could be safer, right?"

"I'm not sure that I completely agree with that, but you do clean up nice. You even smell good."

"Don't I usually?"

Emma giggled. "That didn't come out quite right. You smell even nicer than usual, is that better?"

"A little," he replied, putting on his best pouty face.

"Callie needs a walk before we go, would you like to come with us?"

"Sure."

They wandered slowly up and down the sidewalks around the motel, walking side by side, so close that their arms would occasionally brush against each other. Emma could feel her heart pounding a little harder than it should have been, and realized that his close proximity was really starting to affect her physically, as well as mentally. She wasn't sure how she felt about that, or what she should do about it. Maybe his mother was right, maybe there was something going on between them, something that they were going to have to acknowledge and address, soon.

"So, you haven't been a stay at home Mom all your life, what did you do before that?"

"I was an interior decorator."

"Really, why did you stop?"

"To raise the kids. We agreed that it would be best to have their mom home for them, rather than send them off to a babysitter every day."

"You both agreed or he thought it was important and you went along with it?"

She looked at Scott thoughtfully. "We both thought it was a good idea. I love being with the kids, but I do miss adult conversations and adult activities sometimes. What about you, though? Based on what Venetia charged me, I imagine you two make a very good living at what you do? What do you do with all your money?"

Scott knew that she was just trying divert the conversation away from herself and her family, and when she began twisting her wedding ring around and around her finger, he decided that he would give her a break and go along with it.

"What did she charge you?"

"Holy shit," he exclaimed, when she told him. "And you paid her that much?"

"Of course, we needed help and I didn't know where else to turn. Why, what do you charge? Actually, I probably should have found that out right in the beginning, but I didn't even think about it."

"You have nothing to worry about, we don't charge anything."

"What?"

He gave her his patent, mega-watt smile, and said, "You heard me, we don't charge anything."

"Then how do you support yourself."

"If I tell you that, you'll lose all respect for us."

She watched him out of the corner of her eye. "Try me."

He laughed and stared at the ground, rubbing his forehead, trying to decide if he should share any more information with her. Looking back up in to those shimmering green eyes, he could see that she was sincerely interested.

"Our Mom supports us, believe it or not."

"But, I thought she was also a stay at home mom."

"Technically, she is, however, she is also an author and writes a series of kid's books called Preternatural. She has done very well for herself, and puts most of what she earns into a kind of trust fund for Tim and me."

"Preternatural, I know those books. Between both my boys, I think they have all of them. They're about ghosts and all kinds of creatures, right?"

"That's right."

"But, the author isn't Doris Devereaux, I can't recall what it is, but I'm sure that's not it."

"She writes under a pseudonym."

"Why?"

"Because the stories all hold some truth to them, and we don't need to put that information out there as fact."

"Oh, my god, they are based on things that you've actually done, aren't they?"

Again, the mega-watt smile appeared on his face and his hand accidentally brushed hers as they continued walking.

"Yes, she started writing them when Tim and I were young. I guess it was her way of making what my dad was doing a little safer, by turning them into a kid's version."

"So, he told her about every case he went out on?"

"In detail," Scott replied. "I think, that's probably why Tim and I haven't been able to find the right woman yet."

"What do you mean?"

"My dad could tell Mom anything and she understood. It's not that easy to find a woman who will, first of all, wait at home while we're gone for weeks at a time, and, second of all, believe anything that we tell her about what we really do for a living. We both learned a long time ago that telling the truth is just something that you do not do."

Emma watched his handsome face change expression as he spoke, his jaws clenched in either anger or frustration, she wasn't sure which. It was then that she realized what a truly lonely existence he and Tim lived, and that, although he cared very much about what he did and the differences he made in people's lives, Emma wondered if, given the chance, he would have chosen a different path for his own life.

They arrived back at the motel just then and put Callie in Emma's room, met up with Tim and headed out for dinner. They ate a fairly healthy meal for a change and, since none of them were in a very talkative mood and were each mulling over their own problems, the evening passed quietly and quickly.

CHAPTER 18

"So, what now?" Emma asked, the next morning.

"Well," Tim responded, "I got a little more information about your house the other day, but not much. I know you guys went through some of the books from the spell room, but right now we've got bupkus, nothing, nada. I have no clue who the dead guy was or what demon they were calling forth."

"Let's head back over to the house, we should take another look at that room," Scott said. "We need to check out the warding symbols on the walls and floor again. Maybe they'll point us in the right direction."

"This will just be research, Emma," Tim said sternly, "you don't have to come, we won't be doing anything other than collecting some information, okay?"

Both of them were watching, waiting for her to get obstinate again about being with them all the time, but she had no desire to go back down in that creepy room and she certainly wasn't going to just hang out upstairs without them.

"Okay, will you let me know when you get back?"

She almost laughed at the suspicious looks they were giving her, they obviously hadn't expected her to be so agreeable. "I'll look through some more of the icky books, if you'd like me too, while you're gone."

"Sure," Tim replied, still waiting for the other shoe to drop. But, when none did, he dropped off a few more books to her and he and Scott headed out.

They were back within the hour and Tim was downloading the photos they took onto his computer so he could do more research on the symbols.

While they waited, Scott asked, "What about the girl that survived? The one that got locked in the basement? Did you find anything out about her? Maybe she has some information that might help us out, you never know."

"I found out that she's at a mental health facility in Adams. I called there but they wouldn't let me see her. Family only."

Scott and Tim shared a look, gave each other a half smile and Tim went back to his computer.

"What was her name and the name of the place where she's living?"

"Stephanie Rogers, and I think it was called the Good Neighbor Mental Health Institution, or something like that, why?"

"You two get out of here and let me work my magic. Don't come back for an hour or two, okay?" He entwined his fingers, cracked his knuckles, and started typing rapidly on his laptop. Scott nodded his head towards the door and Emma followed him out into the hallway.

"So, what now?"

"I don't know, looks like we have the morning off."

"Do you mind if I get Callie and we take her to the dog park and let her run around for awhile?"

"Not at all, that sounds good."

Once they got Callie to the park, which was empty at this time of the day during the middle of the week, Emma let her off leash and she took off at top speed to the other end of the field, then loped around the perimeter to check that out and eventually began her exploration of all the wonderful scents wafting throughout the park.

Emma and Scott were sitting on one of the benches, just watching Callie in a comfortable silence. It was a hot summer day, but there was a nice breeze that kept it from being unbearable. Emma did wish she had thrown on shorts rather than her jeans, but she hadn't known what to expect for the day.

"It's probably for the best anyway," she realized, feeling Scott's muscular leg pressed up against hers on the short bench.

"So, it seems like I'm always the chatty Kathy when we're together, it's your turn now. Tell me more about your life, your family."

"What's to tell? I have three kids who I love to death, and I have a husband that I've been with about twenty years."

"That's not telling me about your life, that's just who lives in your household."

"I'm not sure what you want, I thought I had a great life, but I was mistaken. Jeremy is a good man, he really is." Emma emphasized when she saw Scott's eyes narrow in disgust at the mention of Jeremy's name.

"He is a good provider, he is good father and I think, until recently, he's been a good husband. We lived in a great apartment in the city, it was huge and was in an excellent location. The kids loved it there and we all had what we wanted, I had my horses and could ride whenever I felt like it, the kids had their friends and their sports and other activities to keep them busy. Jeremy had to spend long hours at work, but he tried to make it to as many functions for the kids as he could. Now, we're here and everything has gone straight to hell."

Scott watched her curiously and noticed that she started twisting her wedding ring again.

"Okay, so I know who you live with and what you all do, but what about you? What makes you happy? What makes you sad? What do you want out of life?"

Emma stopped twisting her ring and lifted her head and stared into his eyes. Her mouth partially opened, but no sound came out. Scott just watched her patiently, his deep brown eyes reflecting his concern as he watched her struggle to answer his questions.

"What is it?" he finally asked, when he saw her tears build up and threaten to overflow.

She gave him a wavering smile and tried to get herself under control before responding. But, when he gently wiped an errant tear from her cheek, Emma almost crumpled completely, mentally and emotionally. She hadn't realized how close she was to her breaking point.

Unable to come up with the appropriate words, she just leaned her head against Scott's broad chest. He put his arm around her and pulled her close, leaning his cheek against the softness of her hair. He felt frustrated, he hadn't meant to upset her and her sorrow touched him in a way that he couldn't understand. He wanted to fix things for her, but didn't know how.

Callie startled the both of them when she ran over from the side of the bench and gave a sharp bark, letting them know that she was there and ready to play. Scott and Emma slowly disentangled and stood up.

Emma pulled a tennis ball out of her bag and handed it to Scott. "I'm pretty sure this is what she's looking for."

Scott took it from her, his fingers caressing her hand as he did so, and gave it a heave at least half way down the long field. Callie took after it like a shot.

Without taking his eyes off Callie, Scott asked, "So, would you like to tell me what just happened?"

Emma smiled at him, he was so polite and yet so annoyingly persistent.

"I'm not exactly sure. I guess, I just hadn't thought about those questions that you asked me in such a long time that they caught me off-guard. I realized that I don't even know what makes me happy or sad, or what I want out of life. And that made me sad, because I really feel completely adrift right now, aimless, I don't know where I'm going and suddenly, I am not sure about where I've been."

"So, without breaking completely into a soulful country music song, what do you think you want out of the rest of your life?" He grabbed the ball out of Callie's mouth and threw it again, watching in admiration as she charged down the field after it.

"I do sound pitiful, don't I?"

"Not at all." Scott turned and gave her a mega-watt smile. "You are an enigma to me and I just want to understand you better."

"Good luck with that, I don't even know what I'm doing half the time. But, if I really wanted to be truthful about the future, I think I want some adventure. I want to feel like I'm really living my life, not just putting in time, getting the housework done, helping the kids with their homework, making sure everyone has everything that they need."

"That's a noble aspiration, do you think that's why you are so insistent on coming with us while we're working?"

"No, I don't. I think that it is extremely important to me that I know that everything is really resolved, and I also think that I have some things to prove to myself."

She laughed suddenly when Callie came up behind Scott and stuck the tennis ball in his hand, he jumped a foot into the air and let out a little girly scream that she would never have expected from him.

"That wasn't funny." His tone was forbidding, but he couldn't help starting to laugh himself and, after petting Callie's head to let her know there were no hard feelings, he tossed the ball again, this time keeping his eye on her.

"So, what exactly do you have to prove to yourself?"

"Well, for starters, that I am no longer just a little scaredy-cat, afraid of my own shadow. I want to prove that I do have a backbone and I can stand up and take care of myself."

"Why would you think that you have to prove that? You are one of the bravest women that I've ever met."

"And you're full of it, I'm just a trembling mass of jelly every time I get near that stupid house. If it weren't for you and your brother, I don't know what would have happened, I never could have gone back inside without you. I am not brave, and I'm actually scared to death of all kinds of different things in my life right now, particularly, the future."

"I don't think that you have any idea what bravery actually is." Emma got caught up in his dark gaze and turned her head to break his hold on her.

Scott took his finger and trailed it along her jaw, exerting a little more pressure, he turned her head so that she had to meet his eyes again. "Bravery is when you are afraid of something, but you do it anyway, its facing your fears. I saw that courage in you the first time that you went to the house with us. You were petrified, but you did it anyway. I admire you for that, I really do."

His fingers were still resting on her cheek and without even thinking about it, he leaned forward and captured her half-parted lips with his own. She moaned softly and the kiss deepened. Emma's hands snaked around his neck and he pulled her in closer.

The kiss lasted only moments before Emma regained her composure, and her sanity. She pulled back, her hands still resting on his broad shoulders.

"I'm sorry," she whispered. Her eyes were drawn to his full lips, just inches away from her and she wanted to kiss him again, wanted to feel his arms around her, she wanted him.

"Don't you dare say that," Scott replied, running his finger over her lips. He gave her one more chaste little kiss and grabbed her hand. "We'd better get going, Tim will be waiting for us."

Emma was disappointed and relieved at the same, she called Callie over and they headed back, their hands comfortably entwined until they reached the motel parking lot.

*    *    *

"So, here you go."

"What's this?" Emma asked curiously, as Tim slid a couple of business cards over to her and Scott.

"Your pass into the Laughing Academy."

"I don't get it."

"You are now officially employees of Gloucester and Manning, PC, attorneys at law."

"Why?"

"Because," Tim looked quite pleased with himself as he explained, "that is the law firm that handles Stephanie Rogers' financial affairs with the Good Neighbor Mental Health Institute. Other than family, only the representatives from the law firm are allowed in to see her."

"How did you get all of this information?" Emma asked, the card even had the firm's logo on it and looked very authentic to her.

"The internet has a wealth of information on it, if you just know where to look."

"So, why do I have to be Matthew Abercrombie, you couldn't come up with a better name than that?"

"He's an actual attorney with the firm, and Sheila Smythe is an actual paralegal with the firm. I thought that would make you both seem a little more genuine, if anyone checks on you."

"I don't know if I can do this," Emma said warily.

"Trust me, you can, haven't you ever told a little white lie before?" Scott asked.

"Of course, I have, but I don't know if I can walk into the place and actually pretend to be someone that I'm not. They'll never believe me."

"You'd be surprised, people are just putting in their time at work, even at a bug house they generally don't question anyone of authority. You get shit from them, you just give them attitude and they back right down. We do it all the time."

Emma was watching Scott as he spoke and could tell that this type of thing didn't phase him at all, but she wasn't sure if she had the nerve to go through with it, and didn't want to mess up any opportunity that they might have with this woman.

"Maybe the two of you should go, instead of me."

"No chance," Tim replied. "I was able to hack into the facility's computer and the firm always sends a man and a woman, so you're up. You'll do fine, just follow Scott's lead."

It was a two hour drive so they headed out a short time later, trying to plan it so that they arrived just as the shifts were changing at the facility so there would be fewer questions from the staff, who would either be eager to get out of there or just getting settled in for the evening.

Emma thought they should probably discuss what had happened at the dog park, but she was so nervous that she never brought the subject up. Her hands were sweaty and shaky as she got out of the car.

On top of just being nervous perpetrating this fraud, she hated the pants suit that she was wearing. It was navy blue, very austere and professional looking. She hadn't worn it in years and was relieved that it still fit, even after all the greasy diner food that she'd been eating lately, but it was tight and uncomfortable and the heels she was wearing didn't help either.

"Is this your first visit to a bug house?" Scott asked as they walked towards the building.

"Yes," Emma replied, and he could hear the nervousness in her voice.

"No worries, you look perfect, you'll do fine. Just follow my lead and don't talk unless you have to, okay?"

"Okay." After opening the front door for her, Scott briefly grasped her hand as she walked through and nodded at her in encouragement. Emma smiled at him, straightened her shoulders and walked up to the front desk like she owned the place.

# CHAPTER 19

The receptionist was a bit surly, but Scott stared her down and bullied her into getting an aide out to take them back to their client, even though it was no longer visiting hours.

The aide, Thomas, shook hands with Scott, nodded in Emma's direction, and walked them back to the first locked door. He pulled out his key card and swiped it through the slot, let them through and followed only when he was sure the door had closed completely.

"You don't look familiar, have you two been here before?" He was a big man with a deep voice and Emma had no doubt he could handle any of the patients here. She kind of hoped he would be sticking with her and Scott, just in case.

"No," Scott replied, "the account just got transferred to me and I wanted to get a personal look at what we're dealing here."

"I'll take you to Stephanie's room and lock you in with her. You can ring for me when you are ready to leave. Do not, under any circumstances, leave that room before I come and get you, understood?"

"Yes, but what about Stephanie? Do we have anything to worry about from her?" Emma asked, and Thomas assumed that was the reason she seemed so nervous.

"Not a thing, in fact, it's unlikely you'll even be able to get her to talk to you. She usually just sits in her rocking chair and stares out the window, she doesn't talk hardly at all."

Emma started swearing under her breath at Scott because of the silly high-heeled shoes that he had insisted that she wear to fit the part. She was having trouble keeping up with the two men and her heels clattered annoyingly on the linoleum floor.

They passed a few patients, both men and women, in the hallway. Thomas spoke briefly with each of them, just said hello or asked how they were doing. They seemed docile enough and Emma stopped being quite as fearful of them.

Following the men down a long, dim hallway, Emma screamed when someone suddenly grabbed her arm and dragged her across the hallway, she fell out of one of her shoes and struggled to get her arm free as the man continued to drag her across the floor.

Scott appeared out of nowhere and knocked the patient flying. Thomas was right behind him and lifted the patient off the floor and led him back towards his room on the other side of the hall.

"The girl, the girl," the patient kept whispering.

"Sammy, you know better than that, why'd you do something so stupid?"

"The girl, the girl," he just continued to whisper, as if that was the explanation for what had happened.

"Well, you're in lockdown now kiddo, sorry, no treat for you tonight."

"But the girl," he said quietly, giving Thomas a beseeching look just before he was securely locked in his room.

"I'm so sorry," Thomas said to Emma, worried that, of all the people Sammy had to do this to, he chose an attorney. Damn, there was going to be a lot of paperwork to fill out tonight. "Are you okay? Sammy isn't ever violent, I don't know why he did that."

"I'm fine," Emma replied, her voice wavering a little, as she slid her foot back into her shoe. "Are we almost there?"

"Yes, it's just a little further down the hall."

He slid his key card into Stephanie's door and stepped inside, holding it open for the two of them.

"Stephanie, these people are from your lawyer's office, they just want to talk to you for a few minutes, is that okay?" There was no response and the petite brunette just continued to hug her teddy bear and stare out the window.

Thomas shrugged at them and pointed to the call button they could use when they were ready to leave.

"I'll be back in twenty minutes, if you haven't used the call button by then." He stepped back out into the hallway, closing the door and making sure it was locked securely before walking back to his station.

Scott pulled up a chair near Stephanie.

"Hello, my name is Scott. I just wanted to talk to you for a few minutes, if that's alright with you."

There was no response, no indication that she even heard him. "We just wanted to see how you are doing, are you okay at this place?"

Still no response.

"Do you remember what happened, why they brought you here?"

Still no response, but she started rocking a little harder and began to hum. She had to be about twenty-seven or twenty-eight years old by now, but her face was still almost childlike and she could easily be mistaken for someone much younger. Her long hair was held back in a ponytail which enhanced her youthful look.

"Do you remember your home, being in the basement?"

Nothing.

"Emma, do you want to give it a try?"

"What do I say?"

"Anything, just see if you can get any response, otherwise this was just a big waste of time."

"Hello, Stephanie, my name is Emma." She pulled her chair over closer to the girl and rested her hand on the arm of the rocking chair.

"What do you see out that window? The tree is pretty far away, but it looks like there are some songbirds in it, is that what you see? Can you hear them sing?"

The girl reached over and put her hand gently over Emma's and began to hum louder.

"You can hear them, can't you? And you are singing just as prettily as they are."

The girl actually smiled and Emma looked at Scott excitedly.

"Ask her about the house."

Emma frowned, she didn't want to disturb the girls' happy thoughts, but they only had a limited time with her and needed some information.

"Stephanie, I live in your old house, the Creeghan House." The girl stopped humming and missed a beat in her rocking.

"Do you remember living there?"

Nothing.

"Do you remember being there and having something happen to you in the basement?"

She started rocking furiously and stared straight out the window.

"Can you tell me what happened? Did your Mom and Dad do something to you or was it something else."

"Bad, bad, bad," the girl began to whisper.

"What was bad, Stephanie?"

"Bad monster, bad monster, hurt me, hurt mommy and daddy. Bad monster, bad monster."

"Did you see the monster?"

Stephanie had enormous blue eyes and she turned to Emma and stared straight at her. "Always."

"Is the monster still with you?" Emma didn't know why she asked that, maybe because Stephanie still looked so haunted. The girl nodded tentatively, fear filling her features as she looked around the room, almost as if she was looking for it.

"Is it here with you all the time?"

Again the tentative nod.

"We're going to try to help you, we want to get rid of all the monsters, from the house and from here. Can you help us?"

This time she shook her head no.

"Why, don't you want us to get rid of it?"

The girl grabbed tighter to Emma's hand and she struggled to not to pull it away as Stephanie's nails dug deep into the palm of her hand. The girl was whispering quietly and Emma had to lean down close to her to hear what she was saying.

"The attic, it lives in the attic." Suddenly, she let go of Emma's hand, her eyes rolled back into her head and she started a high-pitched keening. It didn't stop, but grew louder and louder.

Emma looked at Scott, feeling very panicky.

Scott pushed the call button and it was just moments before Thomas arrived.

"What did you do to upset her?"

"I don't know," Emma replied, knowing she was lying as she spoke. "We were just trying to talk to her and she started doing this."

The high wailing continued and, after giving the two of them a very disapproving look, he pulled out a hypodermic and gave Stephanie a shot of some type of sedative.

"She hasn't needed that in over two years. You two really messed her up good. Let's get you out of here so I can tend to her properly."

He took them outside of her room, secured Stephanie's door and strode down the hallway. His pace was angry and much faster than when he had brought them in here and Emma had to pretty much trot to keep up with him.

Once they were back in the car, Scott let out a deep breath, raking his hand through his hair as he tried to understand what had just happened.

"So, was this just a waste a time?" Emma asked.

"Not really," he said, with a heavy sigh. "I'm afraid that whatever we are dealing with may be able to attach itself to a person, as well as a place. I think it still comes and terrorizes that poor girl."

\*       \*       \*

They'd given Tim a brief run down about what happened when they returned and agreed to get cleaned up and meet for dinner and then they could go over it in more detail. This evening they would be dining at a nice little Italian Restaurant in town and Emma was really looking forward to it. She practically had to beg them to go to a real restaurant, not a diner or a pub, but they'd finally relented.

Emma went downstairs and saw Tim standing alone in the lobby. He nodded in her direction and, when she got closer, said, "Scott's upstairs on the phone. He'll be down in a few and then we'll get going."

Scott walked into the lobby before the words were even completely out of Tim's mouth.

"Hey, guys, I'm going to have to bail on dinner tonight."

"What's up? Was that Butchie on the phone?"

"Yeah, he's run into a little problem and could use a hand. I'm going to head over there now and help him out."

"You need me to go?"

"I think we'll be alright, it's just, um," he hesitated, glancing over at Emma, "just a little problem. The two of us can take care of it."

"Since you're going to be down that way, are you going to stop in and see Tanya?"

"That's a good idea, I can hit that on my way back."

"Who's Tanya?" Emma asked, ignoring the sharp jab of pain in her chest, refusing to admit that it might be jealousy.

"She's just a witch we know, why?"

"No reason, just curious, and are you being a smartass or is she really a witch?"

"Trust me, she's a real witch. You're going to miss me, aren't you?"

"Hardly," she responded, although she was dying of curiosity about Tanya and hoped that she could get Tim to fill her in later on.

"Alright, I'm out of here, you two behave, okay?"

They both just gave him a dirty look, he laughed and headed out to the parking lot.

"Do you still want to go to dinner?" Tim asked.

"Sure, if you do. I was looking forward to a real dinner, and maybe a good glass of wine to wash away everything that happened today."

"Let's go then. You'll have to drive though because, obviously, I don't have a car now."

Dinner was excellent, the Chianti helped ease Emma's nerves somewhat, and she was able to let go of some of the anxiety from her trip to the sanitarium.

Tim was a much more serious person than Scott, and not very talkative, unless it was about the case. There were long silences over dinner, not necessarily uncomfortable, but Emma felt like she needed to make an effort to get to know him a little better.

"Did Scott fill you in the rest of the details about what happened today?"

"He did," Tim answered, shaking his head. "I don't understand how a demon can travel between locations like that, unless there were multiple demons and one latched onto her and one stayed at the house. We still have a lot work to do to try and find out what we're dealing with. This is bigger than what we usually run into."

"I'm really curious about something," Emma said.

"What?"

"Why did you and Scott come to my house that night when Venetia was there? I know, at the time, you said it was because of Mr. Waters being killed, but you couldn't have known his death would be related to what you do."

"You're right," he said, with a brief smile. "That house had been on our radar for years, on our Dad's too, for that matter, because of all of the odd accidents that happened in it."

He hesitated when the waitress came over with the bill and coffee refill. After she left, he continued. "Once we heard another family was living in the house we decided that we would head over. We intended to come see you anyway, but then we heard the news about Waters' death and we dropped everything to go check it out."

"Why didn't you or your Dad ever investigate the house before now?"

"We didn't have an opportunity. Either we showed up too late and the family had already moved out or they wouldn't let us help."

"That doesn't make any sense to me, they should have been grateful for the offer."

"Back in '09, we got close. I think we almost had the wife convinced, but the husband was a mean drunk and she was scared to death of him. He was not about to let us do anything inside that house."

"That's when the young boy fell down the stairs, isn't it?"

"Yeah," Tim looked down at his cup of coffee, stirred in more sugar and seemed to lose himself in the past.

"That really tore Scott up. We saw the kid when we were there and, I don't know, Scott got it into his head that if we had done something different, or tried a little harder, we could have saved him. It took quite awhile before he let it go, and I'm not sure he ever did completely."

"It's a really heart-breaking profession that you're in, isn't it?"

"It can be, but you have to be able to walk away and know that you did the best that you could, even though it doesn't always go in the win column. But, sometimes that's easier said than done when people's lives are involved."

"I admire you two."

"Don't."

"Why not?"

"Look, we didn't ask for this, we were basically born into it. We do what we can, but we're no goddamn heroes, okay? You have to stop romanticizing all of this."

"Is that what you think I'm doing?"

"Yes, I do, to certain degree."

"Maybe you just don't appreciate exactly how much you do for other people."

"I'm pretty clear on that. Let's get back to the hotel now, okay?"

"Sure, what's the plan for tomorrow?"

"No plan, I'm going to go over my research again to see what I've missed. You're on your own and can do whatever you'd like, except go back to that house."

Emma didn't know what she'd said to turn his mood so ugly. He'd never been quite so brusque with her and, right now, all she wanted was to get back to her room and forget that this day had ever happened.

# CHAPTER 20

Emma ignored Tim the following morning. Instead of meeting up with him for breakfast like they usually did, she took Callie to the dog park for a few hours. Once she was back with Callie, Emma loaded up her dirty clothes and hit the laundromat.

It was late morning when there was a loud banging on Tim's hotel door. He tossed the notes he was looking at over onto Scott's bed, grabbed his pistol and stuck it in the back waist band of his jeans. He walked over to the door very quietly and peeked out the peephole, there was nothing there at first, and then suddenly Emma's head popped into view and she started banging on the door again.

Tim sighed heavily, he had hoped to avoid having to spend time with her alone today. Somehow, Emma managed to get him to share things with her that he normally wouldn't with someone that he barely knew. They were very private people and, although he understood Scott's attraction to her, because it did feel good to have someone else who could understand some of what they went they went through every day, it also made Tim very uncomfortable. He felt like he was betraying secrets best left to just him and his brother.

Tim unlocked the door and opened it. "Come on in."

Emma watched nervously as he pulled the gun out and set it down on the nightstand. She still couldn't get used to exactly how dangerous their lives, and they themselves, could be.

"Hi, Tim, I'm sorry to bother you, but I just remembered something and thought I should tell you about it."

"What?"

"When we were with Stephanie, she whispered something in my ear, she said, 'the attic, it lives in the attic'."

"You didn't tell Scott about that?"

"No, I forgot about it. Right after it happened, all the craziness started and I never thought about it again, until now."

"Let me think for a minute." He ran various scenarios through his head and finally said, "Okay, I'm going to head over and check it out. You wait here."

"No, I'm not letting you go alone."

"You don't get to decide that. Scott will be pissed as hell if I take you in there, so you're staying here."

"I have the key to the house and you're not going without me. We don't have to tell Scott, right?"

He was a tall, strong man and the angry look he was giving Emma almost made her give in and just toss him the keys, but she knew that she'd go crazy just sitting around worrying about him all afternoon, so she stood her ground.

"Fine, but the dog's not going, we can't take her in the attic."

"Okay," Emma replied, a little uncertain of how she felt about going into the house without Callie, but she'd put herself in this position and now she had to follow through.

It didn't take nearly enough time for them to get to house and, once again, Emma felt queasy as soon as they pulled into the driveway, and her insides started to turn to jelly.

She considered offering to wait in the van, but took a deep steadying breath, unsnapped her seatbelt and stepped onto the driveway.

"It's okay," Tim said, obviously sensing her fear. "We'll be fine, just stay close to me, alright?"

Emma nodded and followed him up onto the porch and in the house. She could immediately feel the heavy coldness of the air and couldn't help shivering, but she had no time to think about it as she hurried to keep up with Tim, who was already heading up the stairs.

Tim had no trouble reaching the chain to pull down the attic stairs. Once they were fully extended, he took out his holy water pistol and headed up into the dusty darkness above them. Emma scrambled up right behind him and they both stayed close to the stairs as they looked around.

"Is any of this stuff yours?" Tim asked.

"No, we never put anything up here, it must all have belonged to the previous owners."

They walked around the attic and peeked under the dusty sheets at some of the old pieces of furniture, and the knick-knacks and dishes that had been thrown into boxes that were so old that they were beginning to disintegrate.

"What do you think?" Emma asked. The air was stale and cold, but it didn't feel particularly bad.

"I don't know, nothing looks out of the ordinary up here. Maybe she was confused, she was accosted in the basement, not the attic."

They checked everything out, but couldn't find anything to indicate a demon or ghost had ever been around. Emma was staying close to Tim, but she became distracted by a little jewelry box that she found with a wind up ballerina inside it, just like one she had as a child. She was listening to the music and watching the ballerina spin, when something smashed into the side of her and knocked her flying.

It happened so suddenly that she was unable to break her fall and her head and face hit the floor hard, along with almost every other bone along the left side of her body. She tried to muffle her scream of pain, but Tim heard it and was beside her at once.

"Give me your hand," he yelled, extending his own, but looking up and around for any more danger. He had his little holy water gun out and was spraying it all around them, making a path towards the stairs down to the third floor.

"Go," he said, once Emma was on her feet, and he kept spraying as they both ran towards the steps and didn't stop until they'd reached the safety of the driveway.

\*     \*     \*

"You did what? What the hell were you thinking, Tim?"

Emma could hear Scott's voice through the wall of their rooms and knew she needed to go play referee, so she quickly ran out into the hall and over to their door. She had to knock persistently, because they were both yelling at each and didn't hear her right away.

"What do you want?" Tim bellowed as he opened the door.

"I heard Scott yelling and came to explain."

169

"Yeah, good luck with that. He's in there."

Tim pointed to the open bathroom door where Scott was standing bare chested over the sink washing a piece of clothing.

"Scott, please calm down," Emma said, as she walked towards the bathroom. "It was all my fault, I insisted."

Her words died in her throat when she saw that he was washing out a shirt, and that the water in the sink ran red with blood.

"Are you okay?"

"Oh, this," he said, still looking down at the sink as tried to scrub out the stains, "it's not mine. I'm fine."

He was clearly agitated and it looked like he might just rip the shirt into two. Then he turned to her, and said, "Jesus, Emma, look at you. How bad are you hurt?"

"I'm fine, just a little banged up. But, what's with the blood?"

"Don't worry about that." He unplugged the drain, gave the shirt another quick rinse and thoroughly washed his hands.

Scott grabbed the towel and dried his hands as he walked towards her. For some reason, she backed away, feeling a little frightened, maybe because of the blood, maybe because he seemed so angry.

"You don't have to be afraid of me," he said quietly, reading her expression perfectly. "I just want to be sure you're okay."

"I am, I'm fine."

"It doesn't look like it, nice bruise." He reached out a hand and, this time, Emma did not flinch away from him as he ran his fingers over her tender left cheekbone.

"Thanks, I landed just perfectly on it."

"Alright, you two, it's been a shitty couple of days. I say, let's hit that pub, play some games, drink some beer and get over ourselves. What do you say?"

"I'm in," Tim said quickly.

"Me, too." Emma added, and within a few minutes they were headed off to the pub.

After some food and a couple of beers, both of the men relaxed and were actually a lot of fun as the three of them competed at darts and pool, and even tried their hand at foosball, although that wasn't a pretty sight.

There was no talk of ghosts or demons, or even what had happened with Scott when he was out of town, for that matter. All three of them just needed a break from the craziness, just for this one evening.

Scott and Tim were currently engaged in a game of pool for some serious money against a couple of the locals, so Emma just sat back on a bar stool watching them while sipping a nice, cold beer. She felt more relaxed than she had in quite awhile.

Emma watched Scott as he circled the pool table, searching out his next shot. He was muscular and athletic and had an adorable grin that would just appear on his face instantaneously, whenever something amused him. But it could disappear just as quickly when something annoyed him.

She couldn't help comparing him to Jeremy. Both of them were handsome, Jeremy was more sophisticated and polished and Scott more rugged and natural. Emma couldn't remember the last time that she saw Jeremy just let loose and show his feelings spontaneously, without first thinking them through and putting the right spin on whatever he was doing or saying. Scott, on the other hand, didn't seem to need any reason to do or feel something in particular. He just did it, or felt it, and to hell with anyone who didn't agree with it.

Emma was roused from her reverie by a loud crash. She looked up to find Scott and Tim embroiled in battle with the two guys that they had been playing pool with. They were holding their own, Scott had just thrown one of the men into a table which was what had caused the loud crash. Unfortunately, that crash also alerted other patrons who were now coming over to assist their buddies.

Scott and Tim were seriously outnumbered, but apparently had a little more fighting experience than the other men. They did alright for themselves for a few minutes, but the numbers were starting to take their toll and Scott was knocked back into the wall with a big thud.

Emma watched with wide eyes, gripping her glass so hard that it was close to shattering in her hand, as one big tattooed bruiser walked slowly towards Scott while he was still down on the floor. Without thinking, Emma jumped off her stool and ran over behind the big lug and smashed her glass into the back of his shaved head.

Emma hadn't been able to jump up high enough to hit him solidly, but the glass did break and caused a little gash that immediately started bleeding.

Her heart stopped beating in her chest when he turned towards her, his eyes were just narrow, angry slits and the tattooed snake on his muscular arm seemed to come alive as his raised his fist toward her.

Even though she knew that he was going to do some serious damage when he hit her, Emma stood frozen, unable to move. The man suddenly grunted in pain and fell forward onto the floor in front of her and Emma could see Scott standing there, no longer hidden from her view by the girth of the tattooed fellow.

Scott grabbed her hand. "Come on, he'll be back up in a minute."

He looked around quickly, Tim was doing battle with three guys and was taking some pretty good hits. Scott hesitated, wanting to help his brother, but knowing that he needed to get Emma outside to safety first.

Suddenly, everyone stopped what they were doing as the sounds of approaching police sirens became louder and louder.

All of the patrons started running for the exits and Scott pulled Emma along with him as he headed out the back door.

Tim beat them outside somehow and already had the engine running. Emma and Scott jumped into the car and they escaped the parking lot just as the first police cars were arriving.

"Are you guys okay?"

"Hell, yeah," Scott replied, full of exuberance. "That was nothing, too bad about the cops or we really would have kicked the shit out of them."

Tim nodded his agreement.

Emma had to laugh. "It was nothing? Seriously, have you two actually looked at yourselves?"

They looked each other over, bloody knuckles, some cuts and bruises and a doozy of a black eye for Tim.

"Like he said," Tim replied, "this is nothing."

"By the way, thanks for your help with that tattooed guy, I didn't know you were a brawler."

"I'm definitely not a brawler, I don't know what I was thinking, but that man scared me to death."

"You did great, we can get you tuned up and ready for the next one in no time."

"Thanks, but I think I'm good."

Once back at the motel, Emma was still full of adrenaline and very restless. She made her way over to their room and after knocking several times, she was about to give up and go back to her own room when Scott opened the door.

Emma swallowed hard and was suddenly tongue-tied as she stared at his broad, bare chest and tried desperately to avoid looking down at the wet towel wrapped around his waist.

"Um, yeah, I just, uh, wanted to be sure you guys were alright. Okay, well good night."

"Wait," he said, grabbing her arm as she turned away.

Emma turned back towards him and their eyes caught. She could feel her heart trying to hammer its way out of her chest, but she couldn't break the eye contact or move away from him.

"Would you like to come in?"

More than anything Emma suddenly wanted to be in that room with him, but she hesitated, not sure what to do. Then she realized how silly she was being. Scott shared a room with Tim, so it wasn't like they would be all alone, and she certainly didn't think any one of them were the threesome type, so she was getting herself all worked up about nothing.

"And when did you start thinking about him quite like that anyway?" she asked herself crossly. "I don't imagine he feels the same, so get it out of your head before you make a fool of yourself."

"Sure, for a few minutes," she finally replied, aware that he was watching her curiously.

Scott closed the door behind them and turned, standing so close to Emma that she could feel the heat from his body. He grabbed her hands in his, trying to stop her obsessive twisting of her wedding ring.

Emma swallowed hard, looking up into his dark brown eyes. "Where's Tim?"

"The store, this dump didn't have any ice and he needed some for his shiner."

Scott's voice was low and sexy. He stared down at her and gently pushed an errant lock of blonde hair back away from her face, then slowly, very slowly, he leaned down and captured her lips with his own.

Emma stood motionless, frozen to the spot while her heart began jackhammering in her chest. Then her body began to respond on its own and she leaned into him, returning his kiss and wrapping her arms around his neck.

Not unexpectedly, the towel slipped to the floor and Scott pulled her in even closer against his damp body as their mouths continued to explore one another.

"Emma," Scott's voice was soft and deep, and she loved the way he said her name.

"What?"

"I'm not a halfway kind of guy so, unless you are really sure about this, we better stop now."

Emma stepped back a little and looked him directly in the eye, surprised at herself and at how positive she was of her response. "I'm very sure."

He pulled her in close again and briefly ravaged her mouth, then abruptly released her and stepped back.

"Then get your cute little ass back to your own room."

"What?" she asked incredulously.

"Tim will be back any minute. I'd feel a whole lot better if I knew there was no chance of his walking in and interrupting us. So, go to your room, I'll throw some clothes on, write him a note and join you in five minutes, okay? You won't change your mind, will you?"

"I highly doubt it," she replied with a giggle, trying not to stare at his naked body as she got up on her tiptoes, planted a soft, sweet kiss on his lips and left the room.

As she waited, although a little nervous, Emma realized that she truly did not have any second thoughts about what was going to happen, but she couldn't decide if, deep down, this was just revenge for Jeremy cheating on her or if she did really care for Scott. She came to the conclusion that it was probably a little bit of both, as she continued to twist her wedding band around and around her finger.

True to his word, Scott returned a few minutes later, wearing nothing but a tight pair of jeans. And he looked almost as good in them as he did the towel.

Emma was a little timid initially, but Scott was tender and gentle, and it wasn't long before she found herself completely lost in his kisses and caresses. It was not until the wee hours of the morning that they both finally drifted off into a completely satiated sleep, their arms still wrapped tightly around each other.

# CHAPTER 21

Emma heard Callie give a little whine and opened her eyes to see the big, black dog sitting patiently next to the bed, her tail now wagging spastically back and forth as she realized that Emma was finally awake.

"Morning, baby, we'll go right outside, just give me a minute."

Emma started to move and felt sore and wonderful all at the same time. The memory of the previous night came crashing in on her and she quickly turned over and found Scott rubbing the sleep from his eyes.

"Morning, yourself," he said sleepily, "but I'm good, no need to go outside just yet."

Emma blushed as she stared into those mesmerizing brown eyes and remembered what those hands felt like on her body.

"I think I'll stay right here, I kind of like the view."

Emma blushed an even darker shade of red when she realized that she was completely naked and the thin sheet wasn't coming close to covering much of anything.

"Oh, shit," she said, and sprinted into the bathroom, which was, fortunately, just a few feet away. She could hear Scott laughing on the other side of the door as she shut it.

"Ain't nothing I haven't already seen, Emma, no need to hide it."

But hide it she did, in a big, bulky bathrobe. He smiled and shook his head when she came back into the room.

"Fine, I guess there won't be any morning calisthenics then, will there? No problem, we'll meet for breakfast in a bit and figure out the plan for today, okay?"

"Okay." Her voice wavered a little as he stood up, completely naked, and strolled casually over to his jeans and started pulling them on.

"Emma?" She wondered if her heart was going to skitter every time that he said her name now.

"What?"

"Are you okay?"

"I'm a little confused. I guess I don't know what to make of this."

"You don't have to make anything of it. It is what is. You don't regret it, do you? I know I don't."

"No," she replied with a sweet smile, "I honestly do not regret it. In fact, I think it was amazing."

Scott kissed her lightly on the lips, then pulled her tight against him for one that was much deeper and lingered for several moments.

"Good, me too," he said, pulling away and tenderly tracing her jawline with his finger. "You're something else, Emma. There is nothing for you to be embarrassed about. We had an incredible night together, that's all."

"I know but, I guess now I don't know how to act around you. I haven't been with anyone but Jeremy in,"

He put a finger over her lips to shush her. "Look, the majority of my relationships last no more than a week, so I'm pretty good at doing the dance for a few days."

Emma looked at him curiously, not knowing where he was going with this.

"But, you make me feel like I never learned the steps to this particular dance, so I think we are both going to have to find our way through it. If you want to stay back, out of the rest of the investigation, or more particularly, away from me, we can make that happen. I don't want you to feel uncomfortable."

"I'm not uncomfortable, I just feel a little odd. And I want to continue helping with the investigation, particularly if I'm with you."

Scott smiled and his eyes positively glittered. "Okay then, we'll play it by ear and take it as it comes, does that work for you?"

"Yes, it does."

They shared one last, lingering kiss and he headed out the door.

*     *     *

"What the hell are you doing, Scott? Do you think this is some kind of a freakin' game?"

"No, I don't, and it's none of your damn business."

"Wrong, it's as much my business as it is yours."

"How do you figure?"

"Scott, she's our client, we're supposed to be helping her, not creating a whole new problem for her."

"And how am I doing that?" Scott was pissed, but he was trying not to let his brother see just how much. He continued to get ready, throwing a tee shirt on and then walking into the bathroom to brush his teeth.

Tim followed him. "You know how. She's fragile right now, not only does she have this thing going on with her house, she's also got a pretty big thing going on between her and her dickhead husband."

"I know exactly what's going on and I don't need you to point it all out to me. Stay out of this and let me deal with it myself."

"Obviously, you aren't able to do that if you let it get to this point. Seriously, dude, what did you think you were accomplishing by sleeping with her? Do you think that she's suddenly going to give up her husband and her family for you, just because you screwed her once?"

They were both very angry, their eyes snapping and their jaws set. Scott clenched his fists at his side, trying to get himself under control before he knocked the shit out of his baby brother.

"Tim," he said quietly, "you need to leave this alone. I know what's involved and I know you are concerned about me, but let it go and let me figure it out myself."

"Sure, as long as you actually do figure it out, and quit just winging it and pulling stunts like you did last night."

He knew his brother well, and knew that he had pushed Scott as far as he should for now, so he shrugged his shoulders, put his hands up in the air, and said, "Fine, take care of it then."

*     *     *

As Emma was getting ready, she couldn't help but overhear some of the yelling coming from the room next door. She felt awkward and out of place when they all went to breakfast, knowing that the horrendous row they just had was all about her.

"Tim," she said, after they were settled in and had their meals, "I know you're upset about what happened between Scott and me, but it really isn't any of your business. We're both adults and know what we're doing."

"Do you?" he asked, raising his eyebrows and glaring at her with a snort of impatience. "You don't know Scott, you don't know me, and you've just had a small glimpse of what it is that we do. It's bad enough that you are still tagging along in this investigation, sleeping with my brother just messes up the situation even more.

And it is my business, because if Scott has his head up his ass because of a woman, one, or the both of us, could end up dead."

"So, is your issue what happened between him and me, or that I'm participating in this little adventure?"

"I could have lived with you coming along with us, at least until it got really hairy, but now it's become too complicated. I think it would be best if you ran on home to your husband and kids, and let us do our job."

Emma stewed silently for a few minutes, getting even angrier when Tammy leaned down as low as she possibly could while refilling Scott's cup, so that he had a good look down her top. She calmed down a little when he completely ignored the waitress, who walked away in a huff.

Emma wasn't sure why Scott was remaining silent during her little argument with Tim, but thought it might be to see what her response would be to Tim's concerns.

"This problem with my house was supposedly taken care of twice so far," Emma said, once Tammy was well away from them.

"And, after the second time, my daughter was hurt, all of us could have been really badly injured, but we were lucky. I am not walking away until I know for sure that this thing, whatever it is, is gone from my house. I will not put any of my family in danger again. As for running home to my husband, that's not going to happen and is definitely none of your damned business. Have I caused any problems by being around so far?"

"Not so far, but one mistake is all it takes to get someone hurt or killed."

"Oh, come on, Timmy," Scott finally interjected, "like we both haven't made mistakes before. Are you really going to hold her to higher standards than we hold ourselves to? She's not a problem, she's an asset and so is her dog, you know that. So, I'll be sure to keep my head out of my ass and she'll do exactly what we tell her. Are we good now?"

Tim and Scott glared at each other across the table with their jaws clenched, neither willing to back down, at least until Tammy returned and discreetly cleared her throat as she held out the bill for breakfast.

"Thanks," Scott said brusquely, not even looking at her.

They went back to the motel room where Tim had all of his research spread out. There was still tension in the air, but it dissipated a little as they started concentrating on the case.

"Let's start with the timeline," Tim began. "The house was built in 1894, burnt to the ground in 1918 and the only survivor of the fire, the youngest son, Jonathan, rebuilt it."

"So," Scott interjected, "I think it's safe to assume that it was Jonathan that built the secret basement room, but was that his body that we found? And, if so, who closed it all up and left the body down there to rot?"

"I don't think it was Jonathan. He supposedly developed dementia and died in a sanatorium in 1938, but I haven't been able to find any confirmation of that."

"So, who the hell was that in the basement?"

"One of his buddies, maybe? Every article that I saw about Jonathan included comments about three of his friends, or showed him with them in the pictures. It doesn't look like he did anything without these guys."

"They'd all be long dead by now, so that doesn't help us too awful much. Find any of their relatives?"

"Albert Johnson had children who stayed in the area. I have an address for one of his sons who lives not far from here."

"Well, let's go then."

"Excuse me." Emma had tried to sit quietly and just listen, but her curiosity got the best of her. "But, how does talking with the son of a friend of the guy who used to live here, help us figure out what's going on now?"

They both looked at her quizzically, but Scott responded. "We don't know if it will, but we also don't know that it won't, so we'll check it out."

"Of course we will," she replied, thoroughly confused.

*     *     *

Thirty minutes later they were sitting in Albert Johnson, Junior's living room, sipping iced tea and nibbling on sugar cookies with him. He was still fairly spry for a man in his seventies and he welcomed the company.

"So, Miss," he asked, "how long have you lived in the old Creeghan House?"

"Just a few months."

"I hear lots of stories about that place, any of them true?"

"It definitely has a personality all its own," Scott interjected. "That's why we're here, to see if you might have any information about the house. I understand that your father was a pretty close friend of Jonathan Creeghan."

The old man stared curiously at Scott, and then at Emma. He was quiet for a few moments, almost as if he were trying to decide if he was going to share any information with them or not.

He finally broke the uncomfortable silence. "They were very close, right up until Jonathan completely lost his mind and had to be locked up."

"Can you tell us anything about Jonathan?"

"I never knew him, but my father talked a lot about him in the last few years of his life. Apparently, Jonathan had aspirations to be a wizard."

"A wizard?"

"Yes, he practiced black magic, did it for years before he pulled my father into his ugly little world."

"What attracted your father to it?"

"I don't know how they first met or got involved with each other, but Jonathan always had a small group of guys to help him with his ceremonies. In return, he would do spells to benefit them. I guess that was how he paid them. Anyway, my parents couldn't have children. Once Jonathan took my father under his wing, my mother started getting pregnant every couple of years. I was the fifth and last child. She died giving birth to me."

"So, what did Jonathan get out of all this?"

"Power. He hungered for power, and with each spell he cast he became stronger and more powerful. He wanted enough power to destroy his enemies and all the people that had contributed to the demise of his entire family in that fire. Do you know about that?"

"Some of it, not all the details."

"My father was at the house the night of the party that started it all."

"What happened?"

"There were circus performers and some animals they did acts with, dogs, monkeys, little animals like that. Something happened, I'm not sure anyone knows exactly what, but the animals suddenly went berserk and attacked whoever was closest to them. I guess it was pretty brutal and pretty bloody. It continued until the last animal had been shot and by then quite a few people were also maimed or killed."

"What could have caused them to act like that?" Emma asked.

"Many years later, my father began to suspect that Jonathan may have had something to do with it. He'd already begun dabbling in black magic by then and may have tried something that went horribly wrong, but Jonathan never would admit to it."

"So, what did all that have to do with the fire?"

"They say someone set it in retaliation for a loved one that was killed by the animals. Nothing was ever proven and, in all honesty, I don't think much of an investigation was ever done, even though four people died in the fire. Several high ranking police officers and their wives were injured or killed when the animals went crazy, so there wasn't much sympathy for the Creeghans at the time."

His voice was getting scratchy and he suddenly looked very tired.

"Are you okay, Mr. Johnson?" Emma asked. "Would you like us to come back another time?"

Scott frowned at her, but Mr. Johnson gave her a half-hearted smile. "Bless you for your kindness, Miss, but I'm fine. And there is more to the story that you should know."

"Jonathan began going a little mad after the fire. Once he had the house rebuilt, he got into the black magic in a serious way. He was rarely seen around town any more. Only my father and two other men spent any time with him at all."

"O'Malley and Reinhart?"

"Yes." The old man looked at Tim in surprise.

"Do you know anything about the actual rituals that they performed?" Just as Tim asked the question, the temperature in the room dropped at least twenty to thirty degrees. He and Scott stood up and looked around, trying to find the threat.

Mr. Johnson opened his mouth to speak, but no words came out, his eyes began to bulge and he started to claw at his own throat, as if he were trying to pry something loose from it so that he could breathe again.

"Call 911," Scott ordered, as he ran over to help the old man.

Emma punched in the numbers with a shaking hand as she watched Mr. Johnson pull Scott down close so he could whisper in his ear. Then he leaned back and, after several desperate gasps as he tried in vain to draw air into his lungs, he sighed and closed his eyes, and the life faded from his body right before her eyes.

Emma practically threw the phone at Tim. She wasn't sure if she was going to scream, cry, or pass out, but she definitely wasn't able to talk on the phone. Instead, she sunk to the floor, covered her face and began to cry quietly.

Tim came over after hanging up with the 911 dispatcher and sat next to her, putting his arm around her shoulders. "Did we do this? Did we bring it here?" she asked, choking back another sob.

"I don't know," he answered. "I just don't know."

Scott stood watching them, shaking his head, angry at his inability to prevent this from happening. Without a word of explanation, he ran upstairs and didn't come back down until he heard the police sirens approaching.

# CHAPTER 22

"You did good," Scott said to Emma, as he handed her a glass containing a hefty shot of whiskey.

"What do you mean?" she asked, feeling fairly numb even before drinking any of the alcohol.

"With the cops, you told them the truth, but you didn't share any more than you needed to. That was good."

"Thanks, but honestly, I feel so wiped out right now that I can't even remember what I said to them." She took a hefty sip of the whiskey and enjoyed the warm trail that it left as it traveled down her throat and into her chest, melting away her tension.

He gently tucked her hair back behind her ear and ran his fingers along her jawline, lingering over her lips, and leaned forward, capturing her glittering green gaze with his own.

"Here's what you're going to do. You are going to drink this down and I'll fill it up again for you to take back to your own room, then you are going to sip it while soaking in a hot tub, and then you are going to crash for the rest of the night and not think about any of this, okay?"

"Gee, do I have to?" she asked with a giggle, the whiskey apparently already starting to take effect, or maybe it was just from the shock of watching that sweet, old man die right in front of her.

Scott walked Emma to her room and checked it to be sure it was clear. Then he grabbed hold of her and kissed her long and deep. She moaned and melted into his arms.

"Are you going to take that bath with me?"

"I am tempted, but I can't, not tonight. You get some sleep and I'll come pick you up in the morning, okay?"

"Alright, I'm glad you were there today. I always feel safer when you're there."

"No worries, all right? Tim and I will always make sure that you're safe, no matter what. Now, lock the door behind me and get some sleep."

*      *      *

"So," Tim said at breakfast the next morning, "between Albert's journal and the symbols on Jonathan's robe, I think I know who the demon is that they were trying to conjure."

"Wait a minute," Emma said, trying to brush the whiskey cobwebs out of her head, "how long was I asleep and when the hell did we get Albert's journal?"

Scott just smiled and shoveled a forkful of eggs into his mouth, leaving Tim to reply.

"Albert, Jr. told Scott about it just before he died, and my devious big brother was able to smuggle it out of the house without the cops being any the wiser."

"What else was in it?"

"There were some very interesting spells and incantations. These guys were into serious black magic. He documented pretty much every detail of their spellwork, even the one that granted him fertility early on in their adventures. I guess that's what made him a true believer, but he never saw the dark side, the price that had to be paid, which in his case was the life of his beloved wife."

"Bummer for him," Scott replied, finally joining the conversation. "I have no sympathy for any of them. You reap what you sow. So, who is the big, bad demon that got the best of them?"

"The demon they called up is Eitooheikoh, he is a minion for Moloch, the Prince of the Land of Tears. And Moloch is one bad ass demon. Parents made child sacrifices to him back in the day. Maybe that's why things went awry, because these guys didn't sacrifice a child to get to him and it pissed him off, so he killed Jonathan."

"Wait a minute," Emma interrupted, "the body was Jonathan?"

"Yep," Scott answered, "the journal had all kinds of information in it, including the details of that last night. One of the men, he wasn't sure who, or maybe it was him and he didn't want to admit it, smudged the line of the pentagram, allowing the demon to get to them. They all scrambled to escape but it got Jonathan. They heard him scream, but didn't look back to see what was happening."

"Pretty loyal friends."

"Definitely, anyway, it happened in the middle of the night, so they waited until the next day to come back and found Jonathan dead in the basement with no apparent injuries. They boarded up the basement, left the house and never picked up a magic wand again."

"But why didn't they bury him?"

Tim joined in at that point. "They'd also been dabbling in Necromancy and were afraid his body would come back to life with the demon inside of it. So, they buried an empty casket and locked Jonathan in the basement with whatever demon might be still be around."

"Then how did the demon get out of that room?"

"It was stupid of them to think a locked and boarded up door could keep a demon out," Scott said disgustedly. "They knew better, or at least they should have, but it was the quickest and safest way out of their predicament and once it was done they could just pretend none of it had happened. You can thank those men for the demons in your house, the damn cowards."

"So, what now?"

"It's time to go back to the house and find the portal."

"Wouldn't that be in the basement where they were doing the spells?"

"Not necessarily, but we will check there first."

"And what happens when we find it?"

"We shut it down and send them all back to hell."

Scott's voice was cold, his face, usually so expressive, was closed and indiscernible, and his eyes were a darker shade than Emma had ever seen before. She had to rub her arms briskly to get rid of the goosebumps that had risen suddenly.

"Let's get Emma back to the motel and then we can head over."

"What are you talking about, Tim? Do we really have to go through this again? I'm going with you."

"No, you aren't. This is where it gets really dangerous. We can't be keeping an eye on you all the time, while we are trying to protect our own butts."

"I can help, I am going with you or you aren't going back in there at all."

"That's pretty foolish, don't you think?"

"Why?"

"Because you called us, we can walk away right now and be no worse for it. You, however, still own a haunted house and would be putting your whole family at risk if you go back there."

"Touché, asshole," she replied. "But you can use me, and Callie. We can help, please let me come with you. Whatever happens, I need to see it with my own eyes."

"Please," she added, turning to Scott with a pleading look, her green eyes sparkling with unshed tears that threatened to spill at any moment.

"She's coming," he responded.

Tim shook his head in exasperation, pursed his lips and practically took the diner door off its hinges as he headed out.

*    *    *

"Before we go inside, I need to give you this." Scott pulled out a beautiful turquoise gem with a pentagram etched on it. There was a circle around the pentagram and flames along the outside of the circle. It was stunning. There was a black cord attached to it and Scott slipped it over her head.

"I didn't realize that we were at the jewelry giving stage of our relationship already."

"We aren't, smartass. I picked this up when I ran over to PA the other day, special order, just for you. Do not take this off and I mean that, it's an anti-possession necklace. As long as you are wearing it, the Demon can't take over your body. See, Tim and I wear them, too."

He slid his out from under his tee shirt and then tucked it back away. Emma blushed, she'd seen his necklace before when he'd taken his shirt off, but she'd had other things on her mind at the time and never asked him about it.

Scott led the way in, stepping over the threshold with his gun raised while he scoped out as much of the house as he could see from the Foyer. Emma was close behind him, holding Callie's leash tightly, and Tim brought up the rear. Emma felt like she was in a bad remake of some old action film and almost giggled. That urge disappeared immediately as she watched the hair on Callie's neck rise.

"Um, guys," Emma muttered, then nodded her head towards the dog when they both turned to her. Scott turned quickly back towards the stairs where Callie seemed to be staring, but saw nothing.

"Anything?" Tim asked.

"I don't think so. The EMF isn't going off and she isn't barking."

"Any idea what's setting her off?" Tim asked Emma.

"No idea, should I let go of the leash and see where she goes?"

They all stopped suddenly as a loud bang came from one of the upstairs bedrooms.

"No, stay here. Tim, watch them."

Scott sidled over to the staircase and started up the stairs two at a time. At the top of the stairs, he stopped and tilted his head, apparently hearing something off to his right, and disappeared from view down that hallway.

Emma and Tim heard nothing for a moment and then the loud, thrashing sounds of a serious scuffle filtered down the stairs.

"Scott," Tim yelled. Emma could see that he was torn between his responsibility to look after her and his need to help his brother.

"Go," she urged. "We'll be fine."

Tim had just reached the base of the stairs when Scott came back into view dragging someone behind him by the collar of their nicely tailored dress shirt.

"Jeremy?" Emma called out in surprise.

"Your husband?" Tim asked.

"Yes, Jeremy, what are you doing here?"

He glared at her and she grimaced when she saw that his lip was split and bleeding.

"My children needed some clothes and other items. You wouldn't answer my calls, so I had to drive out to this hellhole myself. What are you doing here? Let go of me." He yanked himself backward out of Scott's grip.

There was an awkward silence as they all seemed to just be looking at each other.

"So, what exactly is going on here?" Jeremy demanded as he started down the staircase.

"We're trying," Scott began.

"I'm not talking to you. I'm talking to my wife."

Emma saw Scott's eyes narrow as he stared a hole into Jeremy's back.

"Jeremy," she called a little too loudly, "these men are helping us get rid of whatever it is that's haunting this house. Please be respectful to them, they've already done a great deal to try and fix this situation."

"I'm not convinced there is anything more to fix, other than your imagination. And, I assume that they aren't really FBI agents and were just perpetrating a little fraud to get into our home the last time they showed up. I certainly hope you haven't given them any money."

"Jeremy, stop it," Emma said impatiently.

"Are you okay?" Jeremy asked, as he reached the bottom step and strode towards her. Emma couldn't help flinching away as Jeremy raised his hand to touch her face.

"Please, don't," she said quietly, backing away from him. She could see the hurt in his eyes, but couldn't do anything to change it at this point. Her own pain from his betrayal was still too raw.

"Well, then," Jeremy said, with an edge to his voice as he stared hard at Emma, "I guess I'll be joining in on the ghost hunt. You know, to watch over my property and make sure nothing happens to it."

"Tim, why don't you take Mr. Draper into the living room and show him what's already happened to his property. And show him what we found downstairs, maybe then he'll accept the fact that this is not just his wife's imagination, after all."

"I'll make some coffee," Emma said, as she headed down the hallway to the kitchen. Scott and Jeremy both followed her with their eyes, which then locked on each other.

"Let's go," Tim said, breaking the silent war between the two of them. Jeremy finally turned away and followed Tim towards the living room.

Emma stood perfectly still as Scott came up behind her and softly asked if she was alright. Their bodies were so close that she could feel the heat emanating from his. She wanted nothing more than to lean back and let him envelop her in his arms, but she knew that couldn't happen, not right now anyway.

"I'm not sure," she replied with a harsh laugh. "I'm certainly surprised, and I feel like I have pretty much each and every possible emotion running through my body right now, and I'm not sure which one is going to win out."

"Emma."

She turned quickly and put a finger to his lips. "Please don't say anything, let me work my way through this, okay?"

"If that's what you need, that's what you'll have. But, I'm here if you need me, don't ever forget that."

Their bodies were mere inches apart and she couldn't resist raising on her tiptoes and giving him a quick kiss. It calmed her and allowed her to step back and quietly continue setting up the coffee maker.

A few minutes later, Jeremy and Tim returned and they all sat around the table drinking black coffee. Emma wasn't sure if it was all in her head or not, but the room felt thick with tension, or maybe just testosterone. Even Callie seemed to feel it as she paced nervously around the kitchen.

It didn't escape Scott's attention that, in between sips of coffee, Emma was unable to keep from twisting her wedding band around and around her finger, it was her tell and indicated how nervous she was, not about the haunting, but about Jeremy, and about him. Scott could see that Jeremy was oblivious about it, but it made Scott furious because there was absolutely nothing he could do to reassure her, not right now anyway.

"So, you've already torn up part of my house, what now?" Jeremy's arms were spread wide on the table, claiming his territory as he looked back and forth between Scott and Tim.

Tim set an odd little object on the table. It looked like a miniature birdhouse made of steel. Inside the cage, sitting on a bed of finely ground gravel or sand, was an odd shaped, azure stone.

"This stone will tell us where the portal is. Once we find that, we can close it."

"How do you do that?"

"With a spell."

"Of course," Jeremy replied, with a smug little smile. "And once that's done, then it's over?"

"No," Scott replied, and Jeremy turned to him with narrowed eyes.

"Why not?"

"Closing the portal just prevents any further spirits or demons from crossing over. We still need to dispose of the ones already here."

"And you have a spell for that too, I assume?"

"We have ways to take care of them."

"What ways?"

Scott hesitated. "Some things are best left to Tim and me. You don't have to be involved."

"Don't give me that shit," Jeremy said. "I want to know what's going on every moment that you are still here."

"That's not going to happen, but," Scott said quietly, his eyes darkening, "I appreciate that, after all this time, you're finally taking an interest in what does go on in your house."

"Get the hell out of here, right now."

"You'd better step back, dude, and ease up on the attitude. You didn't call us here and, until your wife decides that we aren't able to help her make this house safe again for her family, we're staying."

"Listen, you son of bitch,"

"No, you listen." Scott stood so abruptly that his chair tipped over backwards with a loud bang. He leaned down until he was just a few inches from Jeremy's face.

"I don't give a damn what kind of hot shot lawyer you are. You do not have a clue about what's going on here. We do. So, if you aren't going to help, then get the hell out of our way and let us do our job."

Scott's voice was firm but not loud. Jeremy's face paled and, for one of the few times in his life, he was at a loss for words. He glared hatefully at Scott as he tried to hide his discomfiture.

The growing silence began to make Emma nervous, so she started picking up the coffee cups and putting them in the sink.

"So, where do we start?"

Tim gave her a quick nod of thanks for breaking up the mental arm-wrestling match going on between Jeremy and Scott. "With the first floor, I already checked the basement when we were down there. I thought for sure it would be in the Magic Room, but it wasn't."

"How does it work?" she asked.

"The stone will glow a deep, deep red when it is in the vicinity of the portal. Ready?" he asked the other two men, hoping they would mellow out a little bit. If not, it was going to be a very long day.

The four of them slowly made their way through each room on the first floor. Tim held the miniature cage out at arm's length, but the stone never turned red. Then they all headed up the staircase to begin going through the second floor.

Scott was leading the way and Jeremy was bringing up the rear. Jeremy had been fairly quiet while they checked out the first floor, but he was starting to get bold again and make snarky little comments.

Emma was just turning around to tell him to shut up when all hell broke loose.

Scott's EMF meter went off the charts with its noises and lights and Callie started barking frantically. Just as Emma felt a blast of cold air rush by her head, she heard Jeremy scream and watched as he tumbled head over heels down the stairs. The noise and confusion was over as soon as it started and Emma ran down the stairs to see if Jeremy was alright.

He was alive, but moaning and groaning as he slowly moved all of his limbs to be sure nothing was broken.

"I'm okay," he said, smiling up into her worried face. "Banged up a little, but all in one piece."

Emma was so relieved that he was alright, she instinctively threw her arms around him and hugged him tightly.

"You two should probably leave now," Scott said, his voice a little husky. Emma knew why and could see how hurt he was. She also knew that this situation was getting much more complicated and she needed to figure out what she was doing, and fast.

"We can go through the rest of the house ourselves and then we don't have to worry about anything more happening to the two of you."

"That's probably a good idea," Emma replied. "Jeremy, is your car here? We didn't see it when we pulled in."

"It's around back, near the garage."

"If you're sure," she said, "it's probably best that I get him out of here. I'll talk to you two later, okay?"

"Fine," Scott replied, as he turned and headed back up the staircase.

CHAPTER 23


Emma got Jeremy back to her hotel room, gave him a few Ibuprofen and managed to get him to lay down for awhile. He really was banged up pretty good. She sat quietly staring out the window while he slept.

Her only view was the nearby highway overpass, but that's not what she was seeing. In her mind's eye, she was seeing her children as they grew up, seeing Jeremy as he was when they started their life together, and as they shared so many different moments together over the last twenty years.

And then she saw his mistress and their haunted house; she saw her horse break its leg and her daughter once again fall down those stairs; watched Scott do what he does, wearing his long, tough-guy leather coat, or his obligatory tee shirt and jeans, or wearing just a towel and last, but not least, wearing nothing at all and spending an incredible night with her, making her feel worthy and cherished.

Emma's thoughts and feelings were swirling out of control, swinging like a pendulum from the highs and lows that she'd had in her life, and she couldn't get them to come to rest. She still couldn't find any answers for what she was going to do with her life now.

"Hey, Em, you okay?" Jeremy asked after resting for an hour or so. "You look like you're a million miles away."

She smiled wistfully, and said, "I sort of wish that I was."

"Can we talk now? About us. About our life, not the stinking ghosts or demons or whatever the devil is at the house."

"Yes," she replied quietly, "but I'm not sure what there is to talk about. You've been having an affair. I don't know for how long or if this is the only one. I don't care why it happened, only that it did happen. So, what is there to talk about?"

"Emma." Jeremy hissed through his teeth suddenly, as a sharp pain ripped through his right side when he tried to sit up. He took a deep breath and got himself situated as comfortably as possible before continuing.

"Listen, Emma, I want you to know that I love you, only you. I made a terrible mistake. I know that, and I will do everything in my power to make it up to you so you can forgive me and we can move on."

"Why would I want to do that?"

Jeremy looked surprised at her response and, in that moment, she realized just how arrogant he was. He had no doubt in his mind that she would forgive him and that they'd just put it behind them and carry on as usual.

"Because, Em, because you still love me and you love our family, and we all belong together."

"Did that occur to you before or after we found you with your little whore?"

"That wasn't called for, Emma. It sounds like you've been spending a little too much time with your trailer trash ghostbusters."

"They are good men, Jeremy, and you can rest assured that phrase came from me, and me alone."

"Listen, Emma, I don't want to argue with you. I made a mistake, a big mistake. I don't know what I was thinking, I truly don't, but I am so sorry and I want to make this right. I love you so much, I can't lose you. I won't lose you. Please come back to the apartment with me. We'll talk and figure this out, just like we always have."

"No, that's not going to happen right now."

"Why not? Having too much fun with the Hardy boys?" It was amazing how snarky he could be, even as he was trying to woo her back.

"As a matter of fact, it is kind of fun and a little cathartic. I'm hunting ghosts and getting the bejesus scared out me, and I'm able to focus on something other than the pitiful state of my marriage for a little while."

Jeremy winced as he threw back the covers and got out of bed. Emma stared at him calmly as he strode purposefully towards her and pulled her to her feet.

He took her into his embrace and kissed her deeply, wrapping her tightly in his arms. When they stepped apart, Jeremy had a rather smug smile on his face.

"You see," he said, "you do love me. We belong together and you know that we do."

Emma took a deep breath.

"Jeremy, we've been together a long time, we've raised three children together, we've known joy and happiness, grief and sorrow, and have been there for each other through all of it. I know that I will always love you. We've shared too much to ever let that go."

She raised her hand and caressed his stubbly cheek. He was smiling down at her expectantly.

"But," she continued, "loving someone and being in love with someone are two totally different things. I think that a door slammed shut in my heart when I saw you with her, and it locked away so much of the way that I feel about you. And it slammed shut so hard, that I'm not sure if I'll ever be able to get that door open again. And, as of right now, I haven't even decided if I want to try."

"I am being completely sincere, Jeremy, when I tell you that I don't know what I am going to do. I need some time alone, so you need to leave now. I'll call you soon."

He opened his mouth to speak, but changed his mind and turned abruptly.

"You haven't even asked about your children," he remarked bitterly.

"I know."

He turned and looked at her quizzically. "Don't you care about them anymore either?"

"Of course, I do," she replied, tears brimming in her eyes. "But, I knew that it would make me cry if I thought about them or talked about them with you, okay? Please let them know that I'll see them soon."

"Whatever," he replied, as he grabbed his suitcoat and stalked out the door.

\*　　　\*　　　\*

Emma laid on her bed for a long time, just staring at the ceiling, trying make sense out of what she was feeling. When she realized that the sun was going down, she decided to see if the guys were back from the house yet. Maybe they had good news about the portal.

After showering and getting herself back together, Emma headed to their room. There was no response to her knock so she went downstairs. Their car was not in the parking lot so she assumed they must still be at the house.

That worried her a little, but Emma knew there were things they would have to do if they found the portal, so they could still be busy with that. She would give them a little longer and if they still weren't back, she'd try their cell phones. If she couldn't reach them by phone, she would have to drive back to the house. Emma really hoped that wouldn't be necessary, because she wasn't sure she'd have the courage to actually go inside and look for them.

Emma wandered into the bar area, it was small and dark and there were only a couple of people scattered here and there at tables. She sat at the bar where she would be able to see them enter the lobby when they returned.

"What can I get you?" the bartender asked.

"Chardonnay, please."

When he set it down in front of her, she went to pick up the glass, but hesitated when she felt Scott's animal heat directly behind her.

Emma turned into his embrace and he kissed her long and hard, renewing his possession of her.

"Wow," she replied, when he finally released her, "that was unexpected."

He smiled his charming, mega-watt smile and sat down beside her, pulling the stool close enough that their legs were touching.

"Scotch, barkeep, thanks."

"So?" she asked, the suspense was killing her.

"What?" he replied, brows furrowed in confusion.

"Did you find the portal?"

"Oh, no," he replied. "We went through the entire place three times and there was nothing. We can't figure it out, it has to be there. Timmy went back over to the library to see if he can dig up anything else."

"Why didn't you come and get me?"

"I was afraid that you might be busy. And, if you were busy, I might have to break the nose of the dickhead that was making you busy. So, I thought it best to wait for you to come to me."

"And here I am."

"Yes, here you are." He leaned forward and kissed her again, this time, slowly and tenderly.

"I'm very happy about that," he added, as he leaned back on his stool.

"Obviously." Emma smiled mischievously, nodding down at the evidence of his affection.

He smiled back, but then turned serious. Scott was pleased to see that she was not twisting her ring, so she was feeling comfortable and calm, which he hoped meant that they were still good and she didn't plan on running home to Jeremy any time soon.

"So, what happened?"

"We talked and didn't resolve anything. But, I did tell him that I'm not going back until I figure out what I want."

"And what do you want?"

"I honestly don't know. I know that I will never feel the same for Jeremy again. I know how much I love my children and that they will always be my first priority. I know that the decision that I finally make will be the one that is the best decision for them, not necessarily for me. But, I also know that I care a lot for you, a real lot, and right now you are the one that I want to be with."

Scott threw some money on the bar to cover the tab and then held out his hand to Emma. She took it and he helped her off the stool and up to her room, where he needed no words to express the extent of his feelings for her.

\*       \*       \*

Scott spent the night with her and Emma couldn't miss the disapproving looks that Tim was throwing in both their directions while they ate breakfast at the diner the next morning. Even Tammy was acting a bit surly since Scott hardly even acknowledged her.

Emma waited until Scott went off to the restroom to look Tim straight in the eye and confront him. "Is there something that you would like to say to me?"

He was silent for a moment and then set his fork down onto his plate, a piece of his omelet still nestled in the prongs.

"No," he replied, "but I do have something I would like to ask you."

"Go ahead."

"What the hell do you think you are doing?"

"Well, that's simple enough. I haven't got a clue."

"Don't be flip with me. You are a married woman and you will inevitably end up back with your husband and family. And, when you do, you are seriously going to mess up my brother. I've never seen him become this involved with someone. He's in way over his head.

We deal with life and death situations every day. He can't have his head stuck up his ass because he had brief fling with a hot, married lady who got pissed off at her husband. If he does, it could very well get him, or me, killed. You just don't seem to quite get that. You need to think real hard about what you want and be honest about it, with him, and with yourself."

She was silent for a few moments, thinking through what he had said. "Please don't think that this is just a fling for me, I really do care about Scott."

Tim held his hand up to stop her. "That isn't good enough. If you aren't in all the way, then get the hell out before it gets even more complicated."

"I'll do what I have to do, but it's between Scott and me what happens, not you, and you just don't seem to get that." Emma picked up her coffee and started sipping on it when she saw Scott walking back towards the table.

Her response to Tim had been more bravado than truth. Emma was sincerely worried about what she might possibly be doing to Scott, to herself, and to her family. She was not taking this situation lightly, but she didn't yet know what the right answer was, and no one was going to push her one way or the other.

"Everything okay here?" Scott asked, looking curiously at the two of them.

"It's all good," Tim replied.

Scott turned to Emma. "He wasn't sticking his nose where it doesn't belong, was he?"

"No, he was fine," she replied, but she couldn't help but rerun Tim's words over and over in her head. She really did need to figure out what she was going to do, and soon.

Scott didn't believe a word either of them were saying as he sat down and watched Emma twist her wedding band around her finger in a constant non-stop motion.

Thankfully, Tim switched the conversation back to the house right then. "So, I went through everything I could think of last night at the library, but I'm stumped. If there is a portal, it has to be in that house somewhere. I don't get why we can't find it."

"I don't really understand how the portal works, but, since the demons or ghosts or whatever can go from one building to another, could it just be somewhere else on the property, rather than in the house? There's the garage and the barn, and lots of creepy things have happened in the barn."

Both men looked at Emma with interest as they considered her question.

"I've never heard of a portal in one building allowing the entities to jump over into other ones."

"But, Scott," replied Tim, "there have been cases of spirits haunting multiple locations on one property, remember that case down in Georgia?"

"Right, but weren't those bodies all buried throughout the property and that's why they could travel from building to building, as long as they stayed on the plantation?"

"True, but we've never worked a case where we had both ghosts and demons present before either. Or a case where a stupid, creepy, black magician conjured up the crap to begin with."

Scott nodded his agreement. "Well, it wouldn't hurt to check out those other buildings. If there's nothing there, we'll have to come up with something else."

# CHAPTER 24

The day was overcast and the air felt heavy as they made their way to the barn. The garage had been clean, so this was their last hope.

Emma swung the doors open and Tim handed her the miniature cage and raised his shotgun. Scott also had his gun up, and they both stepped inside before her.

"Look," Emma yelled as she followed them in. The stone in the cage began to glow and then turn a bright white, pinkish rose and then bright red. Once it turned a deep, dark burgundy, it did not change any more.

"Okay, Emma, get out of here, now."

"What?" she asked, mesmerized by the stone.

"Get out of the barn, now," Scott said forcefully, grabbing her arm and dragging her outside. Tim was right behind them.

"Why did you do that? Don't we have to close the portal?"

"Yes, but the stone is just our beacon, our guide to where the portal is. We needed to get it out of there before the demon recognized what it was and tried to destroy it."

"Let's get this put away." Scott took the cage gingerly out of Emma's hands and walked towards the trunk of the car.

The stone was placed carefully in a padded box in the trunk and secured with a small, antique key. Scott and Tim rustled through some other items in the trunk, filling their pockets and a small rucksack.

"You have the spell?"

"Yes," Tim replied, "and here's a copy for you."

"How does that work?" Emma asked.

"They'll hear us when we begin the spell and they'll be pissed and try to stop us. We both say it together and, if they are able to stop one of us, hopefully, the other is able to finish it."

"Hopefully?"

"Don't worry, we'll be fine. Fortunately, it's a short spell and we talk fast. You stay here with Callie, okay?"

"No."

"Please do what I ask. I can't do this right if I'm distracted and worried about you."

Emma hesitated, ready to argue her position yet again, but her concern for their safety overrode her need to be involved. "Alright, but please be careful."

"I will." Scott gave her a quick peck on the cheek and he and Tim headed back towards the barn.

Emma waited for a few minutes, but couldn't stand not knowing what was going on. She put Callie in the car and moved closer to the barn.

She could hear the men chanting some Latin words that made no sense to her. A strong wind was swirling bits of hay and other debris all around them, although immediately outside the barn door the air was dead calm.

For some silly reason, all Emma could picture was the tornado scene in the Wizard of Oz and she half-expected that the barn would take off into the air at any minute.

There was a loud bang and a grunt of pain as Scott was lifted into the air and flung into one of the walls. Tim kept on chanting, but the wind was growing stronger and, even as tall and broad as he was, he was having trouble staying on his feet. But, he gripped the paper tight in both hands and kept on reading.

Emma was just a couple of feet outside the doors, frozen in place. Her heart was pounding and her hands were sweaty. She wasn't sure what she should do, if anything.

She watched as Scott shook the cobwebs out of his head and managed to stand back up and begin chanting again. It was just a matter of seconds before he was picked up yet again and thrown against the wall. This time he didn't recover right away and the paper flew out of his hands.

Emma watched it get caught up in the swirl of wind and ran into the barn and chased it down. It was like entering another world, the wind whipped her hair and pieces of debris stung her face and eyes. The air itself felt like it held something indescribable within it, something unclean and rancid. It raised goosebumps on her arms and legs and made her feel nauseous.

Tim was still chanting, but was struggling to keep his feet. He was concentrating so hard that he didn't even know that she was now in the barn.

Scott was lying still on the ground, so Emma sat on the floor and grabbed ahold of the boards in one of the stall doors, hoping she wouldn't get completely sucked into the windy vortex.

With her body wrapped around the stall door, she was able to find where Tim was in the chant and joined him, yelling to get her words out over the rush of the wind.

They were close to the end when there was a piercing scream and Tim was lifted off his feet and flung across the room into one wall and then another, like a ragdoll.

Emma felt something pulling on her hair. At first, she thought it was just the wind but then she realized that something had actually grabbed a handful of it and was yanking her head backwards. She wanted to scream and cry and run out of the barn as fast as she could, but she held tight with both arms wrapped around the board and kept reading, ignoring the pain as her head was repeatedly jerked backwards.

She yelled out the last line as loudly as she could and suddenly everything went quiet.

Tim dropped to the barn floor in a crumpled heap. The wind stopped and the pieces of hay and debris just floated harmlessly down to the ground. Emma couldn't seem to let go of the stall door, although she knew it was now safe to do so.

Emma looked at Tim, then at Scott. Neither looked like they were conscious and she knew she had to go help them, but she couldn't get her arms to let go of the stall door.

Tim moaned, shook his head and slowly got up off the floor, looking around in a rather dazed manner until he saw Emma.

"What are you doing in here?"

"Trying to help." Emma's voice was a lot shakier than she had expected and she worried that she might actually start crying.

"Looks like you were a very big help. Thank you."

She nodded at him with a trembling smile, still clinging to the door.

"Is Scott alright?"

"He will be," Tim replied, as he walked over to check on his brother.

"Scott." Tim tapped him lightly on the cheeks. "Scott, you okay?"

Scott exhaled loudly and a moment later was able to sit up under his own steam. "Damn, that was a nasty one."

His voice was weak and he frowned as he raised a hand up to the knot on his forehead where he had made contact with the wall.

"What the hell are you doing in here, Emma? I told you to stay out."

"Leave her be, Scott. She saved our bacon and finished the spell when they were banging me around like a piñata."

"She what?"

"You heard me, she's an official ghostbuster, for now anyway."

Scott smiled tenderly at her, shaking his head in surprise and disbelief. Emma wished that her lips would stop shaking enough so that she could smile back, but that wasn't quite happening yet.

Later, after they'd finally been able to pry Emma loose from the stall door and assist her to the car, they agreed to meet at the hotel bar once they'd all cleaned up.

*     *     *

"Here, you need this." Scott slid a glass of amber liquor towards Emma as she moved onto the stool next to him.

"What is it?"

"Brandy, it'll calm your nerves, trust me."

The initial burn eased up a little and warmth soon spread through her chest and torso as Emma sipped the brandy. And, amazingly, her hands even stopped shaking.

"Better?"

"Much, thank you."

"So, what did you think about that little adventure?"

"How surreal it was. This whole thing is so unbelievably crazy, I can't get over it. A few months ago, I would have thought you both belonged in a looney bin. I'm just struggling to comprehend all of it. It's like having a whole new reality and my brain just can't completely shift gears and accept what I'm seeing. Does that make any sense?"

"I think it's a great way to explain it," Tim added. "We had the luxury, if you want to call it that, of knowing about these things from the time we were kids, so we never had that reality slap in the face that other people have to have."

Tim was being much nicer and more accepting of Emma since she helped close the portal, but she knew that it was just a temporary respite.

"What's next?"

"Now, we try to narrow down what spirits and demons are still there and get rid of them."

"I know you didn't want to share much information with Jeremy about what happens next. Is it going to involve burning more bones?"

"Most likely," Scott replied.

"You know, some things are starting to make more sense to me now," Tim said thoughtfully.

"Like what."

"Well, I still don't quite get how the entities are able to move freely from the barn to the house, but I do know that the barn did not burn down in the fire. From what I recall from the news stories, the injured people, and animals, were taken to the barn after the incident at the party, at least until they could get those people that survived to the hospital. Most likely, there were quite a few that died there and that's where the strongest pull was coming from. It's probably why the portal opened there instead of in the house. Since the house had been rebuilt when Jonathan called up the demon, there hadn't been any deaths in it at that time."

"Which means what?" Emma asked.

"It means we'll work on the ghosts first and clean them out. I'll go back and get the information on who died after the party and we'll find their graves and take care of them. Then we work on the demon."

"Sounds like a plan." Scott lifted his glass to them in salute.

Tim took off a short time later and Scott walked Emma to her room. The brandy had calmed her nerves and warmed her up, but she still couldn't stop the uncontrollable shivers that were ravaging her.

"It's shock." Scott explained as he sat her down on the bed and started helping her out of her clothes.

"It'll pass, it's just your body trying to catch up with your mind, or some shit like that. Lay down."

Emma did as she was told and Scott removed the rest of her clothing and pulled the heavy comforter up over her.

As she lay there, her eyes trying to slam shut, she heard the swoosh of fabric as Scott removed his own clothing.

"Scott," she said apologetically, "I'm just so tired."

"Ssh," he whispered, climbing into the bed and snuggling up close behind her. "I'm just going to hold you while you sleep."

And that was how they spent the rest of the afternoon, until her tremors subsided against his warmth, and the terrors in her mind finally let loose and allowed her to think straight again.

Her first coherent thoughts were about Scott, who's warm body was still snuggled up close to her, and Emma realized how safe she felt when she was with him. He could be so thoughtful and caring, when he wanted to be. He made Emma feel like she was the most important person in his life and that she was worthy of such tenderness and kindness. It had been a long time since anyone had made her feel worthwhile and it meant the world to her. She turned in his arms and kissed him softly until he was awake. Scott gave her a sleepy smile and they spent what was left of the afternoon in each other's arms.

\*       \*       \*

The three of them spent some time at the library the next morning. Tim was able to come up with a list of people that had died at or shortly after the party. Now all they had to do was track down where they were buried.

"Can't we just walk around the local cemetery?"

"No," Tim shook his head. "There are several in the area and it could be any one of them, and we also need to make sure none of these people were from out of town. At that time, some families had their own burial plots on their property, so we'll have to rule those out also. This will help us narrow down the search substantially."

They reviewed the archived obituaries in solitude, the only sound breaking the silence was when one of them would call off a name from the list that they had located. Eventually they were able to confirm that all of them were buried locally and they knew where each of the graves were located.

Scott and Tim spent the rest of the day picking up all the supplies they would need so Emma decided to stop by and see Lynne, who was absolutely ecstatic when Emma showed up on her doorstep.

"Come in, come in," she said, giving Emma an exuberant hug and dragging her, with Callie in tow, into the living room.

"So, tell me all about it. What has been going on?"

"I don't even know where to begin." Emma hesitated and tried to find the words to explain what was going on. "Even more bizarre than my house being haunted, is the fact that I've developed some sort of a relationship with Scott. I know it's crazy, but everything just feels so right when I'm with him."

"Hold on, what exactly are you talking about? Have you been doing the horizontal mamba with the bad boy?"

Emma couldn't stop the flush in her cheeks or the smile that lit her face. Twisting her fingers together, she replied quietly, "As a matter of fact, I am."

"Don't say another word." Lynne jumped up and ran into the kitchen, returning a few minutes later with a glass of white wine for both of them.

"I'm not sure who needs this more, you or me. Okay, spill." Emma felt a little uncomfortable trying to put her feelings into words, but it was nice to have another woman to talk to about it.

"Well, he's just so," she hesitated, trying to come up with the right word to describe him.

"Manly?" Lynne offered.

"Yes, that's a perfect way to describe him, manly. He's strong and bold and fearless, and yet he cares deeply about things and isn't afraid to show that side of himself either. He's a really good man."

"I bet he's great in the sack too, he looks so damned athletic."

"We are not going there," Emma replied, but Lynne saw her guilty flush and smiled to herself.

"But, what about Jeremy? What about your marriage?"

"I really don't know. I'm not sure that I can ever forgive him, but I still have to think of what's best for my children."

"I know what you mean," Lynne responded solemnly. "Sometimes it seems that a woman's happiness really doesn't matter, at least until her kids are old enough to be on their own and take care of themselves, and sometimes not even then."

Both women stared quietly at the baby monitor sitting on the end table for a moment. Emma reached over and gave Lynne's hand a squeeze. No words were necessary.

Lynne smiled at her. "No matter what, you enjoy every second with macho man until you go back to being a wife and mother again, okay?"

Emma nodded, staring into her glass and wishing she could see the future, because she was nowhere near as positive as Lynne that her life was going to return to what it was before all this craziness began.

"And what about our friendly neighborhood ghosts?"

"We closed the portal," Emma explained excitedly. "I even helped, although I was so terrified that they literally had to pry my hands loose and drag me out of the barn when it was over."

"So, it's done now?"

"No, not yet." Emma wasn't sure how much more information she should divulge. "There are a few more things that they'll have to do, I'm not really in the loop, they just let me tag along sometimes."

"It's like something out of the movies, with the handsome strangers showing up and saving the day." Lynne said, draining her glass. "Would you like another?"

"No, thanks, I'm good."

"I don't think that I could participate at all, I'm too much of a chicken. I'd never be able to set foot back in that house."

"I've been scared to death most of the time, but it's also kind of exhilarating and exciting. At least, when Scott and Tim are with me. But, hopefully, the place will be cleaned out and safe very soon. Enough about that, what's been going on in your world?"

They spent another hour or so chatting about Lynne's life. Emma skillfully diverted the conversation whenever Lynne tried to get more information about Scott or the house, she had shared all she was willing to about those subjects for the time being.

## CHAPTER 25

When Emma and Callie returned to the hotel a little while later, the manager stopped them in the lobby.

"I'm so sorry to bother you, Mrs. Draper."

"It's no problem," she replied. "What can I do for you?"

"I'm afraid it's your credit card."

"What about it?"

He mopped his brow with an embroidered handkerchief, which she might have found amusing under other circumstances.

"It no longer shows as active, so we'll either need cash, another credit card, or I'm afraid we'll have to ask you to leave."

"I have other cards, can you try those for me?"

"Certainly." He went around the desk as she dug through her wallet for the other credit cards. She fumed as one after the other they were also rejected. The cards were all in Jeremy's name and he must have cancelled them.

"I'm very sorry for the confusion," Emma said, flushing in embarrassment. "I will take care of this, but I'll have to make a call first. Can I have a little time to get this straightened out?"

"I can give you an hour or two, but no longer than that."

"Thank you, are my friends back yet?"

"Not that I'm aware of."

"I'll be back shortly." Emma hurried to her room and tried to reach Jeremy.

Over the next thirty minutes she left two more messages for him as she paced the room, but he wasn't calling her back. She knew it was just a power play on his part, his way of trying to regain control of the situation, but that didn't make her any less angry.

Scott and Tim still hadn't returned to their room, so she called Scott to let him know what was going on.

"He did what? What a jerkknob."

"A what?"

"Jerkknob, a much politer version of what I would actually like to call the freakin' bounder. We're still out at one of the cemeteries. We'll be done shortly, wait there and we'll take care of it when we get back."

"Your creative way with name calling aside, alright I'll wait, but I'm not sure how long it will be before the manager forcibly removes me."

"Set the dog after him if he tries. Don't leave. I'll see you in a bit."

Hanging up the phone, she remembered that there was an ATM machine in the bar downstairs and hurried down to try it. That card had been deactivated also. Jeremy was always very thorough in everything that he did and, apparently, that was holding true for his little financial war on her, as well.

A little while later there was a tentative knock on her door and Emma heard the manager quietly call her name. She didn't respond and kept Callie quiet, praying he wouldn't use his master key to get in. He didn't, and Emma was finally able to breathe again when she heard his footsteps fade down the hallway.

Scott and Tim still hadn't returned and it had been well over an hour. Emma was starting to feel panicky every time she heard footsteps approaching in the hallway. Then she remembered the emergency fund that they kept. She had never imagined that it would be needed for a circumstance like this, but there was close to a thousand dollars in it, and that would carry her for awhile. Unfortunately, the jar was in the cupboard above the refrigerator, back at the house.

Emma peeked out the curtains, it was still daylight and wouldn't be dark for a couple of hours. She had plenty of time to get there, grab the jar and get out before the house became shrouded in darkness.

Her heart was jumping all over her chest and her palms were starting to sweat at the thought of going back into that house alone, but she really didn't see any other way out of her current financial predicament.

Emma wrote a brief note for Scott and Tim and slid it under their door, letting them know where she was going, just in case. She left Callie in the room, hoping she would bark incessantly if anyone knocked on the door and scare the bejesus out of the manager if he tried to use his master key.

"I can't believe I'm doing this," she murmured to herself, as she stealthily slipped out the back door and through the parking lot.

It began to get harder and harder for Emma to press down on the gas pedal as she approached the house. She considered stopping at Lynne's and asking her to come along, but she didn't. Lynne was petrified of that house and, if anything did happen, she didn't want it to happen to her friend.

Emma left the keys in the van, in case she needed a quick escape. Standing in the driveway, she looked up at the monstrosity in front of her. Its evilness was palpable, even from outside.

Taking a deep breath, she strode purposefully up the front steps and opened the door. She left it wide open, again, not sure if she would need a quick escape. It was dim and gloomy inside and she turned on every light switch that she passed as she headed towards the kitchen in the back of the house.

It was a hot summer day and all Emma was wearing was a tank top and a pair of shorts, but as soon she stepped inside she felt a chill deep into her bones and had to rub the goosebumps from her arms. There were noises throughout the house, some fainter than others, doors slamming shut, floorboards creaking overhead, and what sounded like voices whispering around her. Emma almost bolted back out of the house, but she was so close now that she had to finish this.

Her heart was hammering so hard in her chest that she thought she might be having a heart attack, but she kept moving forward, breathing heavily through her mouth.

As soon as she stepped into the kitchen, all of the cupboard doors opened simultaneously and then slammed shut, the noise reverberating in Emma's head. She ran forward, grabbed a chair and slid it in front of the refrigerator.

She had to reach up on her tiptoes to grab the jar in the far back corner of the cupboard. Just as she was pulling it forward out of the cupboard, the door slammed shut.

Emma pulled her hand back, but she wasn't quick enough and screamed in pain as the door caught the tips of her fingers. She was able to claw the door open with her other hand and grabbed the jar.

Just as she did, the refrigerator door opened wide, knocking her off the chair and sending the jar flying onto the floor where the glass shattered and the bills started floating throughout the kitchen.

Emma moaned in pain as she landed on her tailbone. She also twisted as she fell and slammed her shoulder into the hard floor. She crawled around the kitchen, ignoring the pain that was screaming throughout her body, trying to grab as many bills as she could and stuff them into her pockets.

Suddenly, her head was jerked violently backward and some unseen force started dragging her across the floor. Uncontrollable panic gripped her when she saw the basement door slowly sliding open, and she knew that the thing was trying to drag her down there.

Emma also knew that if it got her into the basement, she would never come out. She screamed like a banshee and twisted and turned, trying to grab anything that she could to halt their progress but, slowly and surely, they were inching their way closer to that door.

"Hey, asshat, let her go."

There was a terrific boom as Scott let go with his shotgun in the small kitchen. Whatever had been dragging Emma let loose and she scrambled to her feet as quickly as she was able.

"Come on," Scott said, the gun still held high as he searched for any other signs of danger.

"I have to grab these first." Emma winced as she bent down to pick up more bills.

Tim came around from behind Scott and grabbed her arm. "Leave them," he said sternly, dragging her towards the front of the house.

"I need it though," she whispered, tears streaming down her face.

"No, you don't," he replied. "We'll take care of you, but we have to get out of here now."

Tim hurried Emma out of the house and helped her into the passenger seat of their car. "Are your keys in the van?"

"Yes."

"Okay," he said, tossing their keys to Scott, "I'll take her van back and meet you two at the hotel."

"What the hell were you thinking?" Scott asked harshly, watching Tim pull out of the driveway. "You could have gotten yourself killed."

He turned the key and the engine jumped to life, startling Emma who was still more frightened than she had ever been. "I needed the cash. I thought I could run in, grab it and get back out with no problem."

"Well, that didn't quite work out, did it? Damn it, Emma, I told you to wait for us."

She just stared out the window, the terror still had her in its grip and her body throbbed with pain. Silent tears fell unchecked down her cheeks.

"Emma, are you okay?"

She sniffled a little. "I'll be fine. I know I was stupid, I'm sorry. Thank you for coming for me, I think it was going to kill me."

"I think so, too. It's gotten much bolder. Or maybe its scared because the portal is gone, and now it has nowhere to run when we come after it."

Emma remained silent and he looked at her with concern.

"Are you hurt bad? Do you need a doctor?"

She shook her head but didn't trust herself to speak.

When they got back to the hotel, Tim had already squared everything with the manager and had prepaid her room for another week.

She smiled warmly at him. "Thank you, both of you, for everything."

"No problem, come on, let's get you some food."

"No, I'm good."

"You have to eat," Scott insisted.

"I'm really not hungry. I just want a hot bath and a bed, okay?"

They watched as she made her way gingerly down the hall, even Tim, who had his issues with her, felt helpless because there was nothing they could do for her.

Emma felt much better after a steaming hot bath and was even able to fall asleep fairly quickly. She did not rest easy though, her dreams were filled with creatures chasing her, and the terror she felt was all too real. Callie whined at her bedside as Emma tossed and turned.

She woke early the next morning, but felt like she hadn't slept at all. She took Callie for a long walk and grabbed a large coffee to tide her over until Scott and Tim woke up and they all went to breakfast together.

"You doing okay?" Tim asked, when they met up a little while later.

"I'm much better, thanks."

"You don't look it," Scott replied.

"Gee, thanks, you don't look so good yourself."

"We were up most of the night taking care of the bones."

"Burning them?" Emma asked, her eyes widening.

"Yes," Scott replied quietly, although they were in a back corner booth and no one else was seated near them.

"You found them all?"

"Yes, we did, but the worst of it was the animals."

"What animals?"

"They killed each and every animal that was at the party that night and buried them all together in a big old hole at the back of the cemetery."

"Why did they bury the animals in a cemetery?"

"It was actually in a field back behind the cemetery, guess they just needed a place big enough to dump all the carcasses in."

"So, do you think all of the ghosts are gone now?"

"They should be."

"So that leaves just the demon?" she asked.

"Or demons," Tim added.

Scott frowned at Tim, as Emma shuddered uncontrollably. Scott took both of her hands in his. "No worries, we'll take care of whatever is still there."

"And how do you do that?"

"It helps to know who the demon is and we think this one is Eitooheikoh. We summon it and have a special container that we force it into. Then we bury the container where it will never be dug up again, and the place is clean."

"What kind of container, not Tupperware, I hope." Emma said, realizing what a pitiful attempt at a joke that was as soon as she said it.

"No, smartass" Scott answered with a smile. "Our dad showed us how to make them. Don't worry, it'll hold the damned thing."

"How do you summon it? And how do you get it into the container?"

"You can't expect us to give away all of our secrets, Emma. You'll just have to trust us."

"When are you going to do it?"

"Not sure, we're both pretty whipped since we were up all night. This demon is nothing that you want to take on when you're less than a hundred percent, so I think we'll rest up today, be sure we have all the equipment and supplies that we need, and start out fresh tomorrow."

And so, they did, however, Tim ended up getting quite a bit more rest than the other two. They spent the afternoon in Emma's room and managed to find a substantial amount of energy, regardless of how little sleep they'd had the night before.

# CHAPTER 26

Emma finally had a chance to see the actual Demon Box in their room the next morning. It was a small cube, each side was about eight inches wide and marked with various symbols.

The wood was a light yellowish-brown color and the symbols were etched in black, burnt into it.

"What exactly is this?" she asked, moving it around in her hand and studying it like it was a Rubik's Cube.

"It's made of Shittah wood," Tim responded.

Emma smiled, thinking he was yanking her chain.

"Seriously, shitter wood?"

"Seriously, it's Shittah wood," he enunciated it carefully, "a species of the Acacaia tree, which is found in the Sinai Desert. It's dense and strong and resistant to decay, so whatever is made out of it, endures for a long, long time. As a matter of fact, it's the wood that was used to build the Ark of the Covenant, which I'm sure you've heard of."

"It held the Ten Commandments, right?"

"Yes, it did. We use this wood and bury it some place where it won't get dug up easily, and it should hold the demon many, many years."

"Where do you find a place that won't get dug up easily?"

"Best place is a construction site, we bury it in the dirt just before they pour the concrete."

"Clever. It seems pretty small though." Emma added, as she examined it with a frown.

"Oh, honey," Scott interjected with a smile, "everyone knows that it's not the size that matters."

Tim rolled his eyes and Emma giggled.

"What are all the symbols on it, the eye in the pyramid, the wings and all these other squiggly lines?"

"Containment symbols, just an extra precaution to keep the demon in once we've caught it."

"How will you know it's in there?"

"You'll know it when you see it," Scott replied. "Are you guys ready to go?"

Emma fondled the stone around her neck absently. The reality of what they were about to do hit her hard and she shuddered.

Scott put his arm around her. "You don't have to come with us, you know."

"It's okay, I want to help."

"Alright then," Tim said, with a heavy sigh. He was not sold on her coming along, but wasn't going to waste his time arguing against the both of them. "Emma, when we get into the house, things will start to happen that may frighten you, just stay by me or Scott all the time, okay?"

"Oh, you don't need to worry about that," she assured him. "Should we bring Callie?"

"Not this time," Scott replied. "We are going to have our hands full and I can't guarantee that we'd be able to protect her."

Emma remained fairly calm until they pulled into the driveway and she got out and looked at the evil, old house. Her stomach began to quiver and her heart started to trip-hammer in her chest. She wasn't sure if she was going to be able to actually go back inside, until Scott grabbed her hand and gave it a quick squeeze. She took a deep breath, smiled bravely at him and they walked into the house together, hand in hand.

They decided to do the ceremony in the living room, near the stairway to the secret basement. Tim spray-painted a pentagram on the ceiling and then a smaller one on the end table.

"So, once we begin," Scott told her, getting the end table under the center of the pentagram and then placing the demon box in the center of the one drawn on the end table, "we'll all hold hands. You and I are going to repeat the same phrase over and over. It's 'Bono Malum Superate'. Got that?"

"Bono Malum Superate?"

"Yes, good."

"What does it mean?"

"You and your questions, it's Latin and means something along the lines of good overcoming evil."

"And that's all that has to be said to get the demon here?"

"No, Tim has a lot more that he is going to say, he'll be chanting the actual incantation, calling the demon to us and into the box. What you and I are doing just reinforces it. Oh, shit, Tim, its coming."

Tim turned towards them and Emma could feel them both staring at her chest for some reason. Glancing down, she saw the turquoise stone nestled just above her cleavage and watched in amazement as it seemed to glow and then turn from a pretty sky blue to a deep, angry blue.

"Quick," Scott grabbed her hand, "everyone in the circle, now."

They quickly sat down around the end table and held hands. The Demon Box was open on the table in front of them and Tim began reciting the incantation.

"Emma, it can't hurt us inside this circle." Scott lifted his chin towards the pentagram on the ceiling. "We need to start now, do you remember the words?"

She nodded and they both began to chant 'Bono Malum Superate', over and over again.

Somehow, even though all of the doors and windows were closed, a wicked wind storm arose inside the house. Lamps crashed to the floor, cushions and knick knacks blew past their heads, some barely missing them.

Emma's hair whipped around her face, but she just closed her eyes and kept chanting. She had no idea what Tim was saying, she could hear the words but they made no sense to her. The only word that she did recognize was Eitooheikoh, the name of the Demon living in her house.

The wind became even more fierce and destructive, it pushed the TV over and knocked pictures off the wall, it was literally destroying the room around them.

Tim's voice was rising, he had to almost yell to be heard over the wind and choked when something flew into his mouth, but he just spat it out and continued on.

Emma screamed when an ottoman blew across the room and struck her right in the middle of her back. Scott kept chanting but watched her in concern. She nodded over at him, letting him know that she was okay, and joined in with him again.

There was a horrific shriek, so loud and shrill that it was painful, and Emma tried to let go of their hands to cover her ears. But Scott and Tim held onto her tightly, not allowing her to break the circle.

She opened her eyes just as the Demon Box began to glow a deep red, the air inside of it was pulsating. Emma was repulsed and fascinated by it at the same time and couldn't look away.

The blowing wind and the shrieking were starting to fade and, at the same time, the pulsating inside the box increased. Scott and Tim had their attention fixed solely on that little Demon Box, even as they continued to chant.

Tim forcefully let go one more sentence in Latin and at the same time he grabbed the lid and slammed it closed. He made sure the lid was secured and then quickly let loose of it, as if it had burnt his hand.

Scott rushed in with a strange looking key and locked the box tight before removing the key and stepping back away from it.

Emma bit back a scream and jumped away from the end table when the box started moving up and down and all over the table like a living thing.

Scott and Tim just watched it for a moment and then they smiled at each other.

"It's done." Tim sounded exhausted.

"Good job." Scott clapped him on the shoulder and then turned to Emma, lifting her up in his arms and twirling her around.

"It's over Emma, your house is clean."

She stopped giggling when he finally set her back down on her feet and sobered completely as her hands slid down his chest.

"Thank you, both of you. I don't know what I would have done if you hadn't come to my rescue."

Scott hugged her close, holding her tight with both arms, not wanting to let loose of her just yet, because he was afraid he might lose her altogether.

"Tim, what do you say we spend the night here tonight, just to be sure we cleaned everything out? If it's okay with Emma, of course."

"Certainly, I'd like that."

"Scott, we have other places to be."

"I know, but those places will still be there tomorrow, right?"

"I suppose so. "

"Do you think we would have time to go back to the Sanitarium?" Emma asked.

"What for?"

"For some reason, I feel like we should check on Stephanie.  If the demon really was still terrorizing her, she should be better now too, shouldn't she?"

Tim and Scott gave each other a knowing look, which made Emma uneasy. She looked up into Scott's deep brown eyes and saw the uncertainty in them.

"What?"

"Listen, Emma," he rubbed his brow, trying to find the right way to say what she needed to hear, "we can go there and we can see how she is, but I don't think we'll find any real answers."

"I don't understand."

"I know, you just have to realize that even if this demon was still terrorizing her and we stopped it, that doesn't mean Stephanie is going to be alright now."

"But why, that doesn't make any sense."

"Emma, you saw how she is, she's been living with this for what, twenty years or so, even if we did stop it from actually happening any more, in her mind, it isn't ever going to stop. She's been irreparably damaged, Emma."

He watched the tears glistening in her brilliant green eyes and wiped an errant tear off her cheek.

"If you want, we can try to get in to see her, I'm just not sure it's going to ease your mind, and it may even end up making you more upset."

"I understand, it's just so damned sad though. I can't believe the poor girl will have to live with that terror for the rest of her life, even though it's no longer there."

"It won't be as bad for her as it has been," Tim added. "Nothing will actually harm her any more, it will all be just in her mind."

"I guess that's something, at least. Have you guys seen this before, then?"

"Similar," Tim said, "but not quite to the same extent. If you're sure that you don't want to go see her again, let's get back to the motel and clean our stuff out and come back here. That way we'll be ready to take off first thing tomorrow morning."

*      *      *

They cleaned out their things from the hotel and brought Callie home. The house actually did feel lighter somehow, but Emma remembered that she'd thought the same thing after Venetia was here, so she wasn't completely convinced just yet.

Callie checked out each and every room and not a single hair on her back raised and there was not one growl or bark. It had been a pretty stressful day so they relaxed with a pizza and a couple of beers and then retired early that evening. Tim slept upstairs in Shelly's room because there was a double bed. The boys only had singles and there was no way his long body would fit onto them, not comfortably anyway.

Emma felt a little guilty taking Scott's hand and leading him into her bedroom, into her and Jeremy's bedroom. She knew it was wrong, but she really didn't care at the moment. Knowing this might be her last night with Scott, Emma was not going to regret a moment of their time together.

At first, they both felt a little awkward, like it was their first time together and they weren't quite sure how to act.

Emma put on a nightgown and sat on the edge of the bed. Scott joined her, still fully dressed. He slipped an arm around her shoulders, pulled her close and kissed the top of her head. She wrapped her arms around his waist and held on tight, wishing they could just hold each other like this forever. "Scott, I," she began.

"Ssh," he said, placing a finger over her lips. "No words, not tonight. We'll talk about everything tomorrow, but not tonight. I am going enjoy each and every inch of your body and that's all I'm going to think about, okay?"

Emma nodded and he leaned down and kissed her, lightly at first, then deeper, and suddenly any shyness or awkwardness disappeared as they melted into each other's arms.

Somewhere in the darkest part of the night, Callie suddenly started barking sharply while staring out into the hallway. Scott was already getting his pants on when they heard a loud bang and Tim yelled out, "God Damn it."

Scott and Callie were already heading up the stairs by the time Emma got her robe and ran out to join them. She found the light switch in the hallway and they saw Tim lying on the floor.

"What happened?" Scott asked, extending his hand and helping his brother up.

"I had to take a piss, oh sorry," he said, looking at Emma apologetically.

"And?" Scott asked.

"I took a step outside the room and stepped right onto something and fell ass over teakettle."

All three of them looked around for what it could have been. Emma spied a small, partially deflated kickball over near the kitchen stairs. "Could it have been that?"

"Yes, definitely, it was squishy and rolled out away from me after I stepped on it. But, that was not sitting in front of the door when I went in to bed."

"And the dog started barking before you fell."

"Shit, we didn't get them all."

"What are you talking about?" Emma asked, feeling a little panicky.

"I don't think it's another demon or it would have done some real damage. I think we missed one of the ghosts."

"How is that possible, I thought you burned all of their bones?"

"So did we. Come on, let's get a little more sleep and we'll figure it out in the morning. You okay up here, Tim?"

"I'll be fine, thanks."

Emma was feeling very peaceful and content the next morning as she scrambled up some eggs. It felt good to be home again, even though there was still something there, it didn't feel nearly as foreboding or dangerous as it had.

She smiled and leaned her head back as Scott slid up behind her and pushed her hair away from her neck and began to nuzzle it. Emma could feel his desire and turned in his arms. They shared a long, lingering kiss until the smell of burning eggs caught Emma's attention and she quickly turned back to the stove.

"Make yourself useful," she said to Scott with a smile, "and put some bread in the toaster."

"What if I want to stay right here?" He snuggled up against her again and was a little more forceful as he rubbed against her backside.

"Stop it," she said with a giggle. "Where's Tim?"

"He's out at the car, getting his paperwork so we can figure out what we missed." Scott quieted suddenly and stepped back away from Emma with his head cocked to the side. "Did you hear that?"

"Sounded like a car horn."

"Yes, it did." He started moving towards the front of the house when the front door slammed open and running feet could be heard approaching.

"Mom," James called out, running straight into her arms.

"James, what are you doing here?"

Collin and Shelly came running in right behind him and there was a big group hug. Jeremy entered the kitchen a moment or two later and stared hard at Scott, completely ignoring Emma. He was followed closely by Tim, whose face was creased with concern.

# CHAPTER 27

"Listen," Tim said, "I don't want to break up the family reunion, but this place still isn't a hundred percent safe. You might not want the kids here yet."

"Go to hell. Seriously, just how long did you think I was going to let you play 'let's pretend there's still a ghost in the house' with my wife?"

Scott opened his mouth, but Tim replied first. "Listen, we took care of almost everything. But, there is still something here and it's strong. We know it can hurt an adult, so it can definitely hurt a kid. You might want to give us just a little more time to finish this up."

"We're not scared, are we kids? If your mom can do it, then so can we."

The children did not look very excited about the prospect.

"I'm cooking breakfast, are you guys hungry?" Emma looked nervously from Scott to Jeremy to her children, not at all sure how to deal with this situation.

Jeremy looked deliberately at the clock on the wall, then dragged his narrowed eyes toward hers. "We ate hours ago. We're almost ready for lunch."

"Fine," Emma replied. "We were just going to eat, so kids, why don't you run into the library for a little bit. The living room is all tore up right now, so you shouldn't go in there. We have some paperwork to go over and then, hopefully, we can get this last little problem taken care of, okay?"

Emma, Tim and Scott sat at the table, eating their breakfast and going through the paperwork. Jeremy stood against the doorway with his arms akimbo and his eyes narrowed, just staring at them. Emma's stomach was in knots as she absently moved eggs around her plate, struggling to ignore him.

The three of them poured over the notes that they had on the people that died at the party and their burial sites. Shaking his head, Tim said, "I can't find anything that we missed."

"Could it have been one of the animals?" Scott asked, ignoring the snicker from Jeremy, but feeling his blood boil when he looked over to find Emma twisting that damned wedding band again. She hadn't done that in several days and now, with Jeremy back, she was desperately trying to find some comfort within herself. It infuriated Scott.

"Maybe, I suppose we could dig it all up again, in case some of the bones were buried a little bit away from the others. That's a big job though, they could be on any side of where the others are."

Unable to ignore the next rude noise that Jeremy made, Scott stood up and walked over to him. "Do you have something that you'd like to add?"

"No, I do not," Jeremy replied, still leaning casually against the doorway and staring hard at Scott. "I'm just fascinated with this 'expert' dialogue. And, I must admit that I am shocked to think that you professionals may have missed something, that is just not fathomable, is it?"

"You know, I try not to kick anyone's ass in their own home, but if you aren't going to help, then just get the hell out of here, or that's exactly what I'm going to have to do."

"From what I've seen, you aren't capable of taking care of anything, let alone kicking anyone's ass. I think that I've let this bullshit go on long enough. I'm not going anywhere, but I think it's time that you did."

"You need to watch your mouth and show a little respect." Scott's voice was calm and low, but his hands were balled tightly into fists as he tried to restrain himself from throttling Jeremy, for so many different reasons.

"Or what?"

Scott shrugged his shoulders. "Guess I'd start by slapping you stupid, which I don't imagine would take very long, then I'd figure out what comes next."

Emma could feel the tension coming off both of them and knew that a physical altercation was imminent.

"Scott, just ignore him, he's being an ass. Would you please come outside with me for a moment?" she asked, placing her hand on his arm.

Scott continued to stare down Jeremy, but finally relented and turned towards Emma. His eyes were still snapping with anger and his body was tense, but he followed her outside without a further word.

They walked in silence for a few minutes, Scott's hand reached out and took hold of Emma's and just that slight touch helped to calm both of them down. They weren't headed anywhere in particular, but found themselves outside of the barn. Emma opened up the doors and they stepped into the gloominess.

"I don't know what to say, Scott. I'm sorry he's being such a jerk, but he doesn't like to feel powerless and that's what he is in this situation."

They sat on a bale of hay and Scott turned slightly towards her, his eyes still narrowed in anger. "Don't you dare make excuses for him, Emma. He's an asshole, he started the whole problem between the two of you, and he refused to help you with the problems in the house. And, on top of all the other douche moves he made, he cut off your finances and almost got you killed. He is not getting a pass for any of that."

Emma smiled, loving his protectiveness and his practicality. She wished she could be more like that and less like the silly, maternal milksop that she was most of the time.

"Okay, then let me apologize for myself, for not putting him in his place. I will admit that I was completely caught off guard when he and my kids showed up this morning. I was feeling all relaxed and happy, reliving some of our more adventurous moments from last night, and when they showed up, it kind of blew my mind. I should be in there hugging those kids, telling them how much I love them and have missed them. But, I'm having trouble even looking them in the eye, because I feel so guilty."

"You have nothing to feel guilty about, I told you, he started this, not you." Scott put his arm around her shoulder and pulled her over against him, not giving a damn if anyone walked in on them.

"That's what is so hard to explain, I don't feel guilty for cheating on my husband, although I should. I feel guilty for betraying my children, for not being there for them and for seriously considering completely changing their lives in order for mine to be happy."

"Really?" he asked, lifting her chin and looking deeply into her eyes. "Don't mess with me, would you really consider leaving Jeremy right now?"

"Would I consider it? Yes. Would I actually be able to go through with it? I don't know, I really don't. When I'm in a room with the two of you, I feel nothing for him and just want to be in your arms. That's where I feel safe and cared for."

Emma had to stop for a moment and try to collect her thoughts, her voice was wavering and she needed to be able to explain this properly to Scott, so he could understand the full extent of her conflict.

"My kids, Scott, they're a whole different story. I love them so much and I have to do what's best for them. Jeremy also loves them and they love him. Do I have the right to tear them away from him?"

"You have the right to do whatever you think is best, for yourself and for them. If you're miserable, how does that make their life better?"

"It doesn't, this is all just so surreal. A month ago, my God, I can't believe that's all it's been, but I would never have imagined that I'd be sitting here in another man's arms, or that Jeremy could have hurt me like he did. And I have no idea what another month will bring.

How would you and I make it work? You travel all the time and don't stay in one place long. And you'd be an instant daddy to teenagers, it's not easy being even a real parent to a teenager, so this would probably be the scariest gig you've ever gotten involved in. You said yourself that you were surprised that your own parents made it work."

"You worry too much and you try to plan the future too much. Sometimes, you have sit back and just live life as it comes. Deal with whatever happens on a particular day, either enjoy it or try to fix it and then move on to something else the next day. Nobody can predict exactly what's going to happen and you just can't be prepared for everything. If nothing else, that's what I've learned doing this job. It's dangerous and you never know if this might be the monster that takes you down. That's why you can't waste your whole life worrying about what ifs. If that's all you're doing, then you are never really living at all."

"I think it's a little easier for you because you only have to take care of yourself. My kids' lives are in my hands, I can't just wing it day to day."

"That's crap and you know it. I have my mom and I have my brother, and I would never let anything harm either one of them, so it isn't just about me. And having a family doesn't mean you can't live day to day, it's not all about being ready for what might happen, because you can't predict that and you can't prepare for it."

Emma tilted her head towards him and he bent down and captured her lips with his own.

"I care about you, very much," Scott murmured, reluctantly pulling away from her. "If you want us to work, I know we can, but you need to be absolutely sure, because it's pretty much the biggest decision that you'll ever have to make."

"I know and that's why I'm so scared. My fantasy is that you and I just run away together and we make mad, passionate love every day. My reality is that I have to be with my kids, so I know that will never happen."

"All you need to do is take your time and figure it out."

"You make that sound so easy. Will you be leaving as soon as this last ghost is taken care of?"

"Yes, particularly since your family is all back now. We should be able to get it taken care of tonight, so we'll probably head out tomorrow."

"That's too soon." Emma traced a finger around his jaw and his mouth, studying his face, wanting to remember every detail of it. Scott leaned forward for another lingering kiss.

"I know, but don't think that you have to make your decision right now." Scott hesitated, not wanting to say what he was about to say, but knowing, in all fairness, that he had to. "You know, demons are supernatural maggots, they feed off any discord and make it seem worse than it really is. They mess with people's heads and put thoughts into their minds that they might not have had on their own. They create chaos. It is possible that what Jeremy did was all because of the demon. I think you owe it to him, and to your kids, to see what happens with all of you now that it's gone. It's the only way that you'll ever be sure that you are making the right decision."

"You're suggesting that I stay with him?"

"I'm suggesting that you stay together for now and see what happens. When you realize that you belong with me, I'll be waiting for you. No matter how long it takes."

"When, not if?"

"When, not if."

"Boy, you make this so hard." She leaned her head against his shoulder and he tightened his grip on her.

Scott felt his own tears start to burn and quickly swallowed them back, then he began to get angry. He wanted to sweep her off her feet and carry her upstairs to their bedroom, right in front of her dick of a husband, and prove to them all that she was his and his alone. But, he would never do that to her, and he knew that he had to let her find the answers for herself, no matter how badly it tore him up inside.

"I know that we'll end up together," he whispered hoarsely, tickling her ear with his breath, "so take as long as you need."

Emma turned and looked at him tenderly, running her fingers along his jawline, leaning forward in anticipation of another lingering kiss, perhaps her last with him. But, just as she was about to melt into his arms, they both jumped up when they heard, "Mom, Mom, where are you?"

James ran into the barn, breathless. "Mom, something happened to Shelly."

The three of them sprinted for the house and found everyone in the library. Shelly was lying on the window seat with a wet cloth on her head.

"What happened?" Emma asked, rushing over to her side and checking the cut on her forehead. It wasn't deep and had already stopped bleeding, but it had swelled a little and Shelly was crying hysterically.

"Calm down, Shelly, and tell me what happened, slowly."

"I stood up to go into the kitchen and something shrieked in my ear and jumped on my back. It felt like a little animal. I lost my balance and fell and hit my head on the table over there."

Scott and Tim looked at each other and Scott said, "It's that freakin' monkey."

"Watch your mouth around my kids," Jeremy scolded.

"Shut your own damn mouth and get out of my way."

"Maybe you didn't hear me, I said to watch your mouth."

"You really don't want to test me right now, chuckles. Get out of my way."

"Or what?"

"Or this," Scott replied, shoving Jeremy up against a wall and pinning him there with his muscular arm crossed in front of Jeremy's chest.

Jeremy didn't say anything else, but if looks could kill, the one he gave Scott certainly would have. Scott released him and headed into the kitchen with Tim.

Emma made sure that Shelly was alright and ran out after them. "What are you looking for?"

"Somewhere in here is a copy of the newspaper article that has a photo of the monkey. I know we burned its bones, I looked for them specifically because we knew it was here."

"Here it is." Tim pulled out an old photograph and they all looked it over carefully, not knowing exactly what they were looking for. It was a cute little thing, wearing a hat and vest and holding a miniature accordion.

"Haunted object?"

"Probably," Scott replied.

"What's that?" Emma asked.

"Sometimes the ghost stays tied to an object that they had while they were alive."

"What do you do when that happens?"

"We have to find the object and burn it."

Suddenly, all hell broke loose in the library and they heard some kind of high-pitched shrieking, Callie was barking loud and crazy and, to add to the cacophony, all the kids started screaming.

Tim, Scott and Emma ran to them. It was a bizarre scene, one person after the other was either trying to shake something invisible off of them or reaching behind their head trying to grab whatever was holding onto their back. Emma actually saw Collin's head snap back as the imperceptible intruder yanked on his hair.

Scott drew his gun, but couldn't shoot because the ghost seemed to be jumping from one of the kids to another.
Tim ran over and grabbed James, covering his body with his own, protecting him from the creature. Tim pulled out the picture and showed it to James.

"Have you seen anything in this picture? The clothes, the accordion, anything?"

James didn't answer at first, unable to focus with all the drama unfolding.

"James," Emma said sternly, "look at the picture, have you seen any of those things?"

James turned to the picture and stared at it for a moment. Suddenly his face lit up and he nodded his head. "The hat, it was in the back of the shelf in my closet."

"Is it still there?"

"Yes."

"Show me." Tim picked James up like he weighed nothing at all and sprinted upstairs with him.

Scott ran into the living room and grabbed a fireplace poker, then sprinted back to the library and positioned himself in front of Emma and the children, swinging it blindly at the invisible threat, trying to keep the creature off of them. Emma was leaning over Shelly and Collin who were cowering on the window seat together. When it jumped onto her back, she could only grit her teeth and ignore the pain from the deep scratches that it was leaving on her. She spun around quickly and smashed her back into the wall, then went right back to the children, that seemed to have gotten rid of it for the time being.

Jeremy was covering his head and hiding in the corner behind a chair. She would have thought that was comical, but the reality of his cowardice kept it from being very amusing.

Just as the creature landed on her back one more time, it let loose a horrible howl of agony and jumped off of her. She turned and could have sworn she saw a small burst of flame and then a faint dusting of ashes falling onto the carpet.

Callie stopped barking and the room became very quiet. Tim and James came back downstairs and Tim nodded at Scott.

Emma helped Shelly and Collin up and checked them out to be sure they were okay.

"I'm alright, Mom, but is this finally done, for real?"

Emma looked over at Scott who nodded affirmatively.

"Yes, it is, honey. The house is fine now. I think we should all thank Scott and Tim though. It's only because of them. They saved us." Emma's voice was shaking, partially from left over adrenaline from the attack, and partially out of relief that it was finally over.

"Oh, please," Jeremy mumbled.

The three kids thanked them and Tim and Scott walked towards the front door. Emma followed them out.

"I can never, ever thank you both enough. Will you be staying in town tonight? Can I at least buy you dinner or pay you for your time."

"Emma, we don't do this for money, but it was nice getting to know you. Take care of yourself." Tim said sincerely, giving her a hug good bye.

"You, too," she replied, "and watch over your brother for me, okay?"

He nodded his assent and walked towards the car.

"Besides," Scott said, a little half-smile on his face, "I'm pretty sure you don't have any money, remember? Are you alright?"

"Not so much, can I come and see you after I take care of a couple of things here. I think we have more to talk about."

"No, we don't." His tone was gentle, but the words still hurt. Emma wasn't at all sure if she could let him go yet. "You do what you have to do. I told you, I'll be here when you realize that we belong together.

You do have to do me one favor though, don't call me until you've made your decision. It would kill me to just chit chat occasionally, I can't do that with you and I'm afraid it has to be all or nothing. You wait to call me until you're ready and I'll be here, okay?"

"Alright, I'll do that for you, but I'm going to miss you so much. Where were you twenty years ago? If I'd known you then, everything could be so different now."

With the feather light touch of his finger, he gently moved a piece of her hair off of her face and then let his fingers slide down her cheek, brushing away the errant tear that had escaped.

"I wasn't ready for you then," he replied. "But I am now."

It took all of the control that she had to not lean into him and kiss him one more time, she wanted so badly to feel his arms wrapped around her, to feel his body pressed against hers, to help her get past the searing pain blossoming in her chest.

But, Emma could feel Jeremy's eyes burning into the back of her head and knew that he was watching from one of the windows. She didn't think that seeing her share an intimate good-bye kiss with Scott would be the most auspicious beginning for their new start together.

"I'm glad to hear that," she said softly. "Will you please promise me that you'll stay alive until I'm ready?"

"I promise." He took her hand, gave her one last heart-stopping smile and slowly released it as he turned away.

Tears began to spill freely down Emma's face as Scott walked over to the car. She waved at them as they pulled out of the driveway and then stood silently for a few moments until they'd driven out of sight, waiting for her emotions to quiet down before she went back inside to face her family.

When she did, Jeremy met her at the door, looking relieved.

"So, you're staying?"

"I am for now, Jeremy. We'll see what we can do to salvage our marriage. You'll give up the apartment and we'll try to be a family again. But, don't get me wrong, I can't promise that I'll ever be able to feel the same way about you again, and I can't promise that I'll be able to stay married to you. We'll just have to see how it goes, day by day."

Emma turned her back on him and walked inside to find her children.

# THE END

Made in the USA
Columbia, SC
09 July 2017